GHOST WRITER

R. Wesley Clement

20 Twenty
Literary Group

Ghost Writer

ISBN
978-1-961250-88-8 (Paperback)
978-1-961250-89-5 (eBook)
978-1-961250-87-1 (Hardcover)

TABLE OF CONTENTS

The past two years have been as surreal as a ghost sighting. Covid struck just as I was finishing up this story, so I didn't publish. Then life struck and I underwent a health scare that still has me limping along.

It was during my down time that the importance of family took center stage.

I can never thank my wife Carey enough for the care and concern she heaped on me over the past year. She read this story and cleaned up lots of narrative. I love you.

My daughter Shellee and her family provided a healing environment for this old body for three solid months in their home in Maine. Lots of laughter and card games.

My son Khristian and his life partner Pam visited me and buoyed my spirits.

My brother Zane and his wife Debbie came to see me on a regular basis. We swapped stories and books to read.

My sister Nora and husband Dennis stopped in expecting to see a ghost. I fooled them though.

My friend Bernie was in constant contact tracking my progress and encouraging me on a regular basis.

Friends Nancy and Andy Carbone brought me a walker that fit.

Needless to say my mind is still working and I hope you enjoy this story

Ghost Writer published in 2022

When I made the decision to write a ghost story that is placed in the Central Maine community of Skowhegan I had no idea what would come out of the woodwork.

Beginning the story in the spring of 2019, and invited to speak to a small audience at the East Madison Grange in July, I found myself revealing what I was working on. The night was a celebration of the work volunteers were doing to keep the spirit of The East Madison Historical Association alive.

I used the occasion to highlight and sell a few of my latest read, THE HOUSE THAT JACK BUILT. Many in the audience had purchased a number of my earlier titles. That evening I announced a possible new summer read for 2020 with a haunting theme. Immediately hands rose as local knowledge trumped my imagination. It seemed ghost sightings and soundings had touched nearly everyone in the room. I was given ideas and advice.

After leaving Maine for my winter home in Florida, my sister Tricia sent me a Central Maine Sentinel article about a Paranormal Fest to be held in Vassalboro. I read with interest the genuine fervor that surrounds this topic.

I did a bit of research and took note of how often Shakespeare included ghosts in his writing.

Added to all this was a haunting memory that had invaded my dreams years ago when I was just a kid in East Madison, Maine. In the dream, I killed and buried an old woman believed to be a witch somewhere behind the old mill in lower East Madison. It's strange, but the memory of that old haunting dream had not reoccurred until I began this project.

Another memory that as a kid raised the hairs on the back of my neck was one I shared with a number of brothers and sisters returning home from the grange hall in East Madison on cold and eerie Saturday nights. Leaving the laughter, warmth, and good food smells of a grange supper, a tribe of young people began their walk home in the dark. What started out as group of seven or so quickly dissipated with a friend turning up the hill back towards Skowhegan, while two others climbed the hill in the opposite direction towards Solon to the north. What was left were four Clement kids all imaginative in their own right heading to Lower Mills. The street lights disappeared at the top of the first hill. When our eyes adjusted to the new dark-dark of a windy cold late fall night it felt like the wind took on a new harsher voice. The trees added sound while the dead shrubs and grassy roadside offered movement that could be interpreted in a hundred ways.

A patch of woods east of town came alive with whispers, hisses, and howls. When the wind came up and the trees bent their gnarly fingers in our direction and the dead grass swirled we all broke into a dead run. A hundred yards up the road breathless we stopped. We joked about it, but in that moment each of the four of us knew this was no joke. The Clement family prided itself on never showing a weakness so I was left keeping my fears to myself. Later in a bed I shared with my younger brother both staring into the dark and hearing the old house creak and groan, sighs left our lips but we continued to keep silent on the subject of ghosts in the night.

Then when I was twelve my family moved to Skowhegan, a town five miles south where I became scared for different reasons. It was a larger town, the house we moved to seemed larger, all the extra nooks and crannies offered fuel for my fears. Our family of fifteen kids had lost some of my protectors; Marie was gone, Richard and Russell were gone, Loretta and Laura were gone, George was gone. Times were changing.

There were no trees in our new yard to climb, no little bottle houses below those trees that my sisters had played in daily. I complained to Mama.

'You are growing up Bobby look around there are a million things to do. The morning paper doesn't land on our porch by accident, maybe you could get a job."

So at thirteen I began delivering papers in the early morning before first light. The trees didn't dominate the landscape so my ghosts took up residence in pitch black alley ways swung from power lines and peeked over snowbanks. Every darkened porch and doorway found my eyes scrunching as I released the news of the day carefully folded to cover the greatest distance possible. I did a lot of sighing and talking to myself on those mornings.

My sister Marie, married now with kids of her own, lived down the street from us. One morning a ghost in black and white appeared on her porch and before I could release the morning headlines a skunk scored a direct hit, ruining my new winter jacket.

On my route I was confronted with real live demons, liquored up and smelly they emerged from the early morning fog that rises over the Kennebec River. A swinging bridge that I had to cross daily to deliver my papers brought me face to face with adults who were scarier than ghosts.

So for a hundred reasons, real and imagined, I have a healthy respect for things that go bump in the night.

As you read my story perhaps your own memories of childhood facts and fantasies will become unearthed.

Armed with an over active imagination, experience, research, opinion, and an open mind, this is my version of the unexplainable.

PROLOGUE

Late winter 1960

Ryan and Violet were in Violet's bedroom listening to music on her new Transistor radio. Violet's mother said nothing when Violet showed her the radio Ryan had given her for Valentine's Day and her birthday. She looked oddly uncomfortable though. The kids listened to the latest hits, held hands, and exchanged an occasional kiss though the bedroom door remained partly open. Violet's mother kept finding excuses to tap lightly and enter immediately; cookies and milk, a reminder to their daughter she had homework, and at nine pm. the announcement that the show was over followed her mother into the room.

He was actually relieved. He had stayed longer than he intended. Violet seemed to keep his mind away from all the drama in his life but he needed to have a long conversation with his faithful companion. One more hug on the porch and a promise from Violet that she intended to cook him a Valentine dinner sent a very happy Ryan on his way.

He began his five minute walk home. As he came down the street he noticed a car a few doors down from his house parked on the street with its motor running. Ryan had never seen this car before. Curious, but not alarmed, he reached the house where he was staying. He glanced across the street at his own house, no light no movement. No light showed in Marcia's house which in itself was odd. The old man didn't like the dark. The street appeared as a ribbon of black, framed by a ghost-like off-white bank of snow. Ryan paused. This time of night happened every twenty four hours. He checked the time. Six and a half hours from now, at four thirty am he would be up and delivering his newspapers. He was tired. He should go in. He looked back at the car; it was an old bomber, the engine rattled. A wisp of exhaust rose eerily from the tail pipe. No one appeared to be in the car. Ryan decided not to let his imagination run wild. Ryan walked up to the house where he had recently begun staying, he found the door ajar. He opened the door. Inside it was dark. Pluto didn't run to greet him. Ryan snapped on a light. The old man was sitting right where he always sat, in his recliner. Pluto was a few feet away lying down eyes closed. It was what lay near the feet of the old man that shocked Ryan.

CHAPTER ONE

Late autumn 1959

Ryan Trussell moved from Machias, to Skowhegan, Maine when he was thirteen. He moved there just before Halloween, when the school year was well underway, when any newbie would stick out like a sore thumb.

He spent his first weekend unpacking and getting to know a very old house that complained of its age by creaking and groaning even on a calm day. The steps to the porch complained, the stairs at every level in the house creaked, the doors squeaked and resisted opening and closing in equal measure. The kitchen cupboards and drawers offered noisy resistance to intrusion. Ryan had a room on the second floor. A closet door only partially closed while a single floorboard dead center in the room announced to anyone listening that aging is a bitch. Ryan had already introduced the house and all its unique noises to his most trusted friend. The bathroom on the second floor was a story in and of itself. Ryan hadn't shared that story yet.

This morning was show-time. Ryan left the house without comment and began what would become a daily ritual. Ryan studied the trees on his half mile walk to the junior high. He noted their colorful fall clothing now tattered and torn removed by the cold autumn winds. He saw every blighted branch naked and shivering which reminded Ryan that he too would be under a microscope this morning.

A wisp of curling smoke rose from what had been a pile of leaves just a day ago. In the smoke Ryan saw wispy fingers beckoning him. *A ghost around every corner and in every leaf pile thought Ryan*. At four foot ten inches in height and weighing in at just eighty pounds, thin as the clay character Gumby, it might just take that microscope to find him.

Ryan had been living here a week and had made it no further than the downtown, but it was clear this town was larger. The school would be larger, more students to face. Ryan had confided to his best friend and this morning his mirror, that he was nervous about today. So many things could go wrong.

He entered the school yard. Looming was a brick faced cold looking building. The wind came up and as Ryan approached, the glass in the front door shivered and rattled. Ryan all by himself, no parent to guide him, pulled open the heavy door. The familiar smells of a school full of farts, fragrance, and cleaning wax, reached his nostrils. The hallway was quiet. Ryan could hear his own breathing as his footfalls echoed on the tiled floor finding his way to the office. The hallway suddenly exploded with a class change. Ryan was late. His mother had given him the wrong start time. When Ryan arrived at the office door a tearful student was seated on a bench outside what must have been the principal's office.

An hour later, after talking to the guidance counselor and handed a class schedule, he was standing in the corridor outside classroom number nine. The assistant principal, who never did introduce himself but asked Ryan his name, knocked lightly. Ryan Trussell took a deep breath.

Dressed in new starched khaki's that smelled of cigarette smoke and burning leaves rustled when he walked. Another unwanted gift from his mother. As the door remained closed Ryan envisioned a life sentence about to be handed down. His new short sleeved plaid shirt itched like crazy smothered under a really ugly mustard yellow sweater complete with hanger boobs; which further damned him. He silently cursed his parents. Ryan felt like he was already in costume for the upcoming holiday. *At least let me wear a mask,* thought Ryan, as he studied his face reflected in the glass of the door.

In that reflection morning zits appeared around his nose, arriving just in time for the planned move to a new town; extra baggage. Earlier this morning, staring into the mirror in the bathroom, he imagined what he expected would be a terrible beginning. As a kid you just know these things. *Twenty-five pairs of eyes were going to dissect him like one of those damn vinegar frogs in science class.*

What he hadn't prepared himself for was about to make an appearance. Reality sometimes out duels imagination.

Ryan took a deep breath as the assistant principal knocked once more. The door opened as if on a steel spring. Smells of an over-heated room with all levels of hygiene riding the heat escaped. A pair of eye balls peeked into the corridor. A mouth that hadn't smiled in years offered up an opening line in this play. "Well, who do we have here?"

The assistant principal smiled as he announced with a flourish he intended to be light, but to a bunch of kids sounded like the first prize listed on a game show, "Here, we have Ryan Trussell."

Just the grand entrance Ryan hoped to avoid. In that same mirror earlier this morning he pictured himself slinking unnoticed into a seat, never making eye contact. In reality he knew that was never going to happen.

"Ryan has just moved here from Machias." The assistant principal turned and put his hand on Ryan's shoulder, "Ryan, this is Mr. Kneely."

Flowing along on the heat wave that was still trying its best to escape the room was the first comment from the peanut gallery. It came from the back of the room. "Where in hell is Machias?"

Mr. Kneely turned and gave the class, the **look**. He grimaced and looked down at his hand covered in chalk dust. That hand had just put the first problem of the day on the board. He squeezed that hand into a fist, squeezing out a thought.

Wasted effort, that entire back row. If I could eliminate just five seats, I might actually enjoy myself. He looked back shook his head and sighed. Ryan met his eyes and could read his mind. *Christ, another kid, I'm over crowded now, and a boy at that. Girls are easier.* Ryan's immediate future stared at his hand studied it as if the chalk had formed words then dismissively wiped them on his suit pants.

Mr. Kneely stuck out this hand and conjured up as close to an upside down frown as he could muster. "Hello little man." An introduction that was damning in its own right. Four foot ten eighty pound Ryan Trussell shook Mr. Kneely's hand as the assistant principal turned and closed the door behind him; his job done.

Ryan had not yet made eye contact with his classmates. Ryan looked to the lights. With his eyes raised above the crowd he gave the room a once-over, his mind racing. *The flag he pledged his loyalty to hung stoically above the blackboard.* Ryan's gaze continued to move. *A row of windows sat high on the wall, allowing just the tops of a line of naked swaying branches to be seen; windows strategically placed to provide light but not enlightenment. Bookshelves built in below those windows were most likely fully loaded with math knowledge. The front wall was a solid blackboard with today's date tucked in the lower left corner. A message below today's date announced that Friday was test day. Today's lesson in the middle of all this blackness seemed to Ryan to be a work in progress.*

The back wall was blank except for a round clock that would undoubtedly garner constant attention from some of the students. This was not Ryan's first rodeo; every class has their clowns. Ryan completed his visual tour and his eyes returned to the teacher's desk that faced the rows of students. The desk held no softness, as naked as the tree branches outside. In his look around the room Ryan had not viewed a single poster or picture that might signal this man has feelings for his work or his students.

Ryan's mind wandered briefly once more to all that blackness behind the desk. *A worshiper of the dark, Ryan pictured himself arriving here in that blackness, it would be so much easier; he would be invisible. When the lights came on he would just be there, no introductions, no explanations.*

He was brought back by the sound of whispering.

Mr. Kneely turned to the class once again. He made eye contact and the whispering stopped abruptly. He grimaced, the master commanding an audience. He turned back to Ryan and under his breath he said, "So it's you. You made it."

There was no time for this comment to register with Ryan, Mr. Kneely turned back to the class. "This is Ryan, he's a new student and he looks capable, so let's welcome him properly.

He pointed to the problem he had placed on the board. "Ryan what do you see up there?"

Ryan looked for the first time at his classmates. He saw eyes raised, and mouths squeezed tight around the room; here came a test. Ryan was lost. He had no reference point. He wasn't sure what was being asked of him as he scanned the blackness and found the two messages that he could decipher. "Uh, I see today's date." He moved his eyes, "There's to be a test on Friday." He smiled, he could read he had passed.

Knowing eyes widened, snickers began, then stifled laughter. Two thumbs up came from boys in the back of the room.

Mr. Kneely turned back to Ryan, red coloring his face. He studied his hand again. It opened and closed as if talking to itself. He shook his head. He muttered then nodded in agreement with himself. *A smart aleck remark meant to challenge his authority.* His gaze quieted the room once again, he met Ryan's eyes. Without ever clarifying what he was asking Ryan, he turned back and met the eyes of his pupils. Mr. Kneely pronounced his verdict, "So, we have a little wise guy joining our class, a midget comedian."

A punishable offense had arisen. Mr. Kneely then pointed to an array of problems not on the blackboard. Problems that had taken root in the back of the room. He pointed. "Well Ryan, why don't you take that empty seat in the back and join several of these other clock watching wise guys, who, I am sure will teach you all they think you need to know."

You could hear a pin drop. Eyes fell to their books. Ryan slunk to his seat but certainly didn't go unnoticed. The smell of perfume reached him as his starched khakis moved him noisily past girls that dominated the seats toward the front. He heard himself moving, *these damn new pants*. When he reached the empty seat, the smell of a well-aimed fart hovered inviting him to sit within range of a stifled chuckle. He couldn't have stood out more if he had ridden in on Gumby's orange horse, Pokey.

Mr. Kneely straightened his shoulders, the red in his face slowly receded. He took a breath then turned to the board asking one of the young ladies to explain what his original question had sought. With the girl smartly finishing all the parts of the problem, Ryan finally saw it come together. He wanted to raise his hand and say now he understood what was being asked and knew the answer but it was way past too late.

The upside to his academic demise was how the boys in the back of the class immediately embraced him. Being an avid reader and keeper of a private journal, Ryan was already mentally processing what had happened here and how he could record it and include it in a future book. Tonight though, it would join the pages of all that had happened since the move.

Noticing how this unfortunate beginning brought smiles from the wise guys, Ryan thought, *the upside might also keep him from being beaten up in the bathroom.*

The boys up back were sneaking gum even as they continued to break wind and check the clock. All the while never taking their eyes off Mr. Kneely's back.

Ryan snuck glances at various students. The girls remained on task and several boys in the middle of the room seemed to show interest in the work. Every time Mr. Kneely turned from the board he seemed to be focusing his eyes on Ryan; studying him. Ryan assumed his academic records had been forwarded so with any luck at all, this label as a wise guy might be short-lived. *And what did the man mean by that remark, 'I see you made it'.*

The remainder of the morning was quiet. Several classmates looked at Ryan's schedule and beckoned him to follow them to his next class. That single introduction from the assistant principal had left Ryan on his own.

When lunch time arrived Ryan reached the bottom of the stairs the smell of fresh bread wafted over him. He took a deep breath welcoming in the smell of comfort. He turned into the well-lit cafeteria. He picked up a tray and moved to the food line. OH NO! There standing at the head of the lunch line, bantering, was Mr. Kneely. The man was on lunch duty. He met Ryan's eyes and slowly shook his head side to side.

As Ryan walked the line, his tray filling with a slice of canned ham a gob of potato, green beans, a yeast roll, and applesauce, he could feel the man's eyes on his back. Joining a table with his new wise guy friends, Ryan watched himself get pointed out to teachers by Mr. Kneely as they grabbed a tray for themselves. What was he telling them? Ryan closed his eyes briefly and chewed enjoying the little bit of comfort the yeast roll supplied.

All during lunch Mr. Kneely seemed to be adding to and embellishing what had taken place in his classroom. Like the chalk dust and the mustard stain Ryan had noticed on Mr. Kneely's' suit jacket this morning, the man seemed incapable of cleaning up after himself. *Ryan feared he too was about to become a lasting stain.*

'The kid's a wise guy plain and simple,' the teacher was telling his cronies. Ryan was the newest mustard stain in the building. He wouldn't be washed off any time soon.

Ryan found himself being placed very near the teacher's desk in two of the three classes held after lunch. He sat among the girls and their cumbersome pocket books. Bending down and reaching for a comb, or lip gloss, or a tiny mirror their glued on hair styles defied gravity. Sickly sweet perfume replaced the farts of the math class. The girls eyed him curiously.

One girl winked but from the way she had taken it upon herself to dress in solid black, Ryan assumed she was making it her mission not to fit in. Ryan nodded politely but he wasn't ready to go Gothic yet.

It was an afternoon of cool receptions with few teacher smiles of welcome.

Music class held promise but the jury was still out. The music teacher actually smiled as Ryan was asked to take up an instrument. The only instrument not spoken for was the French horn. "Take this home and practice, it makes a unique sound." Ryan rolled his eyes but nodded his head. Wait, watch, and record was Ryan's approach to life. He got plenty of practice at home. He could only hope his new teachers would take the time to check the records from his past school.

Ryan had walked to school in the morning but would be taking the bus to the library in the afternoon. He announced his destination to the driver when he entered the bus for the first time. He was greeted with a stern look and a warning, the driver had clearly heard the news. "Hey little man, I think it best you sit right there in the front seat on my right, where we can get to know one another better."

So my story has reached the bus barn, word travels faster than a cold wind, thought Ryan, as naked branches swayed in the late afternoon sun. Ryan nodded without comment as he settled in his seat and gazed out the window.

Two classmates on the bus snickered when the driver singled him out. *Better him than me* was how Ryan interpreted it. Ryan looked down at the book he had been assigned to read, The Outsiders. He had already read the book. He sighed deeply, all that he had imagined in the mirror this morning had come to pass.

He raised his eyes to the trees once more as the bus began to move. The few remnants of their garments hanging on for dear life shaded in decaying brown. As the bus sped up Ryan watched leaves riding the wind flitting along the roadway piling up against any available barrier.

Ryan felt like one of those leaves, still hanging on by a thread. Just let me go. *Worst time of the year to move to a new place*, he thought once more.

When the bus stopped in front of the library, Ryan was among the half-dozen kids who got off. Ryan looked back, the door still open, the driver seeming to study him. Ryan waved. The door closed without comment.

The group went their separate ways with Ryan the only one looking up towards the Gothic structure. He took a deep breath and climbed the granite steps. Standing on the top step he looked back across the street where a dark and angry river flowed southward. Some of the leaves had made it into those frigid waters. Several groups of birds hovered just above the water, they weren't conversing, intent on making the trip south saving their energy. The breeze intensified. Ryan shivered and thought, *don't blame you birds a bit.*

He tugged on the heavy door and entered a world of quiet. The sun's afternoon rays had found a stained glass window, a splash of color landing on the rug. He looked at the walls of books circling the room. *Amazing what a wall can keep at bay. It was quiet, warm, and peaceful in here.* He held great reverence for what was contained within these walls.

Books had always been his best friends. He realized the friends he had discovered in his reading weren't real, their goodness and badness carefully selected on a continuum. Each word that left their mouth had been constructed on the page, edited, and finally agreed to. Yet he still felt they were truer friends than anyone he had met in real life. Of course, he had his real confidant in his book bag.

He found a corner where another of the last beams of the day was warming the table top. He seated himself. The table darkened when a cloud suddenly passed, Ryan smiled, he looked up *blessed night would soon arrive for real.* He removed his journal from his book bag. He opened to his latest entry. It was from nearly a week ago. Ryan wrote to his journal like he was relaying a story to a friend. He began to read what had been on his mind just days ago.

October 25, 1959.

I am living in a new town. We moved here on the weekend. It's all my father's fault.

Let me explain.

My father ran a paper machine at the paper mill in Machias, Maine where we lived before.

I've never been in a paper mill but my father tells me it is very noisy and men have to communicate with hand signals. He told me that, to explain that after all that noise all day he likes quiet when he gets home. Quiet for my father includes sipping Whiskey. He manages to sip at least four drinks every evening. Two before dinner and at least two after in the basement.

One of my earliest memories is my father holding up his whiskey glass in a mock toast then putting his finger to his lips signaling quiet. So, therefore I am a quiet kid, (go figure.)

While I attend school, pay attention, and get good marks, I still consider myself self-taught. Books are my instructors. In addition I have one good friend, there whenever I need him. I tell them about the good and the bad in my life and they simply listen. Sometimes when I re-visit our conversations I learn something new.

One of the things I have learned over time is that my mother has never gotten father's message; his need for quiet. In response to his need for quiet, or maybe in defiance of the whiskey that turns him into a recluse, (from my earliest memory) she has pounded out one classical piece after another on her piano cigarette smoke rising keeping time with the music.

So my father in his own act of defiance to the music and smoke removes himself to the basement every evening one half hour after dinner. My father needs quiet and whiskey. My mother rebels by celebrating noise and a future bout with lung cancer.

My father hears my mother's pounding from the time he enters the yard. Cigarette smoke riding on mother's rendition of a classic fairly bursts through the front door when he arrives. He pretends it doesn't bother him but I know better. The looks he offers her back border on hatred.

Off he goes to the basement every evening after dinner and a half hour with the paper. I don't know exactly how much he continues drinking when he's down there but several times a week he comes home clutching a brown paper bag with a new bottle.

Those whiskey bottles become the safe harbor for the boats he builds to set sail in. I remember how carefully he packed and placed several boxes during our move. How he keeps a steady hand I can't figure. On the rare occasion I see him before bed he stinks of a mixture of whiskey and glue. When he comes up from the cellar he's wearing a strange smile on his face and he's wobbling slightly, maybe it's the glue the whiskey or both. I do know the smile is not for my mother.

When we sit down together to eat (that once a day time we all have to face one another) it gets eerily quiet. The scraping of dishes and the squeaking of drawers the only sounds.

A blue haze hovers just below the kitchen light. That haze is a new feature at the dinner table. My father is usually into his second drink and is already slurring any words that might inadvertently slip out.

I eat very quickly and excuse myself to my room, no one seems to notice me, I probably could get away without being polite. I keep my bedroom door closed and it's only when I enter and close it quickly that I can breathe freely.

After dinner, Father goes to his recliner (which squeaks by the way) and reads the paper for exactly one half hour. He sometimes adds a pipe to accompany his whiskey, a pipe which I know bothers my Mother. She tolerates it with the same look of disdain that he gives to her music and her own smoking addiction. At the end of the half hour he rises and goes into the basement. Since we have moved here he has mostly taken to sleeping in his recliner in the living room or a similar one in the cellar.

As for me, I'm invisible. I don't have any brothers or sisters and from the vibe I've been getting, for I don't even remember how long, I don't think I'm even supposed to be here. I have never been smothered by attention or affection that much I can tell you. I couldn't tell you the last time I was close enough to my mother to smell the perfume she wears. I can't remember the last time my father ruffled my hair in passing. I am never invited to the cellar. My knowledge of what goes on down there is limited to the few times I was left alone in the house and got curious.

Mother was resistant and resentful when Father got his promotion. She lost her piano pupils, (not that many of them if we're being real.) It was one of the few times they mustered the emotion needed to argue. She lost that one.

Anyway, if it could possibly get quieter than before at the supper table, it is now that. I have noticed mother seems to be smoking even more. Since we moved in she has taken to smoking at the dinner table. Wonderful!

This is an old house we've moved into and it creaks and groans in the wind and cold. I have a limb just outside my window that scrapes the glass when the wind blows. When the heat comes on a rush of air rising through the registers adds a ticking sound raising a cloud of dust that already my mother is choosing to ignore. Sometimes I have to shake my head at my mother. Sometimes when she makes me extra mad, in my mind I see her riding a broom.

When I shower, the water pipes in the wall announce the arrival of hot water. I swear I hear noises in the attic that I am forbidden to enter. Add the attic and the basement that I am not allowed to go down into and you can see I have few escape routes in this place.

The sound of my father's hobby within a hobby rise from the registers and beneath the basement door every night, riding the smell of glue. What my father calls <u>blasts from the past,</u> a never ending number of fifties hits, drop one after another on to his turntable and compete with the sounds of the house for attention.

At the top of the house is an attic I have been forbidden to explore. Father said he opened the door and saw a stairway full of junk stored there and pronounced it off limits. So in this old house, that shakes rattles, and rolls (lyrics from one of fathers records) in the wind the only sounds of emotion come from a different mother; Mother Nature. She sounds pissed. Maybe all Mother's poison smoke filters out into the world from this old place. Maybe my father's glue smells as well

I'm Just a kid but a pretty observant one, and over the years I have figured out why things are the way they are in my world. My Mother harbors the belief that she was some great undiscovered music talent and blames having to birth me as the great interruption to her life.

Of course father planted the seed so to speak, which puts him just a rung higher than me; me being the on-going living proof of her failure. I can understand why they are the way they are but it doesn't make it any more fun to be their kid.

Anyway, Father was recently promoted to what he tells me is a white hat position at the mill here in Skowhegan. We moved to a street a short walk from the <u>library</u> ; (Best Decision Ever!)

I have to go to a new school next week, not looking forward to it. By the way did I mention there is no TV in this house, thank God I like to read.

Ryan closed his journal. There was more to read but the shadows were lengthening. *Don't want to be late to enjoy the silence, nope wouldn't want to do that.*

Ryan stretched and checked the wall clock. It was ten after four. He lived just a five minute walk away. He still had some time. He opened to a new page and began to write about his first day in a new school.

He left the Library at 4:55pm and said good night to the librarian on his way out. She looked at him a little oddly. She nodded but didn't speak. She had been very friendly when he got his library card the other day. *Don't tell me Mr. Kneely got the word out to the entire town this quickly*. Ryan sighed. *Probably just imagining things.*

Ryan entered his street lost in thought. The street lamp at the corner was just coming on. As his shadow from the street lamp lengthened he wished for some of that length added to his puny height. He barely registered that coming the other way was someone carrying what appeared to be a heavy book bag. When they neared he saw that it was a girl who offered a shy smile.

Ryan kept walking. She spoke to his back. "I've seen you before."

Ryan turned, "Excuse me."

"You just moved into that old house." She pointed, "Am I right?" Her smile widened revealing a girl with a very solid dental history.

Ryan nodded. He couldn't take his eyes off all that white. In his head he was already revising the children's story, Little Red Riding Hood; *what very white teeth you have.*

"I have also seen you at the library. I am Violet by the way, Violet Mooney."

Like two boxers ready to mix it up they met in the middle of the sidewalk. The girl sat her book bag down. Ryan did the same and introduced himself. They shook hands. Ryan threw the first punch-line, "Have you been stalking me?"

The girl stood a full two inches taller than Ryan, she smiled. "Not stalking exactly." She moved her head from side to side. "More just curious about the new inhabitants." (She then dragged out) "YOU DO LIVE IN THE ONLY HAUNTED HOUSE IN SKOWHEGAN!"

Ryan raised his brow and straightened up to his full height. He slowly turned to his house and frowned, suddenly all the noises he had tried to rationalize took on new possibilities "I have heard strange noises in the night. I thought it was just the furnace." This time it was Ryan moving his head from one side to the other. "Are you serious? Haunted?"

Violet cocked her head, giving Ryan the eye, "I have lived here my whole life. In that brown house on the corner of Summer and Spring Street." She pointed, "Yep, pretty sure your place is haunted."

Ryan didn't comment. He looked up at his house. Darkness was gathering starting to shadow, he needed more information. He gave her the eye right back.

Violet smiled, she was enjoying this, "There was a murder in that house years ago." She let that sit a moment. "No one has lived in it for very long over the years. Lots of stories have followed people moving out, none of them good. I think you might just be the first kid to move in though, at least that I can remember."

Ryan turned his head to the house once more. The shadows were lengthening, fingers of darkness reaching into crevices. "Mother and Father haven't said anything about it." *Of course they wouldn't,* he thought. Sounds he had heard in the last week filled his head.

Watching Ryan's eyes trace the outline of his house lost in thought, Violet piped up, "I'm not trying to scare you, just stating a fact."

Ryan studied this beautiful girl standing before him.

"Suddenly the girl, feeling the warmth of Ryan's gaze, transformed back into a shy girly girl. She blushed and stammered, "Well I'm pleased to meet you, Ryan Trussell."

Ryan stumbled and stammered over his next line. "Do-do you go to the Junior High, Violet Mooney?"

Violet stumbled right back, "No, uh, I go to the private Catholic school at the edge of town."

Ryan entered his own head for the briefest of moments. *He had lived his life as a loner, just a man and his books. In this moment of warmth he wondered what it would be like to have another friend, a girl at that.* He plunged, "Are you going to the library?"

The girl nodded.

"I could carry those books for you." When she didn't answer immediately he added, "I would like to know more about my house."

Violet smiled. "Thank you, I have a research project." She picked up the book bag. She sighed and grunted handing the bag to Ryan, "I have exhausted these sources."

"What are you researching?"

She smiled, "don't laugh. I'm studying the paranormal world." Then she added, "Which as you can imagine is not endearing me to the Sisters who teach at my school." A broad smile appeared. "Which also by-the-way, makes your house a possible learning lab."

Ryan laughed out loud. He looked again at the cold and darkness enfolding his house both from within and without and in the moment Ryan already knew the answer, but he had to ask. "Are you an only child?"

"How did you guess?"

"Because I'm an only child too."

Silence filled the street. He had to explain himself. "I think when you grow up with no one except adults to talk to, (suddenly thinking of his own situation, *or not talk to*) you create a world where you have to find your own answers." He let that sit a moment. "For you it's ghosts." He pointed to his chest, "For me, it's the dark. I actually love the dark. Most people are afraid of the dark, I embrace it. Do you like the dark, Violet Mooney?"

Violet studied this boy. He seemed harmless.

They stood quietly absorbing what they had just shared. Ryan looked at the shadows that continued to remove the objects that give definition and direction. Violet still hadn't responded. Once more he felt the need to explain. Ryan pointed out into the ever growing orb of darkness. "See all the sharp edges of the houses and trees, see how they are starting to round into the great circle of night."

Violet looked at the shadows, deepening now, a seemingly larger part of each object; soon to be consumed. She nodded. "I do see that."

Ryan smiled turning suddenly, "Let me pop in and tell my mother where I'm going. Believe me she won't care.

CHAPTER TWO

At the library they sat at a table in a corner of the room that had also transformed with the coming of night. Violet found several new sources in the stacks and was busy taking notes.

Ryan continued reading his entry from today, once in a while stealing glances at this beautiful girl who just dropped into his life. *Maybe she's a ghost.* He re-read what he had entered earlier this afternoon about his first day of school. Suddenly it didn't sound so overwhelming. He closed the journal and his eyes. He had thought of his new math teacher enough for one day. He would finish writing all that happened today after the day was done happening. He hoped Violet would tear herself away from her research and give him more details about who else might be inhabiting his house. He sat there re-imagining all those creaks and groans he heard in the night. Maybe some had not come from the walls and windows, maybe they came from something or someone else.

When the two parted, Ryan, having walked Violet to her house with the promise to meet tomorrow same time same place - the sidewalk, he skipped home. Lights from a higher source were winking, competing with the scattered street lights as he stood once more in the exact spot where he had met Violet hours earlier. He looked up once again at the dark house he had moved to. New and competing thoughts entered his head, *a possible new friend and a possible new ghost.* The wind came up, Ryan shivered and walked up his driveway.

He entered his darkened house with curiosity raised. He began staring at walls and listening to the noises coming from the refrigerator, the furnace, and the house itself. He was comfortable in the dark. He found his way to the kitchen.

Mother hadn't saved any dinner. He checked the oven, the refrigerator. He sighed, *so what's new?* With just the light from the refrigerator lightening the dark he made himself a sandwich.

He smelled the air that was just now rising when the furnace kicked on, a hint of his father's pipe mingled with stale cigarette smoke. Ryan finished his sandwich in silence and put his plate in the sink. He glanced at the closed cellar door. Along with light escaping, music from the early fifties danced up the steps riding a rush of warm air and glue from the register. A sour sweet smell of liquor and an eye watering smell of glue joined expelled tobacco in conversation.

It was seven thirty pm. Below, his father was drinking while contemplating building or launching a boat in a bottle. His father, well into a Jack Daniel's bottle by now, would not care to hear about Ryan's day.

Ryan turned to the living room and sighed again. Weak light from a street lamp showed the outline of his father's recliner. In Machias, they had a television. Who made the decision to sell their TV when they moved was anyone's guess. Ryan in his innocence thought as a reward for upending his life, there might be a new one with a larger screen waiting when they arrived. Back then he had been restricted to an hour a day of watching but lots of days the voices emerging from that box were the only voices he heard in that house. He sighed and began his climb up to his room. Squeaking steps the only sound.

Ryan didn't really want to speak to his mother but he did have news regarding a musical instrument. She should be glad about that but who knows? He was spared the conversation when he saw her bedroom door closed with no light leaking from beneath. In his room he snapped on the lamp. He faced his book case. *Thank god for books* he thought. He picked up his most recent fiction adventure read, White Fang, and tossed it on his bed.

The news of a musical instrument could wait till morning. He chuckled as he thought back. *His mother had reminded him ongoing and without fail since he was six that he needed to broaden himself and take up a musical instrument. 'Not the piano, though' she admonished with a tight little smile after forcing the boy to take piano lessons from her for a month. That had been enough for both of them. The final week in which his mother was slapping his hands and rolling her eyes, even as she took a long drag off one of her fags, Ryan's fingers with a mind of their own coveted the wrong keys time after time. The lesson, and the grand experiment, ended with a bang of the keyboard cover followed by a stern look. Following another drag on a cigarette, and a long troubling cough, the subject of music was permanently ended. She eventually stubbed out her cigarette in one of the many ash trays that decorated the house. When she emerged red faced from one last coughing spasm she ceremoniously locked the keyboard. Her tight little smile followed. Then she lit up another one.*

What he was going to tell his mother if he ever happened to run across her was that his music teacher asked him if he played an instrument. Ryan had told her he had taken piano lessons as a young boy. That seemed to be a good enough answer. The teacher, young, pretty, and female, walked him to an oversized closet and introduced him to the only instrument left. Her smile and sincerity offered the only calm to what had been a frightful day; at least till he met Violet. Anyway, Ryan would be bringing home a French Horn next week.

He hoped his mother would be proud. Ryan didn't really know what to expect from the experience but thought his mother might be pleased that he was responding to her constant nagging.

The teacher told him the French Horn produced a subdued, understated sound, offering accent to a music piece. She finished with, 'It doesn't draw attention to itself.' Ryan like that idea.

He washed up, brushed his teeth, and took a long hard look in the mirror. Lot's to write about. But first he needed to review the book, The Outsiders.

Later he finished up in his journal what the first day at Skowhegan Junior High School had been like. He drew an asterisk and in bold letters wrote, **I met a friend today and her name is Violet Mooney. More to follow, I hope.**

Later in bed in the dark, eyes wide open, armed with new information about his house, he listened as the wind rattled the windows and walls. The furnace kicked on and he smelled heat surrounding him. All his senses on high alert he listened like never before. His eyes probed the dark. He heard his father come up from the basement, mix a drink add ice, and settle into the leather recliner in the living room.

Ryan finally closed his eyes and a more active darkness overtook him. In his restless sleep his mind conjured up guns, knives, axes, and chains and people walking through walls.

VIOLET

Just up the street, Violet lay in her own bed thinking she just might have met someone who understood her. Her parents were the exact opposite of Ryan's. The two compared notes at the library table and Violet thought she had a better deal going. Her parents doted on her and one another to an extreme. They carried their faith like Violet carried her book bag— full to overflowing. At least they loved her she determined.

She told Ryan a little of what she knew of the ghosts in his house. Now that she had a possible way into that house they had agreed to meet again tomorrow on the sidewalk. They would walk together to the library to research any written local history on the matter. *Then maybe a field trip*. The thought made her smile.

She breathed in the remaining smell of a well thought out dinner that had been kept warm for her. She sighed. She loved her parents she just wished they lived more in the present. If they couldn't find it in the bible they weren't interested. She was in the final year of the Catholic school here in town. Her parents were already trying to figure out the finances for sending her to a private Catholic high school. Violet had no intention of doing that. That just might raise some pulses in this house. She closed her eyes to the thought of being dragged kicking and screaming into a van with the words, **Mother of Mercy High School**, written on the sides.

Violet had a strong reason to remain in this town. Her mother wouldn't understand or even discuss what Violet was feeling. That might just all change now that she had made a new friend. A friend with a key that just might unlock the mystery that haunted her.

RYAN

Ryan awoke at 2:22 am, moonlight lightening the edges of his blind. He had slept restlessly watching every hour arrive right on time. He sat up and studied the quiet, the old house was finally sound asleep. He put his robe on over his pajamas and stepped into his slippers. The few things that Violet had told him filled his head. The drama that happened in this house would be researched tomorrow afternoon. The who, the what, and the why contained in newspaper records might give Ryan a clearer picture of who else might be living in his house.

For now Ryan simply needed a glass of milk. The whole day had been overwhelming. He walked down the stairs trying his best to keep them from creaking. That same moon offered a silhouette of his father splayed out and fidgeting in his chair; apparently at war with his wife even in his sleep. The single blanket thrown over him rose and fell as if taking on a life of its own.

The dark of night was supposed to be the time that ghosts and goblins roamed the earth. Ryan had Violet in his mind when he climbed the stairs with his glass of milk in hand. He could hear the heat ticking on. A noise descended from the attic. Ryan looked at the forbidden door. He had half a mind to climb up there. Just as he turned to enter his room his eyes widened. The father he had just seen below fidgeting in his recliner seemed to be just now closing the door to the bathroom. Ryan turned back to the head of the stairs, his heart raced. *Holy shit I think I just saw a ghost.* He could feel his pulse quicken. He waited just outside his bedroom door until his father left the bathroom and walked back down the stairs. He heard the basement door open and his father squeak down the cellar steps. Ryan quietly descended the stairs quivering and shaking. When he got near the bottom he craned his neck and peered into the living room. Someone was damn well sleeping in that recliner and it wasn't his father. He took a deep breath and took the stairs back up three at a time his feet barely making contact with the steps. Back in his room he snapped on the desk lamp. He opened his journal and began conversing with his one loyal friend. **Violet did you plant this seed in my head? Am I hallucinating? Or did I meet one more possible friend today. At least I hope they become a friend.** Ryan continued to shiver. He signed his name and dated this particular passage. Why he did this he didn't understand but somehow it felt important. He snapped off his lamp and jumped into bed it was cold even with the furnace running. He continued to shiver beneath the covers. He did not sleep well.

FRANK

Frank having to share the recliner so the man of the house could spend some of his nights there was not pleased. As he fidgeted beneath the blanket he tried to remember, which caused his head to ache. Remember what? His short term memory had been dislodged by the blow to the head that had ended his life. Events came back in painful flashes when they came back at all. He began speaking aloud hoping someone was listening "*Now the little shit knows I'm here. That's a beginning. Hope I didn't scare the bejesus out of him. He might prove useful. Haven't had a kid here since hell I don't remember.*"

Frank's long term memory was more intact and his mind blossomed like a flower all the way back to when it became

lights out. His head didn't hurt as much when he let the distant past take center stage. His son came to mind who was about the age of this new kid when Frank's light was permanently dimmed. *Whining about Christmas and his birthday and everything else under the sun, it makes me want to puke.* The present returned in a flash of pain. *This kid seems way smarter than my ass of a son. I've watched this kid writing in a book. He's always got a book in his hand. He's already made friends with that girl who always seems to be sneaking around here looking in windows.* He had to take a breath his head hurt so much.

ALICE

Alice raised some dust as she entered the living room making her presence felt. "*Alice you always fly into a whirl when that girl is outside. I haven't figured it out but there must be a connection. I wish you could talk to me.*"

Frank's short term memory blinked out in a wave of pain. He was left sitting there holding his head and wondering what he had just been thinking about. He gripped the leather chair arms like he was manning a rocket and sat back with his eyes closed. His mind winked, the pain causing him to wince. "*It's getting cold up in that damn attic. And those damn flies. They want out as bad as we do. Alice in your own way you have made it clear it's time we really get to know this family. Is that young girl going to be part of this?*"

Silence filled the room.

"Of Course I know you can't come right out and say it Alice."* His eyes watered with the effort. The past returned and brought a measure of relief. "*Anyway, I always suffered from

C.R.S. (can't remember shit), that's what my wife used to tell me before she killed me. At least I think it was her who killed me?" **Frank's brain was like a Mexican jumping bean.** ***When his mind cleared he continued, "This boy's mother, just like my wife, has proven to be a whacko. And Christ she's killing herself with those damn cigarettes. Hey news to use sweetheart, dead ain't that much fun."***

Frank went down to one knee, holding his head and closing his eyes.

Alice was listening to all this and shaking her head. ***The boy's mother is not the only whacko in this house,*** **she thought.**

Frank popped back up ***"Now The father he drinks as much as I used to. I kinda like him. He reminds me of the old me, except he ignores his kid, me I used to slap my kid upside the head. So there's a lot of drama downstairs. Which could prove to be a very good thing."*** **Frank rose with a withering headache and painfully climbed up the stairs. He stopped and studied the door to the boys' bedroom. Alice was just coming out. He had never physically seen the woman but a rush of air signified her presence. She must have just put her touch on some things. They re- entered the attic together.**

RYAN

Ryan checked the chair in the living room when he came down for breakfast. It was empty. His mother was not in the kitchen to greet him which also seemed to have become a pattern since the move. His father must have left for work. Ryan ate a bowl of cornflakes. He smelled the bottle of milk before pouring and it was still usable, though it wouldn't survive another day. His mother seemed to be shopping for groceries less and less.

Seemed like she only left the house to load up on cigarettes. The amount of food in the pantry seemed to lessen the day the move to Skowhegan was announced and had continued to dwindle. Ryan checked his belt, it certainly had not loosened since he had arrived. *How am I ever going to get a dog at this rate?* His mother had become more and more a recluse ensconced in a cloud of blue haze. When she did bring food more often than not it was food that Ryan could prepare himself. *Peanut butter must be a top seller down at the market*, thought Ryan as three jars faced him on the pantry shelf. *Tuna was making a comeback too.* No shortage of white bread for all those sandwiches. As he slurped his cereal, his mind turned to last night. *Maybe he did imagine it. Anyway he'd have a story to tell Violet this afternoon.*

The walk to school was a repeat of yesterday but Ryan noticed the river looking angrier this morning. *Do rivers become restless like I was last night?* Ryan was musing as a newspaper on someone's porch step caught his attention. Suddenly he was thinking maybe he'd like to find a source of income, which brought Violet to mind. He might have future need of some ready cash.

His civics teacher had not bought into Mr. Kneely's view of him, at least not yet. Maybe he could direct Ryan on how to get a job delivering the morning newspaper.

A new batch of leaves scampered across his path, ghost like. Tonight was Halloween. I wonder if Violet intends to Trick or Treat. The early morning sun dazzled the frost covered ground.

In his mind, *Crisp* would be one of two words for the day, *cold* the other, Ryan feared the cold just might seep into every classroom he entered, riding the rumors of yesterday. Ryan shivered and took his first deep breath of the day, it left him as a cloud of vapor.

Yeah *crisp and cold* for sure. A final thought as his school came into view was of someone sitting in that chair in the dark.

When he reached his homeroom there was a message for him to go to the office.

The secretary buzzed the guidance counselor. Ryan waited on a hardwood bench watching students move through the hallway to their first class. Several banged on the glass not knowing Ryan, but celebrating someone possibly waiting to be disciplined.

His homeroom and science teacher, Mr. Corey, had dismissed Ryan to the office in a way that was not encouraging. *Cold* seemed to be the right word.

Miss Donaldson ushered him to a small table in her office. A manila folder with Ryan's name on it was ready and waiting.

She smiled. "It seems you have been a very capable student in the past." She let the comment sit. She studied him. "So what's this rumor that has already reached me that a wise guy has joined our student body." Her eyes registered her concern. "Have I put you in all the wrong classes? You trying to make me look bad Ryan?"

"It was a terrible beginning Miss Donaldson, but it was by accident. Mr. Kneely wouldn't give me the chance to explain and now all my teacher's think I have the plague or something.

I'm hoping when they see my records they will see that I am a serious student."

"My experience with Mr. Kneely is you get one chance and he does not forgive or forget. I can move you to a different math teacher but this is a small school." She shifted in her seat, "You have a label as a wise guy pinned to your chest." She cocked her head, "Now I will share your records with your other teachers and in time if you keep your head down and do what's asked of you, this will all pass."

Ryan sat up straight. "I will stay in his class. He'll see that I am capable. Why is he so angry anyway? He acts like he hates his job."

Miss Donaldson cleared her throat, "You need to understand, Mr. Kneely is our most senior Instructor and he wields a good deal of influence. I have been here ten years myself and haven't figured him out so I find it better to just go along to get along." With that bit of counseling she shooed me along to class.

Ryan entered math class late once again, giving Mr. Kneely an opening.

"So Ryan Trussell, will you be arriving late to class on a regular basis?" The class was hearing all this. "Do you keep your own hours?" The kids in the back began chuckling, Mr. Kneely did not admonish them. "Is everything all right at home?" The man actually chuckled when he said this. The kids laughed right out loud.

Ryan didn't speak he merely handed him the note Miss Donaldson had given him.

Mr. Kneely crumpled the note and pointed to the back, "join your cronies Ryan, and try to stay awake."

Several times during the lesson Ryan raised his hand to offer an answer Mr. Kneely posed. He was ignored. Mr. Kneely seemed to take pleasure in the role he had selected for the new boy.

In the rest of the classes things seemed a little less frigid. Miss Donaldson had given Ryan's academic history to his other teachers and it seemed they would decide for themselves which

Ryan Trussell had arrived in Skowhegan, Maine. His Civics teacher seemed to want to give Ryan the benefit of the doubt. Ryan asked him how a kid would go about getting a paper route. He was given the address of the newspaper in town.

Lunch was easier still when a different teacher was on duty. Seeing Mr. Kneely once a day was plenty enough.

Physical Education was held twice a week and this afternoon was Ryan's introduction to Mr. Wyman and full contact Flag Football. Mr. Wyman had played both High School and College football and thought those (girdles) as he called the belt with colored plastic flags attached, was for sissies.

When the whistle blew to gather round Ryan knew none of this.

Ryan prided himself on being quick and elusive though a bit underweight. Mr. Wyman asked him if he had played before. Ryan assured him he had. With that established he was assigned a team. Surprisingly, Ryan was told he would be carrying the ball on the first play. Handed the ball, several quick moves got him into the open. Just as he feinted left he was hit from behind by what felt like a Mack truck. His wind was taken away and he found himself looking up at those bare limbs that were visible from the classroom. Ryan couldn't breathe and couldn't move. Through it all he managed to hear a whistle and assumed someone would be penalized for an obvious infraction. The boy who had hit Ryan was standing over him with the flag in his hand.

Mr. Wyman walked over and studied Ryan for a moment. Then he smiled down, announcing, 'second down.'

When recovered sufficiently to rejoin the game Ryan's teammates looked at him sheepishly. One spoke up, "Gotta watch your back in this game."

Ryan nodded. He managed to limp through the rest of the game but refused to carry the ball again. *Wow*, he thought to himself *new rules for everything in this school it seems.*

Ryan got on the bus without comment and moved to the seat assigned yesterday. His back hurt. The driver didn't even make eye contact. Let off at the library once again it would be an hour or more before Violet would be dismissed from her school and meet him on the sidewalk. Plenty of time to reflect on last night and his second day of class. Ryan looked again to the river, today a bit lighter with fewer clouds dotting the sky. *Let's hope my days get brighter as time goes on*, he nodded to himself. He stretched and winced at the pain in his back then climbed the granite steps.

Seated at the same table as yesterday, Ryan opened his journal. In parentheses **(day two)** headed the page. With pen in hand trying to organize his thoughts they all seemed to run together. What emerged from the tip of his pen as if guided by someone standing outside himself was a clever capture of what his new beginning had felt like. Suddenly all that had happened since he arrived flowed from his pen.

{Introduced to a naked landscape stripped of all I had been before is this my new beginning all that lays beyond that door?

Seeping cold, closed minds and hearts, not a welcome to be found.

But yesterday brightened when on a sidewalk I found common ground.

A new friend perhaps, maybe more who knows, my heart flutters with possibility.

Then in the dead of night in my father's chair someone made themselves known to me.}

Ryan closed his journal after reading what he had written, several times. *Yowzie, things are changing, my writing is even different.*

The sun was sinking on the horizon as he stood waiting for Violet. Ryan found what he thought was the exact spot and braced himself against an ever increasing wind. He couldn't wait to tell her of last night's experience. Violet appeared from a distance seeming to float along the sidewalk the book bag weightless. Thoughts of ghosts and goblins again filled his head.

When she arrived, Ryan had a new bed time story to tell her about even as he added a line to his personal <u>Little Red Riding Hood</u> story. She was smiling, cheeks blushed by the raw wind, and hat-less, her ebony hair defying gravity. Ryan chuckled aloud. *What rosy red cheeks you have.*

"Am I that funny looking Ryan?" Her eyes danced.

"Not at all. I was just rewriting a children's story," Ryan stammered, "By the way I have news fit to print."

She looked at him quizzically.

"Do you remember in the kids' story, Goldilocks, when the bears complain that someone had been sleeping in their beds?"

Violet looked at Ryan quizzically.

"Well, last night, someone was sleeping in my fathers' chair, and it wasn't my father."

Violet nodded excitedly, "See I told you." She danced up and down. She began singing while continuing to dance, "You are living in a haunted house, a haunted house, a haunted house." Then she calmed down. "I have walked past that place for years and even peeked in a window or two, she confessed breathlessly. So tell me all about it."

By the time they reached the library Violet knew as much as Ryan. At a table near the stacks they talked quietly about possible next steps and the irony of tonight being the one time ghosts and goblins were encouraged to roam the dark.

"Let's throw on an old sheet and explore the town tonight, Ryan, I'll show you some of my old haunts, ha ha."

Ryan possibly having come into actual contact with a spirit wasn't feeling the humor. "Maybe I'll just take the night off Violet, I've had enough of ghosts for the time being."

"Scaredy cat," teased Violet, her eyes sparkling.

Ryan couldn't allow what appeared to be a dare to stand. "I'll walk you home and we'll meet in the middle of this very sidewalk at six thirty. And I won't be wearing a sheet."

CHAPTER THREE

Ryan put on one of his father's old jackets and a floppy hat. He covered his face with his mother's cold cream. Violet arrived dressed as a scarecrow. Violet took Ryan's hand and they knocked on doors throughout the neighborhood. He liked the feeling of Violet's hand in his but she seemed to think nothing of it.

He wondered to himself if he might be delivering the morning paper to these porches soon. It all felt so innocent. People opening doors and depositing candy into paper bags, carved pumpkins lining the steps, ghosts and goblins at least for the night treated as royalty. Everyone was smiling as they held out their candy bowls. Ryan took Violet's hand.

When Ryan arrived home in the dark after walking Violet to her door, he noted his house showed no seasonal decoration. His mind conjured up part of an old Halloween verse. *Cold black cat's, witches hats, Halloween*. On his porch there were no wide grinning pumpkins, no nothing. He breathed in the darkness then entered his home.

He went up to the bathroom and removed his makeup. A million thoughts entering his head as the cold cream disappeared. He looked once to the attic door then went down to the kitchen. His own house had not welcomed kids onto the porch. He found his way to the refrigerator and hauled out the makings of a tuna sandwich. The tuna was dried out. Who-ever opened it left it uncovered. Ryan sighed. By the light from the refrigerator, he poured a glass of milk. The whiteness of it entering the glass brought thoughts of white shrouded ghosts that up until very recently had been limited to Casper the friendly Ghost. Ryan continued to have ghosts on his mind as he munched his sandwich listening for sounds that might signal unusual movement in the walls.

When his mother came down the stairs she turned on the light. "Why on earth are you sitting in the dark?" She shook her head studying her son. She lit up a cigarette and sat opposite him, not saying a word but adding smoke and smell to Ryan's meal. She went into a coughing jag and her cigarette slipped from her hand to the floor. Ryan picked it up and placed it in the ash tray. His mother didn't even realize what had happened. Ryan thought, s*he's going to burn the place down*.

When her spasm passed, once again she sat looking at her son. *She's inspecting me*, Ryan thought to himself as his mother seemed to be looking for head lice or some such. Ryan cleared his throat. He told his mother about the musical instrument he would be bringing home next week. He also mentioned he was going to try a paper route if he could get hired.

His mother frowned, her nose twitched like a bad odor had entered the room. Ryan noticed. "*That's cigarette smoke mother.* "

"Well you and your horn can join your father in the basement." A tight knowing smile followed. "We remember the piano and all the success you had with that now don't we?" She smiled once more as more poison left her lips and more entered as she re-lit her cigarette. "Perhaps you two can bond over his records being played in succession. And when you add the noise you'll be making, you two will succeed in truly driving me crazy." Her eyes widened as she took a long pull, then hacking briefly, she brightened. "I have an even better idea. If the basement doesn't work you can take over the attic."

She stubbed out her smoke and moved to another topic Ryan had raised. Once again she had all the answers. "As to you getting a paper route. Hmmph. Don't expect me to get you up at 4:30 in the morning, you're on your own there." Not waiting for a response or missing a beat she rose and added an exit line. "Turn out the light when you have finished and put your dishes in the sink please, I have enough to do around here." She turned and climbed the stairs, a hack competing with each squeak of a stair tread.

Ryan moved his head from side to side chewing his sandwich. Cigarette smoke continued to drift down from the ceiling, lingering. The lack of affection that had just left the room lingered as well.

In the moment a thought of what his music teacher had said, *a subdued sound not drawing attention to itself.* Ryan was feeling like that French horn this evening himself. *He would not be drawing any attention in this house that's for sure.* He rose sighing, moved to the sink and washed and rinsed his glass and plate putting them in the draining rack.

He moved to the basement door with the little bit of light leaking from beneath and thought about trying to talk to his father. The lyrics of the song, Green door escaped from the same breach. The line, 'what's that secret you're keeping' climbed the stairs keeping him from turning the knob. He certainly was not ready to tell his father the secret of what he had experienced last night. His father, lost in his vapors, would belittle him for sure. Anyway he needed more information to verify what he'd seen.

He climbed the stairs, paused, looked at his mothers' door then his own but moved past them towards a door he had not opened; the attic. No one had been up there since his father had announced it was off limits. He took a deep breath and snapped on the light. From above a faint dimness descended the stairs highlighting piles of debris on each step. A buzzing sound reached his ears and rose in pitch. He looked up a staircase steeped in shadow. Boxes and bags of who knows what, filled to overflowing lined each step on both sides. The dim light sent odd shapes and shadows down the stairs. Ryan heard a scurrying sound from above, he took a deep breath. The buzzing sound Ryan could not identify seemed to be getting louder still. A rush of air filled Ryan's nose and he sneezed loudly. The air seeping down over the stairs was cold as though a window might be partly open. Ryan took a deep breath. With one hand filtering his mouth he began his trip to the top. His first step brought a crunching sound of what he imagined as the body of a spider or fly that had died there. Magazines broke away from their captivity as bags disintegrated crumbling around his feet and falling to the bottom as he moved gingerly upward. The crunching of dead insects didn't lessen as he moved. He grabbed the railing on his left for support even as he held his nose with the other. The hand gripping the railing closed on icky webs and dead critters. Ryan shivered.

When he reached the top step he expelled his breath and sneezed into his hand. He stood motionless wiping his hands on his pants. His eyes exposed a long and narrow room. A bare wood ceiling with sharply sloped wall were lined with who knew what. Shadows hung like drapes in the dim light. A single window on the far end offered little additional illumination. The single bulb descending from a cord was dimmed by a coating of dust and fly droppings.

Hundreds of flies were circling the light as if gathering strength. They rushed in a frenzy to the window and tapped on the glass. *So turning on the light caused this,* thought Ryan. Still at the top step, motionless, He scanned the room looking for the unexplainable. A thought, *Could a ghost live up here*? Lining the eaves shrouded by near darkness was more of what he had waded through on the steps, castoffs of all description. *Could one of those cartons harbor a ghost*?

It was a room that seemed built to entice the dark, and in Ryan's newly formed opinion, maybe a ghost. Ryan took another deep breath. *I like the dark so maybe this room won't be so bad after-all.* Ryan began to gingerly walk around. Dead flies littered the floor. He crushed their empty shells with every step. Odd pieces of furniture hiding behind and beneath what appeared to be old rugs, showed themselves. Ryan moved to the center of the room. He looked toward the window where more mounds of old newspapers and magazines some loose some piled sat next to a straight backed chair. The chair seemingly placed as if to look out that lone window.

Ryan walked to the chair. It was coated with dust. He found an old curtain covering a lamp, removed it and wiped the chair seat then sat down. He looked down toward the street. From this vantage a street lamp in the distance offered a view of a darkened sidewalk in front of his house. *Hmm, that's odd* thought Ryan. He let his imagination take over. *Does someone sit here watching from that window? Does someone read these newspapers*? Ryan shook these thoughts away as the buzzing in his ears grew more frantic. More and more of the flies had left their hiding places, awakened their neighbors, and now circled the light. Then like a flock of geese moving south, they joined forces and moved to the window, tapping the window glass in a frenzied dance. Were they too trying to escape? Ryan batted them away. He rose and looked for a switch on the wall. He wanted to end their madness. The noise was deafening. There was no switch that Ryan could find. Ryan studied the light itself then dragged the chair to the center of the room. He stood on the chair and turned the knob on the cord immediately bringing blackness to the room. The buzzing quieted. The darkness was settling to Ryan. He took a deep breath and when his eyes readjusted he followed the sliver of illumination entering the room from the street. He stayed perched on the chair studying the room from a new height. He stepped down and moved the chair back to the window. He looked down once again. The street was deserted. He settled back into the chair. He chuckled to himself, *so this is where I learn to play the French horn.* He continued to muse, *who's been sitting in my chair?* A hundred thoughts rolled through his head. *The form in the recliner, Violets knowledge and belief in ghosts, Halloween, his mother's indifference, his father's drinking, Mr. Kneely what was he all about, his gym teacher, the French horn. Maybe a paper route.* Ryan was suddenly just plain tired. He dozed.

It was in the dark and quiet of the attic that the voice reached him. At first Ryan thought he was still asleep or that the flies had started buzzing again; but it wasn't that. It was a voice that seemed to attach itself to his bones. It was like a voice leaving his own body circling then reaching his ears. It was a man's voice.

An angry voice.

"That was me aggravating your father's favorite chair. I used to have a chair on that very spot. I want my damn chair back." This outburst was followed by a cry of a man in pain.

Ryan shook his head as he tried to take in what had just been said. *If it had even been said,* Ryan wasn't sure. He looked around, darkness still enveloped him. Ryan held his breath not daring to breathe in or out. He looked back out the window. He waited, still holding his breath. No other sound reached him. Scared and rattled he expelled as little air as possible and began counting to himself, a calming measure he had used since mastering numbers. Through clenched teeth he breathed in a bare minimum, numbers leaving his head worrying he might just inhale a straggling fly. He rose and made his way back to the stairs. He looked back a final time at what might be a ghost's lair. He expelled the last of his breath feeling his heart racing. He navigated the stairs in total blackness. He slipped several times on the cascading magazines but caught himself with the railing. He closed the door. He took a deep breath he was sweating. He entered the bathroom and washed his hands and splashed water on his face. Still breathing heavily Ryan studied his face in the mirror. He was ghost white. Eyes wide, sweating, he sat on the toilet and thought of Violet's textbook analysis of a typical ghost. Thinking of Violet seemed to quiet his breathing. *Well this is my first,* thought Ryan, *first possible girlfriend and now possible first ghost.* It all seemed anything but typical. *He hadn't been touched or threatened. But the voice sounded angry. Was it a warning? Something was said about his father's chair. Do ghosts really swear?*

All those thoughts and more were logged in his journal. Ryan lay awake for a long time, sleep was fitful when he opened his eyes it was 2:22am. exactly twenty four hours since his first sighting. *How does that happen?* He retraced his steps down for a glass of milk. He heard his father snoring loudly in his recliner. Ryan sipped the milk not having the words yet to share with his journal. He slept soundly for the rest of the night. Only once did he wake, finding himself suddenly cold, as if the window had been opened or his covers thrown off. He folded his shoulders deeper into his blankets and dreamed. *A beautiful girl was holding his hand and leading him along a busy street of a much larger town. When they crossed the street he looked up at a sign welcoming a rock band to Bangor, Maine. A picture of the band and date of the concert was posted: July 15, 1960.*

When he woke what had happened in the attic was still with him. So was the dream. Why was he dreaming of a city he had only passed though once on his way to his new home? And that girl in his dream sure looked like his new friend, Violet.

Ryan smiled, perhaps there was a future. *If I can just survive the present*, he sighed.

FRANK and ALICE

In the attic the straight backed chair was occupied once again. The weak light from the window brought shape to a form sitting much like the famous sculpture labeled, The Thinker.

Head bowed, fist under his chin, seemingly lost in thought. Actually this thinker had a splitting headache. "*So the boy has found my lair. Did I scare him Alice?" Frank groaned but continued, "What is he planning to do up here?* The pain entered his eyes. "*It's getting cold as hell up here. I don't imagine he'll be doing much for very long. He needs to leave the light off, those damn buzzing flies make me dizzy. They should all be gone soon at least. And hopefully so will I. Or should I say we?"*

In response Alice added her two cents worth in her own airy way. "*You are way too angry Frank. And your thinking is like the flitting of those flies. Let's not frighten the boy away. I brought him a bit of comfort. I had him dreaming about*

***the girl."* Alice's message to Frank arrived in a ruffle of the curtain Ryan had used to wipe the chair.**

VIOLET

Just down the street Violet had spent the evening at her desk in her bedroom opened to an article that reinforced her belief in ghosts.

Some ancient cultures formed the belief that both man and animal had a soul that left the body upon death. There was also the belief that a soul could be trapped between the world of the living and the dead.

Violet believed that in certain situations, especially situations of extreme violence, a soul could remain in limbo. She closed the book and opened her mind.

She had more than research in mind, she had a purpose. If she could trust this new friend she might let him in on her real reason for studying the paranormal.

She thought back to her conversation with Ryan at the library. She had showed him article after article that supported her beliefs. "So don't panic Ryan, I don't believe this ghost will hurt you. In fact he or she might be looking for a way to leave this world." She looked intently at Ryan, "They might ask for your help. In whatever form that's needed."

Violet readied for bed. She just knew she had been right all along. Her head nodded in agreement with herself as she thought back to the first time she had met her grandmother without ever meeting her. She pondered. *How do I convince Ryan that the ghost he's met might have a housemate?*

RYAN

November, can be fickle. In the North Country, November can land as lightly as a small child's kiss or in any given year land as a cold kiss of death for all vegetation.

This morning Ryan noted a heavy frost had landed overnight. Standing on the sidewalk, he looked up at the attic window. He imagined he saw someone looking down at him. He shook his head. *Probably just the frost on the window.* He shook his head again chuckled, and looked once more. The old adage he had heard a hundred times reached his lips, "It's just your father's shirt-tail," he said in a quiet voice.

He noticed things he had not seen before on his morning walk to school. Plastic wrap strangled house borders, wood piles seemed to have grown overnight. Black smoke exited chimneys. *When did this all happen*? Windows were frosted over, vapor was leaving the tail pipes of automobiles. Ryan wondered if his recent encounter with a ghost was making him more attentive to detail.

At school, Ryan began noticing things too. Mr. Kneely should have gotten the message by now that Ryan was not a wise guy. Ryan did his homework didn't horse around. His other teachers had moved past Mr. Kneely's assessment. *What is it about me the man doesn't like?*

At home in the attic the flies had about given up. Ryan scooped up dozens of their bodies' daily; mass suicide just below the window. The glass was stained with these suicide missions. A few battered stragglers continued to berate the window as long as light remained in the sky. The chair had not moved from its place overlooking the sidewalk.

Ryan hadn't heard from his house guest since that first encounter but tonight on his way into his house, he glanced up at that window. Though it was possible the frost was forming early tonight he swore he saw movement and a flash of white appear, staring down at him. When he climbed those stairs later, all he found was more war dead. He swept them up and added their bodies to a cardboard coffin of fatalities.

After spending time trying to coax more than a squawk out of the French Horn, Ryan had begun reading the newspapers on the floor. They dated back to the 1940s. He read headlines signaling the Second World War would be ending shortly after Two Hydrogen bombs leveled cities in Japan.

Pictures of men returning to their families were growing with every hopeful headline, everyone smiling in black and white.

The papers were in chronological order so every night Ryan did in the attic what his father did in the living room; he spent a half hour reading local state and national news. His news just happened to be old news.

He did not find news that supported Violets belief that a death had occurred in this house. Maybe the death took place before someone started collecting these papers. He'd have a day off soon which would give him the time to dig deeper. In the schools, November begins the rush up to the holidays.

Veteran's Day, was soon to be observed. Teachers didn't seem to get the message that on-coming winter signaled a time to slow things down. Homework was being piled on like an extra set of clothing.

Ryan felt he was beginning to fit in; sort of. Ryan wrote in his journal of a mundane day. *A day with Mr. Kneely is like one of the breakfasts my mother dreams up; very unsatisfying. I am mostly making my own breakfast these days. My real day begins when I meet Violet on the sidewalk,*

This afternoon we decided to spend Veteran's day trying to make a connection with the voice that has not spoken since that first night. I have shared what I believe I heard with Violet. We are both stymied by what it might mean. I have not seen the man occupying my father's chair since the first sighting. I am beginning to doubt myself.

Violet is not in doubt and can't wait for the day off. Violet will ask one of her friends to cover for her with her parents and will spend some time in my room. I have assured her no one in this house will be the wiser.

Ryan made it through math class with no comments directed at him on this last day before an extended weekend. He rose with the bell, gathered his book bag, and with head down began to exit the room. Mr. Kneely cleared his throat and spoke to his back. "Mr. Trussell, a word?"

Ryan turned, "Yes sir."

Mr. Kneely's features darkened, his eyes glared then glazed, his voice deepened. "You think you have everyone fooled, don't you?" He let the comment sit like one of the classroom farts that fouled the air daily.

"But you don't fool me." His head nodded, "I rarely misjudge a situation or a student."

Ryan had no clue where this was going.

"I understand you are living in that old house on Summer Street." His eyes lit up strangely. "You know, people don't stay there long." That was it. Mr. Kneely gathered up his planner and exited the room.

Ryan was left speechless.

Mr. Kneely's words haunted the rest of Ryan's day. But he had plans for a brighter afternoon. He stopped in at the down town office of the Morning Sentinel. A woman was sitting at a desk with eyes on what appeared to be the classified section of the newspaper. Ryan wondered as he waited standing at her desk if the woman was looking for a new job. *That wouldn't be a good sign*. The woman finally looked up when Ryan cleared his throat. Ryan asked who he would need to talk to about a paper route. The lady sized him up and smiled to herself. She kept her thoughts to herself and directed him to a desk where an old man with a pencil behind his ear, wearing a Boston Red Sox hat, and smoking a cigar, hunkered down. Smoke curled around his ears. Ryan thought, *do all adults fill their lungs with that stuff?* On his desk was a wooden sign that read, **CIRCULATION.**

Ryan laughed to himself when he read that. He cleared his throat once more and the man at the desk looked up. Their eyes met through the haze. Ryan thought immediately of his mother surrounded by smoke and sighed. The man seemed to study Ryan for a moment, then signaled him to have a seat even as he rose to open a window. The cigar smoke was replaced by a late autumn breeze. Ryan thought, *my mother should try that*. The man continued to study him up and down and Ryan was suddenly self-conscious of his height. Then the man smiled and introduced himself as Scoop Plummer. Ryan told him who he was and the two shook hands.

"So you want a job in the newspaper business, do you?"

Ryan had to smile, "I would like to deliver newspapers, yes sir."

"So, can you handle it?"

"I think so sir, I'd like to try."

Scoop cocked his head and in a very serious tone delivered the company line. "It's not as simple as just delivering the morning paper, Ryan."

Ryan listened. *Was the man trying to discourage him?*

Each bullet of information was delivered with the proper amount of gravity.

"When you leave a Morning Sentinel on a porch you are the face of the company."

"When a newspaper is late, or doesn't reach a porch, who do you think they call?" Scoop didn't wait for an answer.

"Your job Ryan, is the most important job in the newspaper business."

Scoop watched Ryan's reaction as each bullet struck. He noted the boy didn't flinch when each bullet hit him. He spent a full minute studying this undersized lad who wanted to maybe someday take his job.

Scoop decided. "Ok then. Will a parent be driving you around or will you be on your own?"

Thinking of the stress in his house Ryan was quick to respond. "I can do this on my own."

"You don't have a dog do you? They can be good company on those early mornings."

"No sir, though I'm working on that."

The nitty gritty of route size and collection was gone over and Scoop said Monday morning next, a rack of fifty papers would be waiting at the Spinning Mill on the Island next to the Junior High. The night watchman will assist you. "The man's name is Stan Tuttle, just tell him Scoop sent you." He seemed to study his desk then continued. "You can stop by here any day except Sunday with questions. This is also where you turn in your collection money." He reached into his desk and brought out a sheet of paper. "By the way here is a map of the streets you will be delivering to, and the house numbers. You might want to walk them at least once before you start. He reached out and shook Ryan's hand. "Good luck young man, you are now a newspaper man."

When he reached the library Ryan wrote excitedly about his new job. The excitement of the moment disappeared when the strange conversation with Mr. Kneely reentered his head. He wrote about that too. When Ryan met up with Violet on the sidewalk he repeated what Mr. Kneely had said. "How does my teacher know where I live? And why do I have this feeling that it matters?"

Violet listened but had news of her own. She said she couldn't go to the library this afternoon, her mother was taking her to get her hair done. Violet took off her hat to give Ryan a before look. "My hair will be six inches shorter when you see me tomorrow."

Ryan looked at Violet. "I kinda like the way it is."

"Me too, but my mom thinks it makes me look too wild."

Ryan was about to respond when Violet switched back to the question Ryan had posed earlier.

Violet had never met Mr. Kneely but Ryan had complained about the man every day since they first met. "I think you have to trust your gut about the man, Ryan. We may be on our way to a mystery that is bigger than we thought. I'm excited for the weekend. So here's my plan."

Ryan listened and nodded his head in agreement. He had gotten so caught up in the idea of spending real time with

Violet that he forgot to mention his dream where they shared a future. The idea of spending the weekend with Violet and what they might discover together seemed to be taking a back seat to just being with the girl. He did mention he was starting a job in the newspaper business.

The dream of a trip to Bangor, Maine well into the future was never to repeat itself.

Back in his house Ryan walked the steps to the attic. Daylight entered the room from the window. Ryan opened the case containing the French horn. He was trying to muster a sound from the instrument that didn't sound haunting.

A few flies lay huddled on the window sill. When Ryan put the horn to his lips they buzzed the light.

Ryan the researcher had done a little digging about the origin of this beast he held. He rubbed the brass instrument with new respect. With his recent experience he couldn't help but see the horn as a connection that might include the ancient spirit world. The first horns after all were formed from the horns of animals as they called men to the hunt or brought them closer to the fire. Eventually clever people adapted the horns by adding slides. Finally in the 17th century the beginnings of musical instruments began to take shape. The French Horn really emerged when the Germans created pistons and valves.

The sound brought forth would forever be like one of those quiet unnoticed kids, never drawing attention to themselves.

Ryan put the horn to his lips and in his mind produced what sounded like a real note. He had been practicing diligently in the darkened cold and quiet of the attic for weeks now. When he shared with his music teacher where he practiced she commented that a warmer place might help.

Ryan nodded but he knew that wasn't going to happen. Ryan was doing what he had always done with all assignments; his best, no matter the circumstance. When he finished practicing he put the horn away and picked up headlines from the year 1947. The war was over. Celebrations in every headline. The latest versions of automobiles whose production had been interrupted during the war were on full display in every edition. Ryan found a black and white picture of what looked like the perfect automobile. He riffled through copies of life magazine where colored pictures of these cars dotted the ends of news articles. Some were so expensive they probably would never see the streets of Skowhegan. He found a colored picture of an automobile he had fallen in love with. This one just might have sold from the showroom at the local dealership. It was a Buick, a Maroon 1947 Buick Super Convertible. Were these cars still around somewhere? He wasn't sure they still made them, but maybe. He sighed as he thought of riding with the girl of his recent dream to Bangor, in this vintage auto.

He closed the door on the night and entered his room to review his conversation with his journal. Ryan looked at the scrawled writing that recorded his research effort. The articles he had pulled from the library shelves offered a history of this strange instrument the French Horn which seemed to echo early mans need to communicate. Animal horns pointed to the sky brought announcements to community events. Celebrations, decrees, a hunt. It all began with someone putting their lips to animal horns of various description. These were not musical sounds. They sounded more like what was leaving his horn in the attic. Ryan closed his journal, already wondering what new twist in his life he would be writing about, maybe as soon as tomorrow. He slept restlessly.

CHAPTER FIVE

Frank

In the attic, weekend plans were being developed. *"It's obvious the boy is going to practice that damn instrument up here. Probably banished to the rafters by his tiresome troubled mother." Frank was just warming up. "We have the old man sniffing glue, sipping whiskey and spinning that crap music in the basement. And that mother of his mangling one piano piece after another while she fills the air with smoke in the living room. How's a man supposed to get any peace?" Frank rattled on getting more and more agitated. A sharp pain ended all thought. He took a deep breath and spoke to the air. "Alice, do you have any thoughts on all this?"*

Not even a hint of air movement. *"Hmmph, I didn't think so."* He grabbed his head. *"Well I'm going to visit that damn cellar and see what those damn boats are all about."* He chuckled even as the pain in his head increased. *"I used to get my own inspiration from a bottle."* Frank laughed aloud.

"That was a little joke Alice, don't you see the humor? Geez Louise lighten up!"

RYAN and VIOLET

Thursday morning seemed wrapped in crystal. The frost overnight and a light dusting of snow brought sparkle to the world. Bare limbs a day earlier, this morning the trees wearing their best white finery. The sun dazzled the eyes. The temperature hovered at 26 degrees on this 9:00 o'clock

morning. They met on the steps of the library, closed for the Veteran's Day weekend.

"Let me see your new look Violet, I don't want to spend the day with a bad hair day." He laughed at his little joke.

Violet laughed too as she took off her stocking cap with a flourish, then shook her shorter locks side to side.

"Not as good as the original, but your doo will do," quipped Ryan.

"Okay enough about my hair. What would you like to do until dark, Ryan?"

"Have you had breakfast?"

"My Mom fixed me eggs and toast."

Ryan sighed. "Well, I had cold cereal served up dry since the milk has gone bad again." His nose turned up as if still putting his nose to the bottle. "Let's get a hot chocolate at Whittemore's. I have some things to tell you."

Tucked into a booth sitting side by side at Whittemore's restaurant, Ryan began by asking Violet if she would like to walk the streets where he would be conducting his new business.

Violet looked at him oddly.

Ryan chuckled, "I'm going to deliver newspapers Violet, remember I'm a newsman."

Violet laughed out loud. "You are one strange kid Ryan but sure, take me to your place of employment."

Ryan didn't miss a beat. "In citizenship class we are studying our local government so after visiting my paper route I would like to visit all the places where rules and laws are made and the places that enforce them in this town."

Violet had to smile, "You keep the hits spinning one after another Ryan Trussell, so I am taking you to the Courthouse and the Jail this morning am I?"

Ryan who loved to answer a question with a question offered up, "Have you ever seen a jail cell?" Then added, "I would love to sit in the back of a courtroom and watch a trial, wouldn't you?"

Violet nodded, "It just so happens the Jail and the Courthouse look one another square in the eye in this town. I will point out other little bits of history on the way. Let me see your map" She studied it briefly. "Let's take the long way around to your business streets which will include a trip over the river on an old railroad bridge. Have you crossed it yet?"

"Nope, didn't even know the town had one."

"When we get to your business route, there's another little bridge that will hold your attention," Violet laughed.

They began their trek at the restaurant and walked to the old railroad bridge, stopping to look at the Kennebec River below. Pieces of pulpwood dotted the dark cold water. They turned right and entered Route 201 just before the first of two bridges that held the town together. "Lots of bridges in this little section of town. Believe it or not you are about to cross onto an island." Violet pointed to the spinning mill. "That's where you pick up your papers. Five o'clock in the morning is awfully early Ryan."

Ryan nodded, "yeah it is."

"After you pick up your papers you'll cross that swinging bridge"

Ryan saw the bridge but he also viewed his school standing bleak and cold and uninviting. *He had to enter that building every day. And now he would walk by it twice more every morning. Things had to get better with Mr. Kneely, they just had to.*

When they reached the entrance to the swinging bridge Violet took the first step. A creaking and groaning rose. A short distance across, Violet made a sudden movement then jumped up and down. The groans and creaks echoed her jumps. The bridge rose and Ryan had to grab the railing. Violet laughed, continuing every few steps to again jump up and down causing the bridge to add a step to Ryan's normal stride. Laughter joined the squeaks of the hanging cables as the bounce of the bridge kept normal conversation to a minimum. Ryan took a moment to get his bearings when they reached the end of the bridge. Ryan took a deep breath. "Hopefully, I won't meet anyone crossing early in the morning that was crazy." They walked the streets checking house numbers with Ryan mentally tossing a newspaper on every porch. They finally exited onto Route two and walked back to town.

Violet told Ryan he would be crossing that bridge twice every morning. "So you're right. Let's hope no one is up that time of day."

They re-crossed the railroad bridge stopping once again to study the water below. The two remained quiet. Suddenly Violet suggested they visit her favorite spot in the whole town. "My thinking place," she called it.

The gates of Coburn Park were locked for the season but on foot there was no barrier. The two circled the park, snow thick in the shadows but the gravel road mostly melted. On a second go round they sat on one of the benches that Violet claimed as her own. When they were settled Ryan threw out a question he had been mulling but had not thought through enough to ask. "How did you get interested in ghosts?"

Violet seemed like she had readied herself for just such a question and immediately answered, "My Grandmother."

Ryan raised his brow signaling continue please.

"My Grandmother died on my birthday."

Ryan raised his eyebrows.

"At about the same time of night I was born, actually."

Ryan opened his mouth to speak.

Violet put up a finger signaling she wasn't finished. "I was five years old so I don't remember a whole lot about it, but I still remember her smell and the warmest smile and how she was always tickling me."

Ryan waited.

"Anyway, since that night when she didn't show up for my birthday I have carried strange feelings; a stirring inside me."

Ryan waited.

"I know that sounds weird but I know things about my mother and my grandmother that I shouldn't know." She continued, "Since my grandmother's death, I have visited places with my parents and felt, no not felt but rather knew I had been before.

The feeling always starts with a cool breeze where there shouldn't be one. When my parents began taking me to church and the whole religious ritual that governs their life was being taught to me, I felt like I had heard all this before and had spent a lifetime practicing. Eventually this feeling lessened. But lately it's come back. Even stronger."

"So does your Grandmother ever speak to you?"

"I wish." Violet sighed. "No, she is more subtle than that. She communicates through me, not to me." Violet paused, "If that makes any sense at all."

Ryan, whose only experience had been a vision and a voice, sat quietly mulling this over. "What does that feel like when she's communicating with you?"

"It's like a cool breeze surrounds me, envelops me really. Like I said, it kinda went away but it's back now."

"Do you think she wants something from you?"

"I'm not sure but maybe. The feeling I get is she feels guilty for dying and not being here to help me make sense of my life. Maybe she wants to help me avoid some mistakes her daughter made and some of the pain she herself experienced."

"Why do you say that?"

"Because of the way she died."

Ryan didn't dare ask.

"My Grandmother committed suicide."

Ryan was shocked. His face showed it.

"Don't worry, it only gets worse." Violet half smiled, "I only told you half the truth Ryan when I first met you."

Ryan frowned.

"There was a death in your house. And people do speculate it was murder though no one has ever been charged. But what I didn't tell you was that same house where you write in your journal is where my Grandmother killed herself. And I have questions about the truth of that."

Ryan was speechless but Violet was just getting started.

"I think we met for a reason. I have been trying for the last two years to get a look at that house from the inside. The first time I was allowed to walk to school by myself I went by your house. It was always either vacant or locked up or some weirdo had moved in. There was never a kid living here that I saw. But whenever I walked by I felt my grandmother again."

Violet paused, feeling she had left out an important part, "You have to understand my grandmother was Catholic. Supposedly if a Catholic commits suicide they cannot be accepted in heaven. If that's true I think my grandmother might still be in that house in some form, lost between two worlds." Violet took Ryan's hand, "Something tells me I am being directed to look into my grandmother's death. I'm hoping maybe if I can walk your halls and stairs and sit in the room where she died, she might speak through me and guide me to some answers.

Personally, I think my grandmother was murdered." Ryan was shocked. "What do your parents say about any of this?"

"My mother has not been any help at all. When I bring my grandmothers name into a conversation she grabs her bible and starts to wail. I do know they had not been close for years before she died. She used to drop me off with my grandmother and leave immediately. I have a step dad who was not on the scene at the time so he's no help. He loves my mother to death though and if she doesn't want to talk then there will be no talking."

"Do you have a grandfather on your mother's side?"

"Maybe somewhere, but I never met him. Grandmother was a bit wild in her youth my mother has hinted. No one talks about him, either."

Ryan sighed. He checked his Timex. Then he winked, "Well I think we have just enough time to get an ice cream soda at Leakos' and check out the courthouse and the jail. When it gets dark we'll sneak you into my room."

Violet smiled, "So you have already discovered my very favorite place in town for ice cream and soda. The sisters at my school warn us all about that Leakos' place." 'You will come to no good end if you frequent Leakos', they say, but I just love the cherry cokes and root beer floats."

Ryan took Violet by the hand for the first time. She smiled inwardly as they began their walk out of the park.

Leakos was dimly lit on this Friday afternoon. It was 2pm and the place was deserted. Ryan ordered a Lemon coke while Violet stuck with Cherry. Strategies for getting Violet to Ryan's room were discussed and a plan emerged.

"No one but me goes into the attic. It's getting mighty cold up there though so pack some extra warm clothing." He thought a minute then added, "Hey, you can listen to me play my new instrument," Ryan teased. "Not really." Then he switched gears. "There is a pile of newspapers and magazines in that room that might include an article about when your grandmother died here." His eyes suddenly took on a here comes another joke look, "Now that I'm a newsman myself maybe something will pop right out at me." The joke flopped. "Sorry." Then Ryan became serious again. "When did she die?"

"I was born February 14, 1946. Yes Ryan, Valentine's Day. That is the date she died exactly five years later."

Ryan's eyes lit up. "I have already read newspapers from that time. We'll go back and look again now that you've told me this."

Violet nodded. "When did the man die in this house?"

"I haven't found that out either. Maybe an extra pair of eyes will help."

They walked to the Courthouse and though it was closed for the holiday weekend, across the street the Jail was open for business. Ryan mentally made note of what a future visit might look like. As the day began to pull the shade on what had already been a wonderful excursion, they made their way to the sidewalk outside Ryan's home on Summer Street. They agreed to meet once again at what Ryan dubbed dark- thirty, which this time of year was five-thirty pm.

* * *

When the allotted time arrived, Ryan left Violet standing in the garage while he went to clear the way. Ryan's father, with a rare day off, was already in the cellar with his boats and his music and a half-finished bottle of Jack. (No four drink limit an when a man is on a mini- vacation.) Ryan never saw him at all. Ryan's mother was fixing a sandwich from yesterday's meal. She pointed to the fridge. "I'm taking this to my room, there's a little more left if you're hungry." Parting words that was music to Ryan's ears. He nodded and bid his mother a good night.

He put together and wrapped two spam sandwiches and found a box of crackers in the pantry. He checked the milk for freshness. Someone had gone to the store. He grabbed a quart of milk and two plastic cups. He located one more item. *This might make Violet more comfortable and at the same time shed a little more light on the subject.* He chuckled to himself.

He navigated the attic stairs in the near dark. Enough light leaked in from the window to allow Ryan to place the chair just below the light bulb. Thinking Violet might appreciate a little more light he removed the bulb while gazing into the near darkness from a new height. He was struck by what a simple change in elevation does to your perspective. It was not lost on him that he had been experiencing a wealth of new perspectives lately.

He replaced the 40 watt bulb with a 120. Most of the flies had surrendered, but when Ryan made a last turn of the knob suddenly the attic became a different room entirely. He was momentarily blinded but that didn't stop him from hearing the last few survivors go into a frenzy circling the light then attacking the window. When his vision cleared Ryan rolled up a newspaper, one he had read several times to no success and began swiping anything that moved. When finished with the hand to hand combat silence returned. Ryan, fully warmed and with added light, saw new shapes emerge in definition and texture. Another chair showed its backside beneath a rolled rug.

Ryan dug it out and placed it near the window. Ryan found a folding stand which he dusted off and hauled to the window looking out over the sidewalk. He smiled to himself. He had created a nice little seating arrangement for Violet and himself. He placed the sandwiches, crackers, milk, and cups on the stand. He stood on the chair and turned off the light. When his eyes adjusted once more to the darkness, he hopped down and mated the chair to the other side of the stand. The street light offered just enough light to serve as a screen for what might later unfold. It was time. He went down the stairs with a bounce in his step, carefully avoiding a landslide.

CHAPTER SIX

FRANK

Frank stood off to one side watching the activity. *"What the hell is that kid up to now? Hmm, seems we are about to have company."* Frank looked around the room seeing no sign that Alice was there. *"Hey Alice, you want to dust the place?"* He had a little laugh at that. *"Shouldn't take much that kid did a hell of a job with those flies. What are they going to be doing up here? Christ, not music lessons, please!"* With his thoughts jumbled and his mouth spewing those thoughts from a leaky head, Frank put a hand to the pain exiting the dent in his skull. *"Will it ever get better?"*

Alice arrived in a whirl of attic dust, causing Frank to start sneezing. Sneezing hurt his head. *"Sorry I asked Alice. Good talk though."*

RYAN and VIOLET

The house was quiet. The sound of the furnace kicking on startled both kids as they tip toed through the kitchen on their way to the stairs. Violet was three steps up to the second floor when the cellar door opened and Ryan's father poked his head out of the doorway. Violet held her breath.

Words slurring, he announced as if someone might care, "Just coming up to use the bathroom." He made eye contact with his son. "Haven't seen you in a while." He staggered into the hallway, a wry slack look on his face. "Hmmph, I've heard that god awful noise you make up there though." He continued into the kitchen, "Heard you're taking a job. Well good for you." He held up his drink in salute.

Ryan thought, *so they do talk sometimes at least.*

Violet took two steps up the staircase on tip toe. A night light in the bathroom above cast a shadow down the steps. Below, Ryan tried to stall his father. "I'm going up to practice that noise, father but I need to use the bathroom myself. I'll holler down when I finish.

"Keep it down up there will yuh, I can hear that squawk way down in the basement."

"Good night to you too Father."

Ryan scooted up the stairs and found Violet standing at a closed door on the second floor. Ryan pointed to his right and opened the door to the attic. He flushed the toilet then hollered down to his father. Violet had reached the first step to the attic with Ryan about to join her when his mother opened her door and spoke through a smokers rasp. Violet held her breath.

"Well, I see the wanderer has returned." Was that your useless father you were just talking to?" Two sentences not meant to endear, followed by a raging cough of poison.

Ryan waited for the cough to subside, his mother's eyes wet as if from crying. He stepped back out of the doorway and closed it behind him. "Yep he needs to pee."

"I'm surprised he'd tear himself from his precious bottles. Rather thought he might fill one with his salty brine." She went into another coughing jag while chuckling at her little joke. "Well you have no further need of me." She smiled her tight little smile her eyes wet from coughing and entered her room closing the door smartly behind her.

Ryan entered the attic breathing deeply feeling like he had avoided one of those flag football tackles that leveled him in that first gym class. He snapped on the light. Violet had heard the callousness of both parents and looked as shaken as Ryan felt.

He feigned a smile and whispered, "So far so good."

Violet touched his hand and began her ascent. Ryan had wiped down the railing and removed the cobwebs that had taken his breath away but had pre-warned her she'd need to dodge boxes and bags and magazines on every step. At the top Violet looked about. The higher wattage bulb allowed for a slightly brighter assessment of the room than Ryan on his first trip up these stairs. She looked back at the young man she was about to go into battle with. She couldn't let what she had just heard below go without offering her take without judgment. "This must seem like a nice quiet place to be, Ryan."

Ryan caught her drift and simply nodded. Violet began her own walk around lifting and moving things. When she reached beneath a pile of old clothes she suddenly jumped backward and stifled a scream. "I felt something move in those old clothes."

Ryan poked the pile with a curtain rod and a squirrel high-tailed it to the eaves. The two laughed nervously, then Violet, a little more gingerly went back to her search. She emerged with a box of old letters. She took a seat by the window. Ryan was sifting through a pile of papers from the time period of Violet's grandmother's death.

"What was your grandmother's name, Violet?"

Violet looked up from a letter, "Her name was Alice Beaulier. She would have been forty three when she died." Violet held up a letter she was reading. "This one is dated 1944, a man writing to his wife while he was away during the war. I don't know whether his wife was living in this house at the time. The post mark on the envelope was addressed to the post office."

Ryan nodded. They both lowered their heads to the task at hand.

The attic was quiet. The few flies that might have survived Ryan's war were hibernating in the walls avoiding any further battle.

Ryan suddenly became contemplative. What was going on in this house from top to bottom? In his mind he chronicled what would be going on below in his mother's bedroom. He had walked by that door every night and often heard his mother counting out loud. *His mother would be sitting at her mirror counting aloud the hundred brush strokes she pulled through her hair nightly. A cigarette, the only friend she had in the world apparently, would be sitting ash white waiting to regain its glow when she laid her brush down.* In the attic, Ryan imagined all that because he had witnessed it. What he couldn't do was read his mother's mind.

CHAPTER SEVEN

WANDA

Wanda sat in front of a dresser that offered her a good look at herself. She was not pleased with what she saw. She began brushing her hair. The cigarette did in fact smolder out and turn ashen as she counted the strokes. Wanda imagined reaching the magic number and transforming back into the lovely talented girl she had once been. As the brush moved closer and closer to an ending that was not going to happen, Wanda's face seemed to melt into the mirror. She looked straight into the face of a woman with no joy. Sorrow showed itself briefly only to be replaced by blame. Blame took center stage in the mirror. Not her own blame for how her life was unfolding even now, but a blame that began and ended with her husband and her son. She re-lit her cigarette. She took a long pull as if to gather the strength needed to complete her assessment. From below she could hear but didn't recognize, a song riding the warm air from the furnace. *Damn fool,* she thought. *Him. And me for letting it happen;* both *of us. Well, it won't be much longer. Ryan is able to take care of himself and I won't be missed.* "Ninety-seven, ninety-eight, ninety-nine, one-hundred," she counted. Putting her brush down, Wanda abruptly stood and walked directly to the dresser drawer at the head of her bed. She sat down on her bed. She opened the drawer and felt to the back beneath her lingerie. The bottle remained passive. It would be her decision when and whether to open it, count out the required dosage, and swallow. Then just lay down and go to forever sleep. She studied the bottle in the light from her lamp. She could make out the shape of pills through the brown glass. Little rectangles. *These are the only control that's left to me.* She sat a moment longer sighed and put the bottle back in the drawer. Her face fixed in contemplation she lowered the covers got into bed and turned off the light. Darkness enveloped her. She didn't have the energy to try to identify the lyrics of the song sliding under her door. *Damn fool.*

A final thought as she closed her eyes was, *Will this be what it's like, total darkness?*

RYAN

Ryan in his mind couldn't know to the extent his father was breaking down. *He pictured his father applying the finishing touches to a model boat. Slowly carefully trying to lower the boat into the bottle, a half-filled glass of whiskey and water ready to toast his success.* What Ryan couldn't see were those hands, lubricated and shaking, attempting to hold the end of a protruding thread attached to a sail that was folded. If successful, with the pull of a thread the sail would open as if catching the wind. Ryan couldn't see his father with his bleary eyes and unsteady hand keep dropping the end of the thread as he became increasingly frustrated. Ryan couldn't hear the mumbles of frustration that mixed with the ever spinning classics. None of the musical artists seemed to care whether a boat set sail or not. They simply droned on endlessly taking their turn dropping from the spindle ignoring the swearing that was competing with their lyrics.

Ryan couldn't see through walls. He hadn't kept count. How many of these boats had been launched since moving here. He couldn't know that truthfully only one had been added to the fleet. Just like his mother in her bedroom self-destructing, his father liquor bottle in hand, would night after night give up in frustration and move to the old chair then simply drift off on a voyage in his mind.

FRANK

Down the hall in Ryan's room a one sided conversation was taking place. *"Did you hear what they are doing up there? They are trying to find out who we are and how we died. How do you feel about that?"*

There was no response. *"Figured it would all be left to me!"* Frank clutched his head. *"I don't know if my head can take this. If the lady of the house takes it in her head to kill herself before its time we'll never get out."*

He squeezed out a guilt trip. "That's your granddaughter up there. She deserves to know the truth. You know she would want you to help."* Frank waited, at first there was no response, but then suddenly the room chilled. *"Well At least you're paying attention. I'll take your cold shoulder as a yes. You do what you can do with your granddaughter."* Frank lost his train of thought when a sharp bolt of pain hit him. *"I'm not sure which is worse, the sounds and smells from the

cellar, that damn banging on the piano, or the honk of that horn. We need to get out of here! Oh my head."

A cold breeze suddenly moved dust bunnies around. Frank noted the long neglected vacuuming by the lady of the house. Just one of many things she had neglected if you listened. He felt the sudden breeze, "*Well,*" he sneezed, head back in hands, "*I'm glad you agree with me on something.*" The furnace came back on. It was more than warm air and dust bunnies seeping beneath the attic door and climbing back up the stairs, well within ear shot of Violet and Ryan who were looking for a clue. "*Why don't you help them Alice.*"

RYAN and VIOLET

Ryan was looking through an old paper when what felt like a breeze began rustling the pile at his feet. Violet looked up from a letter that had her teary eyed. She nudged Ryan's foot. The two sat shocked and stark still as the pile started to sort itself. The latest papers on top suddenly slid into the shadows. When the rustling stopped, headlines from June 7, 1944 lay face up staring at Ryan and Violet. **Normandy Invaded by allied troops**. Pictures accompanied the headlines. Inside the first section of the paper smaller headlines added to the story line, America was in the war to win it. Ryan and Violet looked at one another, eyes wide, touching hands. Both breathed heavily. *Yes this was happening.*

Violet slid her chair closer to Ryan and the two began breaking the 15 page paper into sections. War news gave way to more personal stories of wounded soldiers, the war effort on the home front, local news, the classifieds, and finally the obituaries.

It was in the obituaries section following a family farewell to a man in his seventies and a woman in her eighties that a simple pronouncement of a death seemed out of place. Violet read aloud, "A man was found dead in his home on Summer Street in Skowhegan. No name was listed. No family mentioned. No funeral announced."

Ryan looked toward Violet. "That's a strange way and place to list an anonymous death. It happened on this street though. Could this be what we're looking for?"

Violet was still shaken by the strangely familiar feeling that her Grandmother was up here, trying to communicate something. She could just feel it in her bones. "Well there has to be a reason this particular paper is staring us right in the face."

Ryan read the short announcement once again, "It's no wonder I missed it."

The two found, organized, and scanned the next weeks' worth of papers but there was no follow-up.

"What do we do now?" asked Violet. "How do we find out who this man was and what happened to him?"

"Well, if I heard what I thought I heard that night, this man's name is Frank. I have no idea beyond that." Ryan went into his head. His eyes opened with an idea. But maybe I do know someone who can help."

He sat back looking at the ceiling thinking it through even as he spoke. "My Civics teacher is always telling us to use our town as a resource. Most of our lessons come from what he tells us local government does on a daily basis. He even serves on the town council. The man knows how everything works. Let me ask him." Ryan smiled, "Of Course I won't tell him we're trying to maybe identify a ghost." That final idea seemed to put a lid on this first excursion and in unison they decided to call it a night.

Managing to get to Ryan's room without incident, Violet stood with her back to the door studying Ryan's room in much the same way she had scanned the attic. An absence of posters lining the wall indicated Ryan didn't celebrate music or movie stars. Along one wall a full bookshelf told Violet all she needed to know about her new friend; Ryan was a serious young man. His blind was pulled, reinforcing what Ryan had told her about himself; he embraced the dark. A sleeping bag, open and laid out in the corner, indicated Ryan had thought things through and there would be no awkward moments. She smiled to herself. After Ryan ran interference, Violet used the bathroom. When she returned she tucked herself beneath the covers of Ryan's bed and whispered good night. Ryan snapped off the light and crawled into his sack.

Around midnight, Ryan's rumbling stomach woke him. The two had been so absorbed in what had taken place in the attic that they had left the sandwiches untouched. He went back to the attic and brought the food to his room. He snapped on a lamp on his desk and looked to the bed. Violet was already sitting up, still fully clothed. She nodded. "I haven't been able to sleep," she whispered.

A little picnic on the rug took place with neither speaking but occasionally reaching out to touch hands. They had shared an eventful evening. With full stomachs both slept soundly.

FRANK

Above in the dark and cold the two chairs remained occupied. Frank was congratulating Alice for revealing her

presence. *"You did your part, let's see where this goes from here."* Alice did not respond but Frank felt a cold draft reach his shoulder.

RYAN and VIOLET

In the morning, Ryan and Violet whispered back and forth. "You didn't say anything last night about those papers moving. Was it your grandmother?"

Violet's eyes appeared bigger as she responded, "That cool breeze didn't start up out of nowhere. And those papers didn't separate themselves. I think she was part of that." Violet stood and spoke in a whisper. "For the longest time, in the strangest places, I have felt a breeze start up when all around me no leaves were moving. And in my house when no windows were open. What seems to follow that breeze is me suddenly knowing something I didn't know before. Does that make sense? Violet breathed in deeply. "What I believe this morning, after a good night's sleep," she yawned and smiled, "my grandmother is here. She is in this house."

Ryan nodded his agreement with her assessment.

Violet pointed to the door. "How about you run interference once more, I think I'm going to go home this morning. I've had enough excitement for one weekend." She smiled then. "Did I tell you I have started a journal of my own? I need to get all this down while its fresh in my mind."

Ryan chuckled, "Very cool Violet." Ryan glanced at his journal on his desk and seemed to be reassuring his oldest friend even as he encouraged Violet. "It's like having a best friend in your room all the time." Ryan took a risk. "Not as pretty a friend as you though."

He blushed. So did Violet. Ryan cleared his throat, "Let me just make sure the coast is clear," he whispered. "My father isn't working but he's probably laying pretty low this morning I'm guessing. I'll just check on my mother."

* * *

Safely back on the sidewalk away from Ryan's house, the two touched hands. "I'll see you on Monday, and if anything else happens before that I'll call you." Their eyes met and they went their separate ways.

Ryan turned and was whistling his way back toward his steps when a car slowed as it neared, facing him. He glanced at the vehicle. Someone was looking directly at him from the driver's seat. Suddenly a cold chill went through him. *Was that Mr. Kneely in that car? What the hell*?

* * *

Bright and early Monday morning before school Ryan met Stan Tuttle outside the main entrance to the spinning mill. Stan checked his watch. "You are five minutes early, that's a good way to begin. I'm here every morning. If you have trouble with anyone you just let old Stan know. I know ever-one in town and they know me." The two shook hands and Ryan went on about his business. It was still full on dark as Ryan removed the string from the stack of sixty papers, tucked them into a shoulder sling that Scoop thoughtfully included, and started his first official trip across the swinging bridge.

On that same Monday in math class Mr. Kneely avoided any eye contact with Ryan. Normally a day without a confrontation of some sort would be welcomed but after being pretty sure that was Mr. Kneely driving slowly by his house, Ryan was flat out suspicious.

That afternoon Ryan told Violet about who he thought had driven by his house and how Mr. Kneely had avoided him today.

Violet, who was a firm believer in cause and effect, offered her opinion in the form of a question. "So Ryan do you believe in coincidence?"

Ryan shook his head, "Nope."

Days passed without incident, on his route, in the classroom, and in Ryan's house. A long slow slog between Veteran's Day to Thanksgiving. On the way to Christmas the laboratory of learning expelling volumes of instruction meant to keep students with their noses in their books and their minds off what might end up under a tree with their name on it.

A thick layer of snow arrived overnight. The world seemingly as muffled by this six inch blanket as the kids in their classrooms. Ryan had been on the sidewalk dragging his boots through unplowed snow since before dawn. Papers delivered on time. He mentally patted himself on the back as he stood under a hot shower thinking about Violet. Breakfast in his household hadn't taken a turn for the better but Ryan was so happy he didn't even care about food.

He was on his way to school his mind in the clouds pondering how to follow up on his Civics teachers' advice when a snowball hit him square in the back. Ryan turned ready to fight. Violet, her mouth open in laughter, put up her hands in defense. Ryan relaxed and Violet caught up to him.

She had news. "No school for me today," she gushed, "our buses got vandalized overnight."

"Well lucky you." He chuckled as his sense of humor kicked in, "what are you going to do today other than start a war?"

Violet had a twinkle in her eye. "I do have a battle plan. I was thinking of going to the Courthouse and researching your house."

"You've been reading my mind Violet, I was having the same thought but not today." He threw up his hands in mock exasperation. "Nobody messed with our buses!"

Violet chuckled. Then she held two fingers half an inch apart. "Do you ever want to break the rules, just a little bit?" She raised her brow. "We could go to that place you mentioned in the Court house."

"It's called the Registry of Deeds. And you want me to go with you, today?"

"It's never open on the weekend and winter vacation is still a ways off. So yeah today Ryan, how about it?"

Ryan tilted his head in thought. *He had never skipped school before. Of course he had never had a beautiful girl in his life or a ghost in his house before, maybe more than one.*

He checked his Timex. He decided. "The place doesn't open until nine." He smiled. "We could make a day of it though."

The two adolescents first stopped for hot chocolate at Whittemore's where they lingered, watching the adults in booths and at tables conversing, reading newspapers, drinking coffee. A quick check of watches had many rising and leaving to reach their jobs. The overnight snow and general grousing about the state of the world moved from table to table. Older couples their work days well past were quieter, they lingered, they chatted with less passion. Ryan kidded, "You see that old guy and woman in the corner that could be us Violet, in about sixty years."

Violet chuckled, her eyes twinkling as she studied the pair. "Ryan, you're cheating on me. I don't own a red coat."

Ryan burst out laughing, choking on his chocolate.

Ryan checked his watch once again, then the two rose to make their way to the courthouse. They spent the day learning how to navigate the giant recorded ledgers. One of the clerks took them under her wing making the learning a whole lot easier. By three in the afternoon they left armed with the name of the man who owned the house on Summer Street at the time the death was listed in the paper of June 7, 1944. They went back to Whittemore's to sort all this out. Hot chocolate once more sparked their questions. Were the owners occupying the house back then or was it being rented out? How could they find that out? The family name listed in the records was Green. Alvin and Edith Green. Records showed the house changed hands within a year of that June date. The house had been sold eight times since. The latest owners were Ryan's parents. Ryan sat back and sighed. *It seemed Mr. Kneely had been correct when he told Ryan no one stays there long. How did he know so much about all this? Was that him in that passing car over a week ago*?

"What you thinking about Ryan?"

"A million things Violet and I need to write them down to sort things out. I'll walk you home and then I need to spend some time with my less attractive friend."

Violet smiled.

The two separated from the sidewalk with a touch of the hands. Violet went fishing, "We need to stop meeting like this or some people might think we are a couple," she smiled. Then she lightened things by adding, "Like that old couple who could be us in sixty years," she laughed aloud. She didn't give Ryan, who had a response in mind the chance to respond. "See you tomorrow afternoon."

CHAPTER EIGHT

Ryan watched her walk away. *Maybe she is feeling what I'm feeling.* It was getting dark and the sidewalks were freezing up as Ryan skipped his way to his porch whistling a holiday tune. There were no police cars in the drive so apparently his day of playing hooky had gone unreported at least for now. Hopefully no one had called his parents.

His mother was in the kitchen. She remained silent upon his entry as usual. Today that was good news. She had not cooked which was normal but still bad news. Ryan thinking about having to make another meal of dried out whatever, lingered with the fridge door open. He sighed as he took off his jacket. He joined his mother who was sitting in the near darkness at the table. After spending the day with upbeat lovely Violet he could not help noticing even in the diminishing light how wasted and wan his mother appeared. She looked terrible. Her eyes were nearly shut, her hair was uncombed, and she had either worn her robe all day or was already dressed for bed.

He didn't want to ask but he did. "Are you feeling alright?"

A low, barely audible gravely response made its way across the table, "Why I didn't know you cared enough to ask?"

Ryan put his lips together and let the comment die. He went to the refrigerator and removed the tuna that had lain there uncovered and drying out since the day it left the can. He shook his head "Do we have any fresh tuna?"

His mother studied him. She appeared lost in her own world. Then moving her head side to side she turned away letting the question sit there unanswered. Ryan watched and heard the labored breathing and labored effort to rise and leave the room intensifying as she climbed the stairs to her room.

Ryan, still standing, raised his hands in frustration. *She's getting worse. Does Father pick up on any of this? Hell, no, he's too busy drinking himself to death.* He rummaged the pantry. There was no Tuna.

Ryan made himself a toasted peanut butter sandwich. When he tried to match that with a glass of milk, he found that the bottle was empty but sitting in the fridge. *Who does that*? A glass of water accompanied Ryan and his sandwich up to his room. Ryan had finally abandoned the attic. It was just too cold. His French Horn lessons were abandoned along with the move. In all honesty he did not like the sounds he produced. He hated to admit his mother might be right about his musical ability. He sat down at his desk and polished off the sandwich. They had what they needed from the newspapers. If the ghost wanted to make contact he could do it down here where it was warmer. Ryan opened his journal.

A cold breeze hit him and the journal pages began to move of their own accord. Ryan sat back in shock. When the journal quieted, a strange scrawl appeared. Ryan shuddered as he began a first reading. He didn't get it. He read the message again. In an odd style and put on paper as if penned by an angry decrepit ancient poet, Ryan tried to cipher the meaning beyond the words.

Dirty darkened dreary winter snow.

Bleak though chances be we have to try to go.

Plans have been made so leave this alone.

Well-meaning yes but we'll do better on our own.

The old man stinks of whiskey and glue

The woman seems addled but that's nothing new

On the girl's special day we'll contact you.

When Ryan finished reading and shaking and shuddering, he tried to raise his own pen. He found his hand seemed frozen in place. Ryan sat there nearly an hour staring at his open journal, reading and rereading the first entry ever recorded by a different hand. He felt numb.

He heard his father come in and imagined him experiencing the same frustration in locating something to eat. A bottle would make contact with a glass full of ice, the recliner would groan, a paper would rustle followed a half hour later by a cellar door slamming. The last time the family had sat down to a silent meal together had been a long time now. Dried out tuna was the only evidence that anyone even attempted to eat here. The numbness finally leeched from his bones and Ryan closed his Journal; the first time he could remember not being able to pen his thoughts. He lay on his bed trying to read but couldn't focus. Too many things were flying around in his head. He felt invaded, but in an odd sense included. *Had he lost control of his long time closest friend? Was he now sharing him*? He burrowed beneath his covers. His final thought was of Violet.

Were they a couple? Yes, he thought they were. Wait till I tell Violet somebody's been adding their two cents to my story.

FRANK and ALICE

Just a day ago Frank and Alice sat in the two chairs in the attic. It was colder still. Frank could just barely see the water vapor hanging in air that let him know Alice had not left the room. It was obvious the boy was not returning. Had the two found all they needed? *"What were we just talking about Alice?"* An air current reached his head and he remembered. *"Can't really blame him it's colder than hell up here. Just made a little joke there Alice. We haven't gotten to experience hell yet have we?"* There was no response. *"Lighten up Alice. Oh well, I think it's time we kiss this room goodbye, forever hopefully."* Frank was feeling a little cocky after writing what he saw as a fine piece of literature. *"The kid didn't faint dead away reading my first attempt at Poetry. It was cleverly written don't you think? Who knew?!"* Alice didn't say a word but raised enough air to cause Frank to sneeze. *"My head hurts enough without you raising a fuss. Smart ass."*

VIOLET

Violet had lived in this town all her life. But it was only since meeting Ryan that she felt she was seeing things clearly. Ryan allowed her to be herself. She realized he was her first true friend. *Maybe more*, she thought. She sat in her room at her desk, her journal open. She had Ryan to thank for introducing her to the pages that recorded the past two weeks complete with emotions that guided her hand. Writing all this down had cemented things and made them real.

Tonight she didn't add a single word but reread her latest entry. **I am growing fond of Ryan. I am sure my grandmother reached out to me in that attic. I am also certain my grandmother did not commit suicide. I am equally certain we will get to the bottom of all this.** She closed the journal. She too tried to read herself to sleep but the same thoughts that were haunting Ryan just up the street seemed to be making a house call. She sighed deeply. Not a word from the dozen pages her eyes had traveled reached her consciousness. She turned out her light.

FRANK and ALICE

Alice flitted about agitated or excited, Frank couldn't tell. Frank feeling the air currents circling like those damn flies had his own thoughts riding the air. ***Alice had quietly roamed this house since that terrible night all those years ago. Frank had felt a breeze start up even as he watched the life go out of her. Tonight she might not be talking but she was up to something. Frank hadn't felt this much movement in her since her sentence to purgatory began with the light leaving her eyes and the air smothered from her lungs.***

Their paths in this house crossed frequently but he couldn't say they were ever entirely on the same flight pattern. **A stab of head pain caused him to wince.** ***For one thing, Frank was harsh and verbal, Alice couldn't speak. Their demises had come about in entirely different ways though they shared the same result. His demise had followed a loud argument that had him screaming, swearing, and threatening, till the end.***

Alice had gone in a shockingly quiet way, totally unexpected, ending in a weak gurgle.

Frank had lived in this house, dominated this house, right up until he didn't.

Alice, had arrived unexpectedly, innocently. A planned night of what might have started out as shared passion gave way to something ugly. Frank felt partially at fault but he wouldn't be telling Alice any time soon. Frank couldn't see in the dark any more than a live person could. He couldn't be sure that was his son who brought the woman here, but something didn't seem right at the time and he had started the walls shaking. Then he heard her die, heard it all. Though she was a complete stranger to this house until that night, over the years he came to know and understand her pain.

Right at the moment his own head throbbed. *He hadn't made the connection between the girl who always seemed to be lurking in the area until the young boy now living here became the girl's friend and invited her inside. Alice in her own way had tried to tell him but the message had never gotten through.*

It seemed now that she had seen her granddaughter in the flesh in this very house she yearned to go further in their communication. Now perhaps finally they could work in tandem.

Frank lost his thread of thought. He grabbed his head in agony. If a ghost can sweat then he was sweating. Alice cooled him down and he went back to ruminating. *Time was of the essence. With what seemed certain to happen downstairs they needed to coordinate the timing. Yes the*

timing had to be perfect. Alice had given him the date, Lover's day, Valentine's Day. Frank scoffed at the date but agreed to help. We certainly don't need a new tenant moving in. These kids are in hot pursuit but can we wait? Things need to come together on the girl's birthday he'd been told. **Frank spoke aloud, *"I hope that kid reads as well as he writes, they need to back off for now. If we need them to intervene further we'll let them know."* A long sigh left Franks lips, then he suddenly felt a brush of air against his cheek. *"Alice did you just thank me?"***

WANDA TRUSSELL

I do have a name. At least I used to. And it wasn't mother. It meant something too. The hair brush fairly flew as strokes were counted aloud in the same frequency as thoughts entered her head. *My days have turned into night. I am brushing my hair at night for god's sake but leaving it a rat's nest during the day. I'm not even changing out of my night clothes though no one in this house seems to notice. No one cares a whit about me. I'm not sure how much more I can take.* Her eyes filled. The brush dropped to her lap without reaching her goal of one hundred. She asked herself, *what is the answer?* She looked to the drawer knowing there lay one possible answer close at hand. When she opened the drawer the bottle was staring up at her uncovered, and uncapped pills littering the drawer. *How did that happen?* Wanda panicked. *Had she been discovered? Was her husband encouraging her? My god it's not Ryan, is it?* She struggled to get her breathing under control even as she began a coughing jag. It was one thing to have the means to an end ready and waiting, it was something altogether different to be directed. She sat on the bed letting every possible scenario enter her head. *Do I ask? Who do I ask? Could I have done this and not remember?* Wanda eventually turned off the light but she did not sleep well. Cold troubling air seemed to filter right through her blankets. She shivered and dug deeper into her quilt.

ALICE

Alice entered the room and watched the woman toss in her sleep. She smiled as she thought of the look on the woman's face when she found the opened bottle. It would be hours before her husband put a stopper in his own bottle and turned off his damn music. For the longest time now he slept as far away from his wife as possible, either the cellar or the chair in the living room. Alice had studied this family since they moved in. The boy was the only normal one from what she had observed. Alice thought she could certainly live a more useful life than this wreck of a woman twisting in her blankets. She had to admit Frank seemed to have things under control. She watched a troubled sleep pattern shaped by blankets moving in the darkness. *I'll just send a message. See how she reacts.* The room suddenly chilled further, Wanda burrowed deeper into her blankets. Alice chuckled to herself thinking, *just a few more weeks honey and you'll experience what real cold feels like. Stay cool now. Keeping the woman off balance thinking she might have been found out will hopefully keep her from doing anything foolish until we're ready.*

CHAPTER NINE

RYAN

Thanksgiving recess arrived just in time. Flu season had announced the holiday with sneezes coughs and white handkerchiefs waving about in surrender. The ever growing snow banks and a howling wind seemed to be declaring an early winter. Five kids were missing math class on this last day before vacation. The class with three of the worst acting yahoos absent had been unusually quiet. Ryan, as was his practice in this class, kept his head down and his pencil moving. The bell rang. *Thank God that's over,* sighed Ryan to himself. Ryan had one foot out the door when Mr. Kneely once again spoke to his back. "Mr. Trussell a word."

Ryan turned. Their eyes met for the first time today.

"Well you have been with us for a month now and you seem to have survived." He smiled. "How is your family settling into this little town?"

The calmness in his teacher's voice was not one that Ryan had experienced. For most of every class Mr. Kneely was belittling a student or generally being sarcastic. *Where is this going*? Asked Ryan to himself.

"I don't really know what they think of Skowhegan. As for me, I love the place, especially our house."

Mr. Kneely seemed to struggle with what he offered next. "You know, you have been doing good math work. Perhaps I misjudged you. I'm rarely wrong but when I am, I admit my mistakes."

Ryan was shocked but kept silent.

Mr. Kneely wasn't finished. "There are parent teacher conferences right after the holiday. I would like to meet your parents. I would like to tell them how far you have come in this class."

Ryan was further shocked.

Mr. Kneely grabbed a pad off his desk. "Wait just a minute. I'll write them a personal invitation." Mr. Kneely began whistling at his desk as he jotted down the invite.

Ryan fairly swooned with this unexplainable development.

When Mr. Kneely handed him the note Ryan made eye contact and just had to ask, "Did I see you go past my house a while back? At least I thought it was you."

Mr. Kneely's face got red and his calm demeanor dissolved for a moment but he recovered. "So, that was you I saw. I wasn't sure so I didn't wave." He smiled tightly. "Have a nice Thanksgiving, Ryan."

Ryan spent the remainder of the day trying to piece together Mr. Kneely's turn around and interest in meeting his parents.

When he met Violet on the sidewalk a full two hours earlier than usual on this early dismissal day, he immediately told her of the encounter with Mr. Kneely.

"Maybe with your charm and wit you have finally won him over," Violet giggled. "Hey it worked on me. Heck we're bedroom buddies now aren't we?" Violet took his hand.

Ryan blushed. "Thanks Violet, but something is off with that man."

Violet sobered, "Well we have the next few days to explore all possibilities Ryan." She patted his hand. "I think another night in your house might be just the ticket don't you?"

Ryan smiled. "I certainly do."

* * *

Very early on Thanksgiving morning Ryan stood outside the spinning mill's entrance watching an elderly Stan Tuttle amble down the brightly lit corridor. When he reached the door he opened it with a holiday greeting.

"Happy Thanksgiving to you too, Mr. Tuttle. Do you have a minute?"

"Sure, come on in and get out of the wind and cold."

Standing just inside the door, Ryan began, "I don't want to trouble you sir, but you said if anything or anyone caused me a problem I should tell you."

"I sure did what's up kid"?

Ryan's first thought was to tell Stan about the ghosts in his house but thought better of it. "Well sir, there are old two guys who are sometimes on the swinging bridge early in the morning when I am crossing. Sometimes they are going across from this side and other times they are coming back across."

"And that is a problem how?"

"When I get on the bridge they stand together and make the bridge move up and down. Then they dare me to try to get by. They smell like Whiskey."

"You don't know who they are?"

"I have asked a couple of my customers, they think it might be a guy they called Pop another called Whitey. They own a little shop beside Peanut's Pool Hall. They harass kids who have to pass their business on the way home from school. I don't go that way so I have never seen them. Mr. Tuttle, they scare me."

Stan Tuttle cupped his chin. "I know those two yahoos. They live on one of those streets you deliver to. I think they are harmless but I'll just stop in at their business and have a little talk with them. Not to worry Ryan, but what you've told me might be why that paper route changes hands so often. Let me see what I can do."

"Thank you sir, I would appreciate that."

When Ryan lingered, Stan asked if he had anything else on his mind.

Ryan thought once more of telling Stan about his house guests but decided against it, for now anyway. "Nah I just wondered if you knew where I could get a dog? If I could convince my mother that is."

Ryan wandered off without waiting for an answer, he knew his mother's answer.

* * *

The two Thanksgiving meals could not have been more different. Violet's parents doted on the meal and their daughter. The warm and comforting smells of a shared holiday filled the house. Violet excused herself after the homemade pumpkin pie and went to her room to store up some nap time. The weekend promised to be one that would offer little rest. She napped and dreamed, felt her grandmother entering offering support, enthusiasm even. There was a part of the dream that seemed even more revealing but Violet couldn't make full sense of it. She got the feeling that being with family around the holidays had broken through. Violet included her grandmother when saying grace at dinner. Her mother gave her a stern look but said nothing. In Violet's mind, her grandmother had joined her in her bedroom and crawled into her dream, seeming to promise an even closer bond. Violet woke confused but determined. The plan moved forward with Violet gaining her parents support to spend the next two days with a friend; though they were not told which friend. Violet had never lied to her parents. They agreed Violet would be home for a Sunday morning church service with Thanksgiving leftovers for lunch.

* * *

At Ryan's home when he delivered Mr. Kneely's invitation to attend a parent teacher's conference, his mother's response foreshadowed how the Thanksgiving meal would be approached. 'Why should I bother?' His mother promptly ripped up and put the note in the trash.

So predictably, Thanksgiving in the Trussell household was sketchier than just up the street. Tom turkey had been cooked, cooled, and smothered in plastic before he arrived at the Trussell household. A Pumpkin pie too had been conceived and born in a bakery. The table was bare of any decoration. Called to the table, Ryan sat watching his mother move about the kitchen in a slatternly manner, bitching under her breath about the foolishness of all this effort. Canned peas and carrots were the only part of the meal that reached the stove and they spent little time being warmed to the task. As they were placed on the table Ryan was struck by the word that had appeared as one of the vocabulary words just this past week. <u>Perfunctory: performed merely as a routine duty; hasty and superficial, indifferent.</u> Ryan tried it out aloud. "Perfunctory." He said it again. "Perfunctory." Ryan's father with several rare days off during the week had already broken the seal on a celebration purchase of a half-gallon of Jack Daniels. His father was already planning to fill what would soon be an empty jug with a larger boat. Normally satisfied with a fifth occupying shelf space, four days off in a row called for reinforcements. He looked at his son through blurry eyes. "What the hell you saying Ryan?"

"Just practicing my vocabulary words father. One of them is the word, <u>Perfunctory,</u> the meaning just became clear to me."

His father shook his head at a son he just couldn't understand, but he raised his glass, "Let's drink to your new found learning."

Cranberry sauce was overlooked entirely until Ryan asked. "Sorry" his mother fairly shouted. Neither was there a fresh roll or gravy or potato to be found. The turkey was served cold. Since Ryan had mentioned the absence of Cranberry sauce his mother continued to glare at him then rose and slatted around in the kitchen. Her hands seemed to protest as she proclaimed the uselessness of the can opener. She looked over at the two men at the table who offered no help and shook her head. Exasperated she finally gave up and brought the half opened can to the table. "Happy Thanksgiving," she uttered as she passed the can with sharp edges to her son. His mother lit up a cigarette and watched the two of them as she coughed quietly into her sleeve. Silence accompanied this pre-packaged attempt at normalcy so it didn't take long for Ryan to finish and excuse himself. His father, well into his third drink toasted his leaving the table after throwing up his hands. "Go practice your new words. That's a better idea than the noise you've made in the attic."

"I guess you haven't been listening lately father but all noise from the attic has ceased."

Ryan stood in the doorway leading to the stairs. He looked at his father and mother sitting there in a blue haze of shared misery. As disappointed in his parents as he was, Ryan couldn't hide the excitement of the upcoming weekend and actually walked back and gave his mother a peck on the cheek. Looking ahead to Violet's arrival He genuinely meant what he said aloud, "This is the best Thanksgiving ever."

VIOLET

Just up the road apiece Violet had her own thoughts filling her head. She too had a dual purpose for the weekend. Ghosting might be top of the list but spending time with Ryan in his house, sharing a secret that needed to be shared, was near the top. Violet was soon to be fifteen and her feelings for Ryan were quickly moving past friendship, that had to be revealed this weekend. How she would do that and what that would look like and where that might lead was as much a mystery to Violet as who or what haunted Ryan's home. After watching Ryan scribble in his journal every afternoon at the library Violet had made the decision to start keeping an account of her own life in this her final year of childhood. She opened to the first page where she had signed in as the owner and read through the last two weeks of what she had considered important enough to write down. Tonight she opened to an empty page and simply wrote,

This just might be the best Thanksgiving ever.

Not knowing what the ghosts were up to or clearly understanding why they were being warned away, the kids did not back off. If anything they seemed more determined. They decided to do research away from the house however, "No sense stirring things up," Ryan quipped. Tonight sitting on Ryan's bed, heads back on the pillows staring at the ceiling, avoiding the feelings they were beginning to have for one another they planned to review what they had learned.

First though Ryan rose and took Violet by the hand. He turned in his journal to the poetic entry that had been made.

Violet's eyes gleamed with excitement. "Whoever wrote this was writing for two people. I'm sure my grandmother is here Ryan." She looked around the room trying to conjure up her grandmother. Nothing reached her. They went back to sit on the bed with their backs to the headboard. Ryan began a review. They had found a list of owners of this house in the years 1942 till 1955. They met directly after school at the courthouse spending an hour in the registry before the building closed down for the day. One fact had emerged that still had them puzzled. The owner of the house that matched the time frame for Violet's grandmother's death, owned several other properties and had bought this house to rent out. The man still lived in Skowhegan and was willing to talk to them.

They had gone to visit. Violet told the man she was doing a paper on the paranormal.

The man had opened up immediately, 'I was aware of a death in the house years earlier. Didn't think much about it. I was able to buy the property at a bargain price. Didn't think much about that either.' His eyes opened wide. 'I had no idea what I was getting into. I couldn't keep a tenant for more than a month or two. My phone was always ringing off the hook.' The man stood and began to pace. 'I went over and tried to find out what they were complaining about. I never heard anything in the walls but every one of them said the same thing. This place is haunted.'

Violet had asked, "Did you ever see a ghost?"

'No, but less than a year after I bought the place someone died there.' He cupped his chin in thought, 'It was supposed to be vacant. Just two weeks before, a tenant moved out said the same thing as all the others, kept hearing noises in the walls. Scared the bejeezus out of him, he said.'

The past owner returned to his chair. 'I told him I didn't believe in ghosts and refused to give him his deposit back. I was expecting a fight about that. But the guy was so shaken he didn't even demand his deposit back. He just wanted out.' The man rose again. 'That got me thinking maybe there's something that isn't right with the place.' The former owner looked directly at Violet. 'When I went to make sure the tenant hadn't made a giant mess when he left, well I came across a different kind of giant mess and it scared the bejeesus out of me this time.' His eyes widened even after all this time, 'A woman was lying dead on the floor in a bedroom. I ran out of there and called the police.' Then remembering even more clearly he added, 'It was two solid weeks before I was able to get into my own place. I kept calling but nobody would tell me anything about anything. Two weeks later I drove by on my own and the yellow tape is off the porch railing.' He shook his head remembering how upset he'd been with the police. 'They didn't even have the courtesy to let me know I could go back in there. Anyway, I cleaned the place and put it up for sale.' One last shake of the head ended the man's recollection. 'Word around town about the place being haunted made it impossible to get my money back on the sale. Had to let it go cheap.'

Violet spoke up, a quizzical look on her face, "So the woman who died there didn't live there?"

'The place was supposed to be vacant. It was locked. No breakin is the only thing I was told. The renter had returned his keys to me when he left. I had the only keys.'

"Was any of this ever in the local paper?" queried Ryan.

The man cupped his chin once more. 'You have a lot of questions for just a term paper.'

"I like to be thorough," offered a smiling Violet.

The man nodded going back in time. 'As I recall there was a big snowstorm early part of that week. The town lost power. Everything shut down. The papers were full of that storm. I never read a word about the storm that happened in that house.' He stroked his chin looking into a middle distance that brought back a final painful memory of that time. 'So no ghosts for me, just bad memories and a bad business deal.'

When Violet left Ryan's home on that Sunday morning she had not made contact with her grandmother, which was frustrating, but she was carrying a whole heart full of knowledge about her feelings for Ryan.

* * *

When Ryan walked to school on a magical Monday morning following Thanksgiving, he was at peace with his world. The two men had not been on the bridge for the past few days. Maybe Mr. Tuttle had already gotten to them. He could hope.

He no longer feared the ghosts in his house. What they wanted or needed didn't seem to be threatening Violet or himself personally. Ryan didn't feel alone in all this either. He breathed in the fresh cold air. The one takeaway from the three days in near constant company with Violet was there was no doubt Ryan was in love. He couldn't explain what that meant but he sure could feel it. What he and Violet might discover or not discover he knew for certain would be as a team. Ryan looked around at the sparkling snow that painted everything except the roadway. It seemed it was here to stay, Ryan noticed and projected. He began to hum, I'm Dreaming of a White Christmas.

When he entered math class, before he could even take his seat, Mr. Kneely called his name. The same opening line he had used previously, "Mr. Trussell, a word."

"Did you deliver my invitation?"

"Yes sir, I did."

"Does your mother plan to attend the slot I planned for her?"

Remembering his mother tearing the note into pieces, Ryan took the high road. "I can't honestly say but I wouldn't plan on it."

Mr. Kneely frowned. "Perhaps I should give her a call."

Ryan, thinking of his mother slipping away to nothingness, thought it was probably a waste of time. On the other hand, what could it hurt and for the time being at least Mr. Kneely was being nice to him. "That might be a good idea Mr. Kneely. It couldn't hurt."

FRANK and ALICE

They had heard the kids discussing all their research and their theories. The kids didn't seem any closer to figuring any of this out which at the moment seemed a good thing. Newspapers past or present weren't going to unravel this mystery. So Just as one school day follows another leading up to Christmas vacation, in the Trussell household, a trudgetrudge of sameness was setting in with the resident ghosts. They were counting the calendar while holding the fort with a particular date in mind, just over two months from now. They did not want to set too high an expectation or get too low with the thought of possible failure. They had taken a position backstage in this drama just trying to manage the situation. They had warned the boy, and he had shared that with the girl.

Wanda was the problem. Twice they had to step in when she attempted to end it all. On one occasion when it seemed Wanda might get the job done Frank intervened. When she lost consciousness after taking a handful of pills, he pumped hard on her stomach, causing a violent upheaval. That slowed her down. And who could she tell? They had

scared her and for now she seemed to have put the brakes on the idea. Frank and Alice watched her closely.

RYAN and VIOLET

Ryan never heard whether Mr. Kneely called his mother or if the two had met. Something was going on with his mother though he had no idea what. One afternoon she was ghost white and lying on the couch with terrible pain in her stomach. With the flu hitting the school, Ryan thought it might be that.

Her weird ways were increasing in frequency and she seldom spoke to Ryan or his father.

He decided to record all this strangeness in his journal. Parts he had written about earlier but after reviewing it some things were coming together.

Mostly though he was concerned with Mr. Kneely who seemed to dislike him, but seemed very interested in where he lived. Now he was showing an interest in meeting Ryan's mother and was serving up a new kinder gentler approach to Ryan. The fact that he had actually driven by Ryan's house made all this stranger still.

* * *

Ryan was introduced to Violet's parents as her new best friend and was accepted immediately. He was welcomed into the warmth of a home steeped in both religious and main street holiday tradition. Ryan saw the very real lyrics of a Christmas song right before his eyes, <u>Candles glow and mistletoe toe and presents under the tree.</u> Violet's parents could not have been nicer. Pictures of our savior watched his birthday celebration from a wall in every room.

Homes all along the street were lit up in Christmas colors as Ryan made his way home. Looking up at his own house bathed in blackness, Ryan, who normally embraced the dark felt a little bit wistful. No outside Christmas lights framed windows or doors. No colorful lights showed from within. When he entered it was like entering the office of Dickens' Scrooge, dark and gloomy, shades pulled, cold and dismal.

Muffled music drifted up from the cellar as if it too were on a voyage with a boat in a bottle. Ryan unconsciously went to the refrigerator though he wasn't in the least bit hungry. Violet's parents had made sure of that with a feast of their holiday creations. Ryan sighed.

His mother was apparently already in her room for the night. Ryan, not ready to abandon the night just yet went in to sit in his father's chair. He closed his eyes thinking of the fun he and Violet would have over the holiday. He had been invited for Christmas dinner.

Was he asleep and dreaming? It was pitch black so he couldn't tell if his eyes were open or closed. He felt a cool current of air reaching him, wrapping itself around him, not cold but comforting. After becoming enveloped in this cocoon of cool something reached right inside him. He felt it first in his bones then as an electric current raising the hairs on his arms. No words reached his ears but with the same clarity Violet had expressed in her communication with her grandmother, Ryan knew now for certain his mother was not well. He was suddenly drained. Was this fatigue brought on by the current of air or the sudden knowledge that his mother was sick? So much had happened in such a short time. *The move from Machias to Skowhegan, the big change in his school life, the animosity of Mr. Kneely, the excitement of meeting Violet, the strange goings on in his house, the challenge of his new paper route;* Ryan felt overwhelmed. He couldn't raise his arms or move his legs. He remained in that chair well into Christmas morning. He remained awake and did not observe any one come down the chimney with a bag of presents.

The only thing morning brought was a very clear memory of what had been conveyed and a feeling that he had met Violet's grandmother.

FRANK and ALICE

"I think your message was received Alice. The boy didn't panic though." Frank chuckled, "Did you notice, he never moved a muscle. Kinda like my first year after I was killed." Frank took stock of the situation. "So, we have his mother chasing her tail. The boy more confused than ever, and…" **Frank suddenly looked like he had been struck with a good right hook and went down in pain. He was up at the count of nine and continued his commentary** ***"Now give the boy some concrete evidence that his mother is not well. You can do it. We're almost home."***

As if struck with a distant thought he offered, "Merry Christmas Alice. I don't think I could offer you a finer gift than the chance to begin again." **Frank teared up, but then his memory winked off like a C*hristmas light.* He held his head,** ***"Remind me again Alice, why do I suddenly want to sing a Christmas Carol?"***

Alice looked at this man she shared space with. ***He had made it through four or five coherent thoughts in a row. Still, I don't think with a dented head like that he can make it in the real world. I won't be telling him that though.***

Seems the two co- inhabitants were both keeping secrets from one another.

CHAPTER TEN

WANDA

Wanda had been cold all night. She pulled the covers up around her chin leaving just her face and head exposed. She felt like an ongoing cold breeze had washed across her face, waves lapping a shoreline. She awoke feeling physically exhausted. Wanda could barely lift the bed-covers to get up and face another day. She put on her robe and moved to her mirror and sat down. Without another thought she lit up her first cigarette of the day. The smoke reached her lungs then bounced off the mirror facing her. When her head turned, her first thought was the smoke was distorting the mirror. Through the haze the right side of her face appeared drooped. Her breath caught. *Oh my god, have I had a stroke?* Her breathing quickened. She began coughing. Her eyes watered as she struggled to stand. She barely dared to look. The image in the mirror remained. Panicked, she stubbed out her cigarette and fairly flew down the stairs. Ryan was at the kitchen table. When his mother breathing heavily, entered the room he saw sheer terror in his mother's eyes.

"Ryan look at my face!"

Ryan looked. His face showed puzzlement.

"Can't you see how half of my face has drooped?!"

Ryan looked again. "Honestly mother I don't see anything different."

Not ready to accept this verdict she demanded, "Where's your father?"

"He's gone out. Believe it or not he said he's feeling guilty this morning."

Ryan's mother was totally flummoxed.

"Father came up the stairs whistling. He wished me a Merry Christmas and said he was going to try to find a store that might be open." Ryan threw up his hands, "Nope, not whiskey. He said he remembered a tradition his family used to practice on Christmas. Something to do with eggnog." Ryan opened his hands in confusion. "Anyway, he's not here."

Wanda Trussell continued to rub her face. She was as white as a ghost.

Ryan was worried about his mother. "Mother, there's nothing wrong with your face."

Ryan's mother took a deep breath. She seemed to forget about her own troubles for a moment and slammed her husband. "You can be assured if your father craves eggnog it indeed has everything to do with his whiskey." She coughed into her sleeve. "Are you sure you don't see something wrong with my face?"

"It looks the same to me." Ryan fed up with family drama announced his plan for the day. "By the way, my friend Violet has invited me to spend Christmas with her and her family. I was just about to leave you a note."

Wanda Trussell couldn't believe her son was being so insensitive and it suddenly showed as her face darkened and her eyes blazed.

Ryan beat her to the punch. "Mother, there is not even a Christmas tree here." He spread his arms, "There are no presents. I am going to enjoy the day with people who get it," he said with a bit of anger. Then he softened slightly, "I'm sorry you aren't feeling well but your face is fine. If you see Father tell him I'll try his eggnog when I get home; without the whiskey."

Ryan left his mother sitting there rubbing her face. He closed the door with a bit more energy than necessary. He skipped down the steps with a purpose, entering the sidewalk then looked back at his house while shaking his head. *Yes, it was just a house, certainly not a home.* A winter breeze started up and stung his face reminding him of last night. *A different breeze that carried a message. Then this morning his mother was certainly acting strange. Was she becoming desperate? How could he help? What would bring her peace? Is my father thinking about leaving? He has pretty much left already. Am I leaving? The ghosts seem to know more about what's happening in my house than I do. What will Violet think of all this?*

By the time Ryan ended his reverie, he was standing in front of Violet's house. He had his hand in his pocket fingering the small package he was bringing Violet. He took a refreshing breath, *now this is a home: A real snowman on the lawn he and Violet had made, decorations on each window, lights strung along the porch, smoke exiting the chimney, and all around a bed of snow. Well Merry Christmas, Ryan Trussell.*

Ryan listened to the crunch of his boots as he trudged up the walkway he had helped shovel. A smile lit up his face. *Yup, I'm home*

WANDA TRUSSELL

Wanda rose and went to the window. She parted the blind and watched her son on the sidewalk, glancing back and slowly shaking his head.

For just the briefest of moments she understood her son's disappointment. *It was Christmas morning, how could she have forgotten that.* She went into an eye watering coughing jag and when she emerged her concern for her son had disappeared. She spoke aloud to herself, "Now he knows how alone I feel every time I take a step down those stairs. I just want to stay in that bed forever. And how could he not see my face for god's sake." She coughed into her hand climbed the stairs and entered the bathroom, eager to give a different mirror a try. *The damn droop was still there.* She fairly ran to her room and dove beneath her covers.

Below, the door opened and a whistling Mr. Trussell sailed right into the kitchen. From above, Wanda hearing her husband return screwed up her face. *Eggnog! What is wrong with that man!* She turned over in her blankets. *Well I won't share my misfortune with him, hell he probably couldn't see the damage either.* She continued to twist in her sheets. *Two peas in a pod those two; Ryan with that damn journal he always has his head stuck in and his father drinking whiskey, sniffing glue and building boats in the basement.* Wanda groaned and pulled the blankets up over her head.

In the kitchen, Ryan's father had returned empty handed. He found his son's note and stopped whistling. *Of course there were no stores open this time of morning on Christmas, bah Humbug.* He made a cup of instant coffee and headed for the stairs but not before grabbing his bottle of Jack Daniels. He still craved eggnog, thinking, i*t's crazy what the holidays does to our head. I'll get some this afternoon.* With cup and bottle in hand he went down the steps.

FRANK and ALICE

In Ryan's room on Christmas morning a celebration of sorts was taking place. "*Alice, how did you manage that? She's chasing her tail. Seeing herself in that mirror with a bent face, that was genius. Did you see the look on the boy's face?"* Frank suddenly went blank. Seconds passed, then as if not missing a beat, Frank continued, "The *idea that his mother is becoming more and more deranged is taking root. When this is all over that boy will be witness one if anyone asks about his mother's state of mind."* Franks' face slacked once again, lost somewhere in his head.

Alice thought he had finished but no, he brought his head back up and there was more. "*I just love the different ways the wind blows with you, Alice, sometimes you are soft and gentle and cool, then suddenly you turn cold and calculating, Who are you? I hope you never get mad at me*".

A very cold breeze began moving the curtains. *"Ok, I can take a hint. I'll just shut up now. Merry Christmas by the way."* A blank look crossed Frank's face. "*It is Christmas isn't it?*"

RYAN and VIOLET

After a prayer involving the birth of the baby Jesus, followed by a pancake and ham breakfast the two were excused to her room. In this house presents were exchanged at exactly 10:00 am.

Violet's parents were downstairs preparing a family tradition. Joke gifts for each of them were among the pile of presents.

Violet showed Ryan the ugly ashtray she had found for her dad. She placed it in an empty cigarette carton. "The joke is he doesn't smoke. So he will have to come up with a creative way to display and use the ashtray for the entire year. Then he can ditch it." Ryan looked as if he didn't understand. "He wouldn't want to hurt my feelings now would he? With all the thought I put into it," Violet added, laughing. "Now here's what I got my mother."

Ryan decided he wanted to give Violet her present in the here and now. This was no joke gift. He handed her the box. Violet took her time and slowly unwrapped the box then opened it. A charm bracelet with one charm attached. A little silver ghost looked up at Violet. She looked at Ryan.

"We might never have met if it weren't for our own ghost story. So Merry Christmas, Violet."

Violet teared up.

Ryan added, "I hope I can add a lot more charms to that bracelet if you'll let me."

Violet, with eyes wet, gave Ryan a first hug. And a first kiss. No more just touching hands. When the two separated, Ryan was blushing. He covered it by offering, "wait till I tell you what happened last night."

FRANK

Frank had his nose deep in Ryan's journal. He was thinking aloud. He hadn't had a decent sleep in all the years since

his death but for some reason he was feeling chipper this morning. He couldn't remember why though.

"Seems the boy is being bothered by one of his teachers, a Mr. Kneely, his math teacher. The man has spoken to the boy about this house like he has an interest. The boy writes that this Mr. Kneely has driven by this house. Now he is trying to get the boy's mother to visit him at school. We don't need anyone upsetting our plans. Handling the woman of the house is going to be difficult enough. I still haven't figured out what to do with the drunken sailor in the cellar, but that can wait." **Frank couldn't believe how good he felt this morning, he was fairly bouncing around.**

Alice in a moment of cool clarity knew very well who this Mr. Kneely was. She didn't know his real name back then but she could still feel his hands and arms smothering her. She could see out of windows as well as Frank. She had observed the man staring at the boy from his car. Now it all began to make sense. A violent rush of air rattled Ryan's bedroom windows. Frank got the gist of it. ***If Alice knows this man, it can't be good.***

Frank made a decision. The journal page turned. His hand began to move. ***There is danger lurking, keep your eyes wide open!***

RYAN and VIOLET

The air was crisp but filled with sunshine on this early Christmas afternoon as the two sat rocking on a swing bench on the front porch at Violet's home. Violet was thinking about what Ryan had told her earlier. "So you believe something made you feel your mother was ill but would be feeling better soon? And you believe it was my grandmother sending the message?"

Ryan stopped the swing. "That's not exactly what I felt. But yes it was your grandmother speaking to me in the way you described she speaks to you. I could just feel her warmth through the coolness. It was like I was being assured my mother would soon be at peace. Things would be better." Ryan scrunched up his face. "Of course in the morning my mother came down claiming something was wrong with her face." Ryan was feeling exasperated. "So I'm not sure that means the same thing as feeling better soon. The only thing I'm sure of is that it was your grandmother sending the message.

"Well what else could it mean?"

"I have no idea but I do know my mother is getting worse. She is seeing things in her mind. It scares me."

"What does your father say?"

"He doesn't have a clue. I don't think their paths cross much anymore. He's sleeping in the cellar at night and when he is up he's either gone to work or at work in the cellar, if you catch my meaning."

Violet nodded her head. "Do you think you can sneak me back into your room?

I agree with you that the spirit of my grandmother is there. I could feel it last time I was in that attic. Maybe she'll convey something more through me."

With the decision made to get Violet back into his room Ryan asked, "How do you convince your parents to let you spend a night at my house?"

"I'm not going to your house silly I'm spending the night with my girlfriend again." Violet winked. She had told her parents a first lie. She thought about that for a moment then shrugged it off. This was all just too important to miss.

The two met just before dark in front of Ryan's house. The street lights were on, stars just emerging. Ryan's famous and fabulous shadows were just now completing their evening crawl. "You stay right here. I'll make sure the coast is clear." The house was already in the dark. He looked across the street and noticed a for sale sign on the lawn. He had never spoken to the old lady who lived there he was told she was an invalid. *She must have passed,* thought Ryan. He turned back to Violet and put his finger to his lips. When he entered, the usual music was coming from the cellar. Ryan climbed the stairs and used the bathroom. The light under his mother's door was on. He knocked and called out his mother's name.

"Don't come in I look a fright." She sounded drugged her words stilted. "Your father managed to find a market. **Egg nog,"** she fairly shouted. "He said to tell you," Her voice faded like the end of day.

Ryan uttered thanks and went down to retrieve his house guest.

With Violet tucked safely in his room he went downstairs and poured two glasses of eggnog, all dressed up in a red and green carton, a good portion already missing. Ryan mused, *I bet father didn't drink that straight. A new old family tradition. Merry Christmas.*

Back in the room with Violet the two sipped and planned how she might reach out to her grandmother. With Violet on the bed lying back eyes to the ceiling thinking, Ryan went to his desk and opened his journal.

The latest message stared up at him.

There is danger lurking, keep your eyes wide open!

Violet heard Ryan gasp and joined him at his desk.

Ryan pointed to the message written in scary handwriting.

Violet's eyes opened wide. A breeze seemed to suddenly envelop the message. Violet felt it. "I knew it. My grandmother is here, I can just feel it," she whispered. She began to look around as if her grandmother might materialize from thin air.

The two moved back to the bed and lay down side by side staring up at the ceiling. After a lengthy silence Ryan said, "Let's talk this through. How do we get to the bottom of all this?"

Violet studied the light as if seeking enlightenment. She suddenly turned her head toward Ryan. How about using your Journal? You write in it. Now someone else is using it. What if you start asking questions in writing?"

"You mean kind of like a Ouija board." He nodded then affirmed, "Yeah, I like that."

MR. EDWARD MOLUNKUS KNEELY

Mr. Kneely turned on a pan of water to boil then rummaged through his refrigerator knowing full well there was very little to find. A tin foil wrapper produced a pork chop fried up a week earlier. He broke two eggs into a fry pan on the stove and cut up the chop into little pieces adding them to the sizzle. He added butter then busted the yolks and let the whole mixture congeal. He drizzled horseradish sauce over the top then blanketed the whole mess with two slices of cheddar cheese. He removed the pan of boiling water and spooned instant coffee into a cup. His mind wandered as he stirred the blackness round and round, round and round, round and round. *There was so much that needed doing.* The concoction on the stove left unattended began to smoke. The toast popped up, the sound bringing him out of the fog. Smoke reached his nostrils he turned and grabbed the handle on the frying pan not thinking. He yelped as he burned his hand. He dropped the pan on the stove spilling some of the contents directly onto the burner. Swearing aloud while shaking his burned hand he managed to turn off the heat. He went to the sink and turned on the faucet. Still swearing he ran his burned hand under the cool water. He was sweating. He grabbed a dish towel and wrapped it around the handle of the fry pan. He salvaged what he could. The top of the stove would be getting the best of this meal. He opened a window. He dumped and scraped what appeared edible onto a plate then turned to the toast buttering his hand as well as the toast. He took a deep breath calming himself. He looked at the mess he had made of the stove but chose to ignore it. With his meal on the kitchen table and his coffee before him he opened yesterday's paper and began to re-read old news. His mind was not on old news. The real headlines remained in his head. He chewed and swallowed as one thought after another accompanied each bite, his hand continuing to ache. He reached the classified section before the fog in his mind lifted. Through smoke still hovering above the kitchen table it suddenly became clear as day what he needed to do.

Ed Kneely had an inkling when he first met the boy that he was living in his old house. He traveled past that house twice a week and thought he had seen the boy leaving. First kid he'd ever seen in that house. When the boy gave him an opening by appearing to be a smart-aleck, he just naturally pounced.

Edward Kneely had kept a keen eye on his old house since he returned to this town, driving by weekly. He had observed a young girl walking by the place for the past three years. He didn't recognize her so he was certain she didn't attend his school. He'd seen her peeking through the windows on occasion. She appeared curious about the place. It was by accident that he observed this same girl walking with the boy, Ryan who now inhabited his classroom and his old house.

Edward Kneely still had a key to the house and had found it useful over the years to be an unwelcome voice in the walls, a thump in the night. He had heard the stories of the place being haunted since coming back to town and did his part to keep the rumors alive. At times he felt cold breezes himself but was so busy scaring the occupants that he was never truly troubled.

So over the years he had managed to keep the place mostly empty. He welcomed the stories of the house being haunted and if any man could become a haunt it would have been his father.

Edward had another and more recent reason to want to keep people out of that house. He had felt the presence of both his father and the woman he had lured into that house and strangled. To his mind the woman's death had been an accident but the police would never see it that way. He thought back to his good luck at the time. A long and lingering winter storm kept the death from getting any air time.

The last time he had spent the night in the house he had felt the anger of both his father and the woman gaining strength, seeping through the walls. If he could get this latest family out he would end all this. *I'll just burn the place down.*

Then a thought struck him perhaps there was a way. He remained at the table with his head in his hands blowing on his burned fingers. He had seen the boys' mother walking to the market on several trips down this street looking lost and forlorn, definitely not happy. The woman of the house just might be an answer. His first attempt to meet the lady had gone unanswered. The boy Ryan, reentered his head which brought Mr. Kneely back to his own childhood.

{When his father died a violent death Ed was about the same age as this kid Ryan. He had cheered the death of an abusive alcoholic who terrorized both he and his mother. No one had been charged in his father's death because in reality the whole town had been abused by the man and whether someone had killed his father or not no one seemed very interested. His death was ruled a suicide since the man had conveniently choked on his own vomit which offered a simple diagnosis. The blow to his head could have happened when he passed out and fell. Only Edward knew the whole story.

Edward's mother left for a warmer climate within a week and did not include fifteen year old Edward Molunkus Nadeau in her travel plans. When found living alone in that house, Edward was placed with the state. He eventually landed in a foster home in Augusta, Maine and at that point was still a relatively stable young man. He was adopted when news of his mother's death in Florida reached the family he was living with.

So at the ripe old age of seventeen he had a new last name, Kneely. A new name but with troubling memories that were just now bubbling up. Edward kept to himself, but there was a rage beginning to smolder and brew inside. His new parents, the Kneelys', were good to him and he managed to keep it together long enough to graduate high school but still hadn't come to grips with the anger just below the surface.

He left the state and worked construction in Massachusetts. On the job doing manual labor, at one end of a piece of wood or drywall, he had plenty of time to bring his anger to a boil. A coworker seeming to tug the board or sheet rock in an opposite direction caused a series of arguments and later on fist fights. When one argument got out of hand he used a survey stake on the guy and landed in jail for the first time. The judge directed him to anger management.

A counselor saw enough in him to arrange enrollment in a junior college when he was released from the program.

Ed Kneely did not want to go back to jail so he really tried. One of his new classmates spoke of getting his real estate license and the two seemed to get on well. He sat a couple of open houses with his new friend and saw how easy it was to enter a vacant house. Wandering room to room in empty houses imagining living there, Ed found an outlet that would not have him back in the can. The rage continued but was transformed. Edward saw the usefulness of getting into empty houses.

He passed his Real Estate license on his first attempt. He joined a firm and began entering vacant houses as part of his work. Why he was drawn to these houses he didn't understand at first. If a prospective buyer was with him he was able to resist the urge that would overtake him when alone.

When alone he would enter a bedroom and lie down on the floor or a bed if available. He closed his eyes and imagined himself in his old bedroom back in Skowhegan. His father's voice reached his ears. A mean and abusive voice that would raise in pitch when striking his mother.

To the world he showed a bright young man with an affinity for math and with a Real Estate license and a part time job. He stayed in school to get his two year degree. One of his teachers suggested he continue his education. 'Use your affinity for math and become a teacher.' When Ed thought about it, school had been the one safe place in his life.

He enrolled in a four year institution and ended up with a teaching degree. After graduation his proud adopted parents offered him a place to stay temporarily. With a trunk full of clothing and not much else he drifted back to Maine. He spent the summer in Augusta, back doing construction.

By late August he was sick of the construction business but had managed to keep his temper in check. On a Sunday morning over a cup of coffee he scanned the classified ads. A teaching position for a math teacher was advertised in the Sunday Telegram in his old home town of Skowhegan. Edward applied, was hired and returned to the same school he had attended

years ago. At age twenty three all grown up, he was about to become a math teacher in Skowhegan Junior High.

Was is fate that brought him back to the house he was gazing up at? At first he simply walked past the house on Summer Street. Reminded of how easy it had been to legally enter houses he obtained a new Real Estate license for the state of Maine. Ed visited his old home in his official capacity the first time. The fifteen minute walk-through with the prospective buyer had him pointing out all the homes flaws. During that walk-through memories percolated up and Ed, in the moment, knew he did not want this house sold.

He continued to visit his old room when the house was for rent and later when it was occupied. He couldn't afford to buy the place at least not yet but needed from time to time to lie on the floor in his old room listening, remembering the sounds and stoking his anger. Keeping the place empty became a part-time job. He lied to prospective buyers and renters alike. When it was occupied he stoked rumors of the place being haunted. For the most part it worked. The house changed hands frequently and no one stayed long. Periods of vacancy allowed Ed to spend many a night in his old house fueling his obsession with the place.

Then one night following a day of working with what he termed morons, he was angrier than usual. Of course Ed was now a professional and so he attempted to keep the pot from boiling over. It began in the most unlikely of places, a shopping aisle for Christ's sake. Ed didn't drink but the lady bent over picking up oranges that had toppled, looked like she could sure use one. He bent to help, not speaking just being helpful. A conversation that began as a simple thank you found the two of them necking in Ed's car an hour later. Ed got her name, Alice, and the easiest date he had ever been on. They shared a sandwich. The lady suggested a six pack of Ballantine Ale might wash down that sandwich. She had a gleam in her eyes. Ed viewed this as promising He sipped his coke and listened. Alice dialed up an easy listening station and talked and talked and talked. One bottle after another dropped onto the rear floor. Light left the sky.

When Ed suggested they go to his apartment, which was not really his apartment but rather his old house, at the moment vacant, the woman readily agreed. Ed had actually begun to relax. The anger seeped out of him and he began to think this could be fun. Sleeping in his old house raised anger but also brought a sense of peace. When they entered the house and went to his old room peace settled over him.

They had just laid together on the bed when Ed turned to embrace the woman. Suddenly the pipes clanged in the bathroom the heat came on and the walls began to tremble. The woman half in the bag overreacted. She sat bolt upright and began to scream. In an effort to quiet and silence her Edward Kneely panicked. This was not his house he should not be found here. He tried to calm her but she was having none it. Ed wrapped his arms around her chest and squeezed the air out of her trying to quiet her. She struggled still making noise. He continued to squeeze. All his pent up anger took on a life of its own and he imagined he was squeezing the life out of his abusive father. Time passed. When he returned to his right mind the woman was dead still in his grasp.

Shocked at what he had done Ed left her where she lay. He cleaned up any possible links to himself and he ran.

For several days he worried. Every morning he scanned the headlines; nothing. His students took the brunt of his worry. A frayed temper had him throwing chalk at a student who was talking rather than listening. He stalked the rows of his classroom looking for trouble

Nature intervened when a once in a generation snowstorm arrived. Classes canceled for days and businesses closed. Ed wanted in the worst way to drive past his old house but resisted the urge. During the week of canceled classes he started his day with headlines first then the obituaries. There was no mention of a death on Summer Street. By sheer luck he seemed to have gotten away with what he would have termed an accident but would surely be construed as murder by the authorities.

That was all behind him now. He needed to get back into that house once again. He needed to lay again in his old room; alone. Even beyond the anger it was the only time he felt at peace. He needed to get this latest family to leave.

The smoke still hovered around the light. The smell of burned pork still stung his nose. His burned fingers still smarted; anger bubbled to his eyes. Noisily he dumped his plate and the frying pan into the sink. He looked out the window above the sink. He took a deep breath today was Christmas. Edward Kneely shared his own special day with the birth of our savior. He snorted at the idea. The whiteness of the snow outside was like an empty movie screen. That screen suddenly filled with child hood memories of a day that should have been celebrated. For two special reasons actually. A sudden memory of years of special days passed before his eyes. His abusive father appeared, even after all this time causing his body to suddenly shake involuntarily.

Frank Kneely appeared like a ghost of Christmas past. Christmas was simply an extra day he could terrorize his family. Edward was never offered a birthday party. Christmas was simply a time for his father to return from a night of carousing and fighting in local watering holes. Bruised and battered he entered knowing he could win the war at home. When faced with a tearful boy displaying disappointment that his father did not return with a gift, he would lean his whiskey breath close to the boy and bellow, 'we all get older,' what's the big deal?' He grabbed the boys chin. 'How about a beer?' Then he would wink and grab his wife and take her to their room. Edward just a boy of five was left to try to make sense of it.

His mother suddenly appeared in the snow outside the window. He unconsciously nodded his head. In her own feeble way she had tried to fight back. *He pictured a cake. His birthday cake. He had helped frost those cakes year after year. And year after year his father spoiled things. When the sweet smell reached the old man's sniffer, his father tracked it to its source. Laughing like a fool, year after year he poked his grimy fingers into the frosting right to the heart of the cake, ripping out a piece and filling his mouth.*

As for the Christmas season, again year after year, a naked scrawny tree made it into the house. With mother and son proudly standing by the lighted tree his father stood glaring at them. By the time Christmas day arrived Frank had pissed in the tree stand several times and the tree was already on the porch. When Christmas music arrived via the radio, dear old dad began swearing, throwing his arms out in disgust while switching to his favorite country station.

With one more withering look at his son Frank grabbed his wife around the waist and forced her to their bedroom. Edward was left alone to navigate a peanut butter sandwich and little else.

When Edward thought back to those days he found a father who when he was speaking to him, asked Ed to pick sides in the constant screaming and hollering taking place between his parents. Whether in the house, a grocery aisle, a parking lot, or on the street when Edward refused to support his father he would feel the slap across his face and the admonition that followed, *'See that's why you don't deserve a thing from me you little shit.'*

As he grew older worse memories replaced celebrations missed. Memories of blows he didn't see. His mother received those behind closed doors. Edward could hear them land and the whimpering that followed. In his room lying on a rumpled bed never tucked in like a normal kid but rather balled in a fetal position, Edward held an invisible knife. In those moments with each cry of pain that exited those walls a knife entered his father's heart.

Since his return to Maine the visits to this house offered moments of peace even as his anger festered. Over time lying there on the floor before finding peace, his anger would flare. His mother came back to him in his mind. He had tried to be protective of his mother but she wouldn't stand up for herself. Some of Edward's anger was directed at that weakness. She constantly made excuses for his father. Edward here now as an adult saw her as a weak woman and an ineffective mother. At this very moment he could see himself standing behind her in the kitchen as she did dishes. Their eyes would meet in the mirror above the sink. Blackened eyes and bruised lips looked back at him.

'Why don't we just leave? He implored his mother each time his father assaulted her.

The big sandstone building at the edge of town seemed to control his mother's mind and words. *'The church doesn't abide with divorce.' She would sigh aloud grabbing a dish towel and kiddingly snapped it at him. Chasing him across the kitchen then ruffling his hair she spoke just above a whisper, 'You'll understand someday Edward.'*

Edward snorted aloud. Still staring out the window in the here and now, he had known even way back then he'd never understand and he hadn't gone to church with his mother to pretend otherwise.

Edward Kneely found himself sweating and shaking. A final satisfaction reached the screen in his head. *The old man laying lifeless on the floor.*

The bitterness of the past had taken its toll, shaped him, and hardened him. In his public life he became a man in a profession where he could show his anger by demanding respect. Demanded not earned. He continued over the years to brood and his anger was usually on full display in his classroom. A safe place to exercise it with no repercussions.

Between owners he had easy access to his old house and when it was rented he managed to frequent the place often enough to keep it haunted and empty. He was at his happiest when he could enter his vacant house and curl up on a bed or the floor and pretend he lived here happily with a wife and a dog.

Remembering his own child hood, there were never any other kids or a dog. Now he worked with and hated kids. He loved dogs though. In his public life as a member of the teaching profession he saw no need to consider the kids feelings. His father's words had unknowingly become his own silent mantra and his teaching philosophy. *'Get over it. We all get older. What's the big deal? How about a beer?'* Each remark a knife cut meant to demean and discourage. So like his father he had become a bully. What better place to bully than from the front of the classroom.

But now he had a different plan in place. Kill them with kindness was a whole nother philosophy and one that just might work in this situation. He had not only driven Ryan's street recently intending to be seen but had watched and learned the pattern of when Ryan's mother left her house. Just last week he had walked right up to her on aisle 8 in the supermarket and introduced himself. The woman looked troubled but tried to smile through it when he mentioned he was Ryan's teacher. Probing gently it became obvious Ryan had not mentioned the problems he was having in Mr. Kneely's class. That provided just the opening Mr. Kneely needed. First he commented on what a nice polite boy Ryan seemed to be. "What a good example you must have set, Mrs. Trussell. I'm sorry you weren't able to make the parent teacher conference." A genuine smile followed.

He held out his hand, "It's so good to meet you Mrs. Trussell."

Wanda shook hands shakily and announced, "My name is Wanda no one calls me Mrs. Trussell. There is no Mrs. Trussell. Actually no one calls me anything at all."

"Well Wanda that's unfortunate. I would like to become a friend."

Before Wanda could respond he continued, "I know I said Ryan is doing well in my class and academically he is.

But he seems to be a loner and at this age that is not a good thing. I don't mean to pry but is everything good at home? I watch Ryan sitting in class with his head in the clouds and he's not smiling. Can I help in some way?"

In aisle 8 Wanda with a public face being put on her demons, began a melt-down.

Mr. Kneely ushered the distraught woman right out the front doors of the A&P market and into the front seat of his car where Wanda's sad dismal life, like a boat in a bottle, sent out a distress signal. It wasn't lost on Edward Kneely that his last meeting in a super market hadn't ended so well.

Wanda's trips to the supermarket increased to twice a week at a time which fit a concerned math teacher's schedule.

CHAPTER TWELVE

WANDA

Wanda bundled up for her half mile walk to the A&P. She had changed the hundred brush strokes, to the mornings. Nobody in this house noticed and now that callousness seemed a relief. Nothing to explain. In her mirror the only contortion she was seeing lately was an ongoing smile. She kept it hidden as best she could but it was there if anyone had chosen to see it.

This morning the wind was up and she was feeling the full brunt of a Maine winter. Her hair blew freely in the wind but she was too happy to notice. The municipal parking lot appeared and she quickly spotted the car at the edge of a giant mountain of snow.

The engine was running, a white plume of exhaust rising quickly into a clear sky. The minute walk from sighting to reaching the car had Wanda unconsciously falling from a plane her life passing before her eyes. *All her life she had played by the rules. First she had worked hard to become an accomplished musician.*

In a moment of weakness she had succumbed to the charms of a man ill-suited for her. Becoming pregnant with Ryan forced her to follow a different set of rules. Well she followed those damn rules to the point of hating herself and everyone around her, even thinking seriously about ending it all. Now a professional person, one much like herself, was showing a genuine interest in Wanda the person. Free fall over and landing safely, her feet took an unconscious little dance step which brought her to the passenger door already being opened from within.

FRANK and ALICE

Sitting in the recliner in the living room of a now empty Trussell residence, Frank was thinking aloud. *"Did you see the look on her face when she left? She looks happy for god's sake. Hell she was humming while she was fixing her face. What's going on? Any Ideas Alice?"*

Alice had watched the same transformation. In her own experience and observation it could mean only one thing. Wanda had a lover. But who, and how could this be blunted? All this thinking had her flitting about the room. Frank could sit and remember and forget again all he wanted, she needed to act.

RYAN and VIOLET

Back in school for the first day since Christmas break Ryan was pleasantly surprised that Mr. Kneely was extending his holiday. The substitute handed out a worksheet that took maybe ten minutes to complete. Ryan spent the next half hour thinking about all that happened before and during the break. Violet had been a constant companion for a dozen days and a couple nights. Ryan had arrived at feelings that moved beyond friendship. He was in love but had no one to talk to about any of it so he wrote about it. He also had taken Violet's advice and was asking the guest Ghost Writer, to give him more help in understanding what if anything was being asked of him. Five days had passed.

Every morning Ryan opened his journal first thing; nothing. He had not seen Mr. Kneely at any point during the holidays and he wasn't here today so everything in Ryan's life except Violet seemed to be on hold. His mother was acting even more peculiar than normal. Just a week ago she had been sure her face was distorted and disfigured. In the last week she was applying lip stick combing her hair and going out frequently for hours at a time. She did not appear any happier with Ryan or his father but maybe happier with herself for some reason.

Ryan would be meeting Violet on the sidewalk and they would do their homework at the library. It was always the best part of Ryan's day.

When he arrived on the sidewalk Violet was already there. Her eyes sparkled with excitement. She moved from foot to foot swaying, carrying news of some sort. She gushed, "I had a dentist appointment this morning, Ryan."

Ryan looked at her strangely not knowing how to respond.

"On my way back to school I walked by the A&P."

Ryan held out his hands begging for something he could hang his hat on.

Violet smiled mischievously, "I saw your mother get into a strange car. She paused then added, "Wait for it, wait for it, there was a man behind the wheel." That drew Ryan's full attention.

"So that's it," said Ryan aloud.

"What's it?"

"The reason for my mother acting weirdly, she's seeing someone. Did you recognize him?"

"It was hard to see through the window from a distance so no I didn't recognize him."

Ryan sighed deeply. "Do I let my mother know what I know or just wait and see what comes next?"

"If it was my mother I would stay out of it."

"Yeah you're probably right but I would like to know who he is. I just might do a little detective work on my own. This is a lot to think about." Ryan sighed deeply. "I'm going in Violet. I need to think and I do that best when I am writing down my thoughts. I'll see you tomorrow."

It was at the end of a long lingering warming hug that would keep them both safe for another twenty four hours that Ryan said it aloud, "I love you Violet."

Violet looked right into Ryan's eyes. "Well of course you do."

An awkward moment where Ryan could think of nothing to say in response hung between them. Finally Ryan managed, "I guess I'll see you tomorrow then."

"Well of course you will." She gave Ryan's hand a squeeze and left him alone on the sidewalk.

The house was quiet both parents in their respective places. Ryan climbed the stairs snapped on his lamp and began to let his mind kick in following the movement of his pen. First he noted there were no new messages from the (Ghost Writer) as he had dubbed him.

He began by writing what had just occurred on the sidewalk and what he was feeling. He had said those words aloud and inside he knew what they meant to him. Did they mean the same to Violet? She hadn't responded the way he'd hoped but maybe it was different for a girl he'd just have to wait and hope.

He turned to a new page and began asking his resident ghosts as well as himself a series of questions. *When could his mother have met someone? She seldom went out. More lately though.*

How long has this been going on? Is it possible this someone is just a person to talk to?

How would his father react if he knew?

What does this mean for me? Will we move if my father finds out? What about my friendship with Violet? What about the two of you?

Thoughts flooded his mind faster than he could record them. He closed the journal and snapped off the light in one motion. No dinner for him. He was exhausted. When he closed his eyes a cool breeze sifted through his blankets. Tonight the breeze was not comforting but rather demanding that he stay awake and figure this all out.

ALICE

Alice was not only invading Ryan's sleep she was storming the house in a frenzy. If what she had just read in Ryan's journal was real, her plan for escape might just be in jeopardy. She blew into Wanda's room. Seated at her dressing table Wanda now brushed her hair twice a day. The brush moved through

her hair with a new sense of purpose. A smiling relaxed posture reflected a sense of new serenity in the woman. The look on her face was of one who had mentally at least already made a decision. *This isn't good,* thought Alice. *This isn't good at all.* Alice had never left this house. She would be defenseless out there, blown about by any breeze that chose to rise. There had to be another way to end this.

FRANK

Frank sat in the dark in the living room. The possibility that Alice might escape this eternity had him ruminating his past, his present and what might be his always.

His past he had no problem remembering if he was being honest with himself. *He was never a good man, at least never a good man measured by normal standards. But he worked, held a job, came home at night, slept in his own bed with his wife. Helped raise a kid.* He smiled. Thinking about the distant past didn't make his head hurt so much. So he remembered. In his memory all the rough edges had been removed and he was the victim. He could smell the power the devil's brew held over him. But he had handled that and to his mind liquor had not led to his downfall. None of it his fault really when you thought about it. He sighed, his head turning to the cellar door. The man of the house was even now toasting himself two floors down. Frank began mentally comparing stories. *This man has a wife and kid. He holds a job, he drinks to excess. Yet he's down there now putting a damn boat in a bottle and will get up in the morning put on his pants and go back to work. No one is threatening to kill him. How did I come to this? I don't even know for sure who bludgeoned me to death.*

And why am I a prisoner in my own home? The here and now brought on a migraine. He felt the stirrings of a breeze entering. *What will I do without Alice?* Her cold breeze sent a chill through him. He followed the breeze up the stairs to Ryan's room where the pages of Ryan's journal ruffled open to his latest entry.

PART TWO

Author aside: Sometimes when it seems a situation is nearly overwhelming in its own right something new and unexpected throws a wrench into the mix. Just such a wrench, (a family of wrenches actually) arrives to Summer Street in Skowhegan Maine, in the early part of January 1960.

CHAPTER THIRTEEN

BEDFORD DENNIS, wife MARCIA, her invalid FATHER, and PLUTO the dog

Marcia stood on newly shoveled front steps frantically moving her hands trying to direct her husband to a spot near the front door. A foot of snow that covered the driveway had not been plowed. The family dog, Pluto sat with his back to the storm door leading into the house. To a casual observer it would appear the long haired mixed breed mid-sized dog, had his paws over his eyes.

Bedford Dennis, eyes glued to the left outside mirror did not look like he was enjoying himself. The truck's rear tires spun up snow and slid sideways, perilously close to the house. Bedford watched his wife's mouth move as she held up her hand signaling stop! Bedford breathing heavily, stress pulling his eyebrows into what could be mistaken for a flock of geese flying south, took a deep breath and put the vehicle back into Drive. He pulled back down into the street. A run on sentence reached his mind. *It was Sunday morning and it had snowed and the driveway wasn't plowed and it was cold and he didn't want to be here anyway. Damn it!*

He sat in the middle of the street looking out the windshield at the power line all dressed up for winter in a coat of white. In the moment he followed that power line all the way back to Vermont. *That power line was the very reason for being uprooted and forced to leave his native state. He had begged Marcia for more time to find a new job. Marcia had responded that he'd have to get up from their couch and put on proper clothes if that was going to happen.*

Marcia had been promoted. Bedford had lost his job. Simple math equation. To Bedford's mind his wife's exit line was made to induce sympathy. "My father is not well and his insurance doesn't cover near enough. We need two incomes, this promotion will hold us till you find something."

Well he couldn't stand the old coot anyway, hell the man can't even talk.

A flurry of new thoughts reached his mind as those power lines reached right to the top of the mountain where he had worked. *Bedford's job as a sales manager for a ski resort had disappeared quicker than the snow on the slopes in a spring rain when the resort changed hands pre-season. By November just as the first lasting snow hit the ground it became clear the company was moving on a different path. Bedford had worked with area radio stations to get the word out. This new company had decided it was going to use the power of television on a nationwide scale to draw customers. Bedford had never done television advertising. He found he wasn't very good at it. When confronted with the reality of losing his position Bedford refused to believe this could happen to him. Right up until the last day of his two week notice Bedford believed they would see the error of their ways. Radio wasn't dead he insisted.*

Marcia listened to the griping and blasphemy that emerged from the couch for a month after that final day. She then took the hitch in Bedford's professional giddy-up as an opportunity to better herself. As of tomorrow she would be the new office manager of the Central Maine Power office in Waterville, Maine.

Bedford, unemployed, had taken up residence on their cozy couch and watched the last leaves fall and disappear under the cover of what had been his livelihood. When the first mountain snow appeared and stayed and men began grooming the trails he remained on that couch. Along with the griping and swearing, snatches of optimism emerged giving Marcia hope. Marcia noticed Bedford always brought a beer to their discussions. She also noted that there were no wet boots in the entry. He couldn't even take the dog out for a walk for god's sake much less go look for a job. Every evening her father somehow communicated a full description of Bedford's efforts, or lack thereof. If their dog Pluto could have talked he could have added to that communication.

They didn't own the condo they were living in, (it was part of Bedford's benefit package, belonging to the new owners of the resort.) Marcia commented on the dwindling number of days they would be allowed to occupy the place. Bedford seemed unmoved. Something will turn up he assured his wife as he rose to get another pop. With daddy dear giving daily reports, Marcia finally came to a decision.

Bedford looked into the trucks outside mirror. Marcia's decision was staring him right in the eye. Plumes of heat exhaust and oily smoke exited the chimney. Daddy had arrived with Marcia a week ago.

Pluto not being able to tell his owner how he was being mistreated had stayed and endured the time alone with the man of the house. It hadn't been pleasant. Freed now from the rental truck and the careless way Bedford treated him while Marcia and her father had come to settle the new place Pluto sat at the foot of Marcia tail wagging. The mutt looked at home already. Bedford had yet to see the inside of the place, but as sure as night follows day one stick of furniture was sure to be sitting in his favorite chair as soon as he unloaded it. As if thinking in tandem the blind in the living room moved, Bedford could just make out the hand holding the slats apart. He began maneuvering the truck back up the drive, grumbling to himself, *Christ she could have had the driveway plowed at least.*

With her mind made up and a job offer Marcia had laid out what she intended to do, no ifs, ands, or buts. Bedford was finally forced to face reality. He was to stay behind in their condo packing their belongings, take good care of her beloved dog, then rent a truck and drive the icy roads of Vermont onto the equally icy roads of Maine to the town of Skowhegan. In the mirror a world of white surrounded him, he chuckled at the irony of the street name; *Summer Street if you can believe it.*

Marcia hollered, her hands sending clear signals to get on with it. Pluto sat quietly on the porch, not wagging his tail with excitement any longer. He recognized the look in his master's eyes in the driver's seat. He had experienced the best and the worst of the man.

Bedford eased up the grade. This time he feathered the gas and the truck followed his lead. He came to a stop sat back took a breath and turned off the engine. Marcia gave him a big smile and hollered, "Come on in I have coffee ready, let me show you the place."

Bedford let the stress seep out of his sore tired muscles, he stretched and breathed deeply. Exiting the cab, slipping and nearly falling, he managed to grab the porch railing. He climbed the steps. Pluto did not move forward to greet his master, he remained a barrier at the door. Bedford gave a smiling Marcia, a peck on the offered cheek then turned his head to survey the street.

At the foot of the driveway on his immediate left a small stream cut a slash in the snow and disappeared into a culvert under the street. To his right was a similar building to his own. Christmas lights still hung along the porch. Directly across the street an older house that had seen better days showed no signs that it had received the seasonal treatment. The blinds were drawn in every window. Standing on the porch was a boy looking at him, seemingly taking in these new tenants. The boy waved tentatively. Bedford ignored the gesture and turned to enter the house. Pluto moved away from the door allowing entry. When he tried to follow, Bedford pushed him away with his foot and closed the door. Pluto remained a pooch on the porch.

RYAN

Ryan watched the man and woman disappear inside. He waved and spoke just loud enough to be heard by the dog. Ryan had watched the man nudge the dog with his foot.

The dog turned and studied the boy. Ryan picked up his shovel from the porch and began to clear the walkway to the street. As he shoveled he reflected on a hundred things. Now he had new neighbors to ponder. And they had a dog. Which brought on further pondering and wistful thinking. He thought back to when he was just six and had first asked for a furry pet. They were living in Machias and had a large back yard and no close neighbors. After throwing a ball in the air, muffing it then retrieving it time after time, he thought what fun it would be to have a dog fetch and bring that ball right back to his feet. He remembered entering the kitchen. His father was at work.

Suddenly he was reliving the conversation. *"Mother I would like to have a dog for my birthday, I'll be seven and I promise to take care of him."*

His mother had looked at him oddly, scrutinizing him, then declaring, *"So you already know the gender of the animal then why are you asking me? Where does* ***he*** *live now? Have you seen* ***him****?"*

Ryan was left stumbling and stammering over words that did little to better his case.

"Exactly. You have no idea of what you're talking about. And in addition to confusion have you forgotten I am allergic to pet hair. Of course you've forgotten, all you think of is yourself." She left the room momentarily only to return with a possible solution. She looked her son up and down. She held up a tape measure. She coughed for a full ten seconds and then red faced delivered her punch line. "Tell you what when you get your weight up to 140 pounds and you hover at a height of 5'7" you can have a dog." With that she lit up and left the room Ryan was left to fetch for himself, in all manner of things.

Ryan threw the last shovel of snow onto the banking. Thoroughly warmed and ready to go in and make a little snack for himself, Ryan watched the dog leave the porch and make a beeline for several small trees on the edge of the property. When he finished staking out his territory he looked directly at Ryan and wagged his tail.

"Hello boy, welcome to the neighborhood."

The dog wagged his tail with enthusiasm. Ryan invited him over to shake hands. Pluto looked both ways crossing the street and approached putting his nose directly into Ryan's glove.

Ryan patted him and spoke softly to him. The door across the street opened and the lady of the house looked over and saw boy and dog enjoying one another. She waved and announced that she was Marcia and the dog was Pluto. Ryan introduced himself from across the street.

"I'm sure we'll be seeing a lot of you, Pluto seems to like you." She called her pet inside. Pluto left reluctantly but Ryan nuzzled his nose promising aloud they would get to know one another.

Ryan made himself a very unsatisfying sandwich and began a walk to Violet's house. The dog was still inside. Ryan sighed thinking once again of how much he would like to own a dog.

They did a crossword puzzle together on the dining room table then went to Violet's room to talk strategy. Ryan still had his pronouncement of love on his mind but had decided to let things slide for now. He mentioned he had made a new friend. A dog named Pluto. Violet who had no pet in her own life said that was cool and she would like to meet Pluto sometime. Then it was back to business. No mention of mutual love.

"As far as a strategy to figure out what's going on in my house. I don't have a clue. I'm hoping our resident ghosts will get back to me on that."

Violet yawned and got up off the bed where the two had been studying the ceiling once again. She checked her non-existent watch and declared, "Let's plan an afternoon trip to your house and walk right in. You introduce me as your friend and see what happens. I'm betting they won't care a whit. From what you have told me and I have seen for myself, you are invisible." Ryan, still lying on the bed turned his head to study this girl who had changed his life. He nodded. "Why not, maybe that will shake things up around there." He nodded once again. "Let's plan it for Wednesday afternoon. The dog might be out, you can meet him." The kisses goodbye were growing in length and intensity. Their bodies seemed to melt into one another. Ryan's heart was finding a new gear. The light had come on, so this was what love felt like. He could only hope Violet was feeling the same.

* * *

Ryan spent another mundane day at school. Mid-winter blues seemed to dominate classes. Two weeks til mid-year exams and everything was review. To Ryan it all felt like watching a movie for the second time. You might pick up a line or two but in reality you hadn't enjoyed the show that much the first time.

Mr. Kneely was absent again so math was worksheets so simple it reminded Ryan of the coloring books handed out in elementary school when a teacher was absent.

Another day ended with a bell and mad dash to be first out the door. Ryan took in a lungful of fresh air. Walkers were dismissed first. Bus students stood in line waiting their turn. A circle of bus drivers stood outside their busses, engines running doors open, swapping tales of how this generation of kids weren't measuring up. By the time bus students were dismissed the busses had filled with noxious fumes. Seated in their respective buses, drivers and kids wore the same perpetual frown the day started with. It seemed neither student nor adult was too excited about their workday. With the churn and crunch of the bus tires Ryan turned to look out over snow that had settled over the weekend changing from pure white to a shade of gray that matched his mood. Ryan held his breath for as long as he could, then through gritted teeth breathed in another failure of adults to give a damn about kids.

The river channel to his right looked cold and forbidding, dotted with ice chunks that had broken away from its banks. The bus traveled the busiest part of down town before taking a left at the soda shop. Ryan thought suddenly of Violet and the ride seemed easier. At the intersection of route 201, Hight Chevrolet showcased the newest models of Chevrolet and Buick. Ryan briefly thought of that Buick convertible in the magazine with Violet's new doo waving in the breeze as the two headed to Bangor for that future concert.

He and the rest of the students were thrown forward when a blare of horns and swearing from the driver indicated someone had stopped suddenly in front of the bus. The bus turned left from Madison Avenue passing the savings bank and pulled up alongside the library. The driver was still swearing under his breath when he opened the door. The man actually glared at him when he left like he was the cause of the problem. Ryan took a deep breath as he exited the bus. He had intermittently held his breath the full twenty minutes it took to get there. He checked his watch. He shook his head, *I can walk this distance in five minutes but it takes twenty on the bus breathing in poison from the exhaust and the driver. That's it I'm walking to the library from now on.* His eyes rose up those granite steps. Today those steps didn't seem inviting, they just seemed steep. He couldn't think of a single hero in the books he had read that could solve any of the situations on his street. He decided in the moment not to go in.

His walk home started out as a trudge. With an ever changing mother, and a father lost in the cellar he was about to add further laments when his thoughts suddenly brightened. Just ahead would be the dog Pluto and Violet would arrive on scene soon. He began skipping along the slippery sidewalk trying to avoid patches of ice. Suddenly he was just a kid in love with a girl and a dog. He realized it was too early for Violet to be there but the dog might be out. He hurried his pace. Indeed the dog was tied up outside, Ryan could hear him barking from down the street. The dog did not sound happy. He hurried the last few yards and looked across at Pluto. The dog had tangled his rope and was wrapped up like a Christmas package, looking and sounding miserable.

Ryan sat his book bag down on the walkway and ran across the street to ring the bell. Time passed. Pluto continued to bark. Ryan was just ringing once again when the man of the house came to the door. The rush of air trying to flee smelled of whiskey. Glazed eyes and a slack mouth looked down at Ryan. Ryan recognized that dazed look from what he saw on a regular basis emerging from his own basement.

"Your dog has tangled his rope. Would you mind if I help him?"

Bedford rubbed his eyes, burped and sighed as if in physical pain. He gritted his teeth and slurred a response. "That damn dog is more trouble than he's worth." His face reddened, "If I'd had my way he wouldn't have made the trip."

He looked back into his living room at the man occupying what should be his own chair. He continued muttering under his breath. He pointed back into the living room, "him neither." Bedford threw his hands up. "Go for it. Just see that he doesn't get loose."

As he began closing the door he added, "Not my mutt. I don't need her harping at me." He finished by hollering to the barking dog. "Shut your damn yap, dog."

Before the door slammed shut, Ryan heard, "Friggin dog," followed by the man shouting, "What, you got something to say? I didn't think so." A loud guffaw was cut short by the door slamming.

Ryan turned away and took charge. He followed the footsteps that had tied up the dog in the first place. The dog had managed to circle several small saplings losing all slack in the rope. The dog quieted as Ryan approached. His barking became a whimper. Pluto began to wag his tail. Ryan bent down and patted him. After talking soothingly he began to unwind the mess, walking the dog back through the tangle. Ryan looked around and thought aloud, "You don't have shelter out here do you boy?" Ryan looked at a series of droppings some partially covered, the latest right where the poor dog had become entangled. "You must have spent most of your day out here." An empty bowl sat knocked over. Had it contained food or water, certainly not both? He got the dog untangled and wondered what he should do next. *Tie him back up or go back and ring the bell again.*

Violet arrived on the sidewalk at that moment. She hollered a greeting. Ryan took the leash and untied it from the long rope. He walked Pluto back to the sidewalk to greet Violet. "Meet Pluto, my new neighbor." Ryan didn't immediately mention what the dog had just been through.

Violet patted the dog who licked her gloved hand.

"I have to return him but let's take a walk first. His owner doesn't seem to want him around anyway."

On the walk Ryan explained what he'd found when he got to his street. Violet agreed with his assessment that not all people should have pets. They made plans to meet at the library at 5:30. Ryan checked his watch, it was nearly 4pm.

Just as the two parted Violet broke into the kind of shy smile that only a teenage girl could muster. "By the way Ryan the answer is yes." Then she walked away.

Ryan was left to walk the dog back across and wonder what she meant. Yes? Yes about what? Then he got it. Violet was finally responding in her own crazy girl way. Yes! Yes! It was a floating above the ground Ryan Trussell that walked the dog back and rang the bell.

The owner with bleary eyes and still stinking of liquor begrudgingly accepted the leash dragging the dog inside and once again slamming the door. Ryan stood a full minute listening to the one sided shouting going on within those walls. Shaking his head and wondering if all adults acted like this he returned to his side of the street. The door across the street almost immediately re-opened. The man wearing a parka and an uncertain gait walked a reluctant dog back to the small tree and re-hitched him. He glared across at Ryan. Still, Ryan couldn't shake the happiness he was feeling. Yes!

CHAPTER FOURTEEN

FRANK

Above, in Ryan's room Frank was busy putting pen to paper once again. He cringed in agony as he thought of what he wanted to write.

Well boy since we haven't managed to leave this hell hole on our own maybe you and the girl can help. All this drama needs to end. Tell us what you're planning. Alice is going to try to shock your mother back to her senses.

WANDA

Two hours earlier

Wanda was busy ironing a blouse. She tilted her head thinking, *when was the last time I ironed anything in this house.* She had bought several new outfits for Ryan when they moved but they had worn out their stiffness. Now she simply let anything she laundered dry on an indoor rack. The iron had remained cold and unused since the move. She was struck with a thought and grunted. *Much like myself.* Well cold and unused was overrated and she was about to change all that. As the iron moved along the sleeve, in her head she imagined the warmth of the iron was coming from a different source. As the iron smoothed the cloth around each button she imagined those buttons being slowly undone. In her mind the man's nervous hands added to the excitement.

The dog across the street was barking furiously breaking into Wanda's imagination. She tried to ignore it.

Lost once more in the movement and warmth of the iron she went back into her reverie. She would be holding those capable hands this very afternoon. They hadn't been together anywhere but the heated car. That would change today. She could hardly contain her excitement. Mr. Kneely was going to show her his place. She finished ironing her skirt with her imagination following the same story line.

The remainder of the laundry in the basket at her feet belonged to Ryan and her husband. She carried this afternoon's outfit on a hanger hooked to the side of the basket up the stairs.

That damn dog across the street continued to howl. She stood on the landing the barking starting to piss her off.

Remembering suddenly how her son had wanted a dog, she nodded in agreement with herself that she had made a wise decision in nixing that idea. She turned to enter Ryan's room. A violent burst of air suddenly hit her in the face full force. Wanda flinched, her breath caught. She turned her head quizzically. She was struck with a gale of wind from a different direction. Her blouse rose like a kite, covering her face. In that moment Wanda panicked. At the same time, a voice reached her ears. Her son Ryan was hollering to the dog. Her mind muddled.

She couldn't find her breath. All those cigarettes caught up with her. She began hacking. Her eyes now covered with the blouse her cough increasing, Wanda spiraled out of control. She began tearing at the blouse. Her feet with a mind of their own, tangled. She stumbled backward hitting the basket of laundry at her feet and tumbled the length of the stairs, arms flailing, blouse, skirt, and basket of laundry following, littering the steps all the way to the bottom. Wanda hit her head on several steps while her arms, hands, elbows knees, and rib cage scraped their way to the bottom.

Wanda landed sitting sprawled on the bottom step dazed and in terrible pain. She tasted a coppery flavor in her mouth. She moaned aloud. She managed to raise one arm to her face finding blood from her nose. She sat facing the front door as if planning for a visitor. She tried to get up. She couldn't manage it. She groaned. She sat back her breathing ragged, it hurt to breathe. She heard her son's voice across the street. The dog had quieted. *Ryan hurry.*

MR. KNEELY
4pm.

Mr. Kneely sat in the parking lot at the A&P. He checked his watch. Wanda should have been here over an hour ago. The sun was going down and there was a call for snow overnight. The weather man had apprised him of this impending storm over and over during the hour he'd sat there motor running, radio competing with his thoughts. He had a cooked chicken ready to be heated up and a salad he just needed to add tomatoes to. Pillsbury frozen rolls sat thawing ready to bake. He checked his watch, it was two minutes past the last time he'd checked.

He'd taken a series of days off from teaching. Today he spent shopping and getting his house in order.

Normally Ed, a typical bachelor might get to cleaning when he had to step over things. Today he vacuumed rugs, dusted, and polished, the place was spit shined. There were fresh sheets on his bed. The table was set, wine glasses gleaming in the afternoon sunlight when he closed the door.

All that was left to do was to gather the reason for all this effort. He checked his watch, the weather report seemed to keep time with his impatience. "Yes it's going to snow I heard already," he shouted to the radio and snapped it off. He took a deep breath. It was obvious she wasn't coming. He took a long look at himself in the rearview mirror.

For some reason those little bastards in the back row of his classroom filled his mind. They didn't give a shit about anything and it seemed Wanda didn't either. Ed turned the key and shifted to drive. He spun his way out of the lot. The clouds were already delivering on their promise, bunched up like sheep's wool on the horizon, mirroring Ed's anger.

FRANK and ALICE

"You came on a little strong there didn't you Alice?" Frank looked to the bottom of the stairs at the crumpled woman of the house. She seemed to be breathing. "Ok, it's fair to say she won't be leaving the place and entertaining for a while. Do you think she's at least three weeks wounded, that's all we need?" Alice seemed to be out of breath. Frank was left to speculate on his own while holding his head.

RYAN 4pm

Ryan climbed the steps of the porch shaking his head and mumbling to himself. Competing thoughts filled his head. Upset about the poor dog but happy for himself, Ryan opened the door and found his mother staring up at him from the first step of the stairs. She was covered in blood. Ryan hurried to her. His mother appeared dazed and couldn't speak. For all the distance the two seemed to travel in avoiding one another he did love his mother. She began mumbling incoherently. He rushed to the kitchen and checked the emergency numbers. Grabbing a dish towel and running it under cold water even as he dialed. After giving the ambulance service directions he returned to his mother and tried to wash off the blood but she refused to be comforted. He could barely make out her words but the withering look she gave him was one of accusation.

Ryan's father came on scene just as the stretcher bearing his wife was being carried down the walk by two oversized men. Ryan walked just to their rear. His father looked at Ryan questioningly. Ryan shrugged his shoulders. Wanda lay there with her eyes closed. "Did she say anything?" asked Ryan's father.

"From what I could make out between groans something was said about the dog barking and me not being here. She didn't say what happened or how. But I think she's mad that I wasn't here."

John Trussell had stopped for a drink himself and whiled away an hour or so to avoid the woman. He couldn't muster up a response for his son. He did touch the boys head. Ryan's father thought, *there goes a night on the high seas down the drink.* He couldn't help chuckling to himself at the thought.

Ryan feeling that hand but not able to read his father's mind was left thinking what a weird world he inhabited.

Back inside, his father told him to rustle up a sandwich for the two of them. "We'll eat then go to the hospital."

Ryan looked quizzically at his father.

"I'm sure we can't see her immediately no sense going hungry."

Ryan, a boy of fourteen was in semi- shock. On auto pilot he spoke. "I'm not hungry but I'll make you one." Ryan rummaged and found a can of good old reliable Charlie Tuna. He opened, drained, and checked the mayo. He mixed and spread it on the last two pieces of bread in the loaf.

He climbed the stairs used the facilities and went to his room. He sat heavily on his bed. *What could all this mean?* As if in answer he looked at his desk and saw his journal open.

He read the message the ghost writer had left. What could that mean? Did they see this happen? Could they have caused this? Ryan went back to his bed and lay down breathing heavily. He was overwhelmed. He didn't move or twitch or even allow a thought until his father called to him. It was a very confused and conflicted young man who walked down the stairs his mother had fallen down a short time ago. There was still blood on the first step. Ryan joined his father in the car and sat quiet as a mouse on his way to the hospital. He knew more about this than he could share, at least for now.

PLUTO

Pluto gazed out the front window at the red lights across the road. His owners were seated at the kitchen table. Marcia was describing her day, avoiding the confrontation that was sure to follow. Marcia's father in his unique way let Marcia know what had gone on earlier. Her husband pretended to be listening while holding his head. Marcia rose and looked briefly out the window when the lights and sound appeared. The boy was following the attendants.

Pluto continued to gaze across the street growling quietly to himself. The boy had helped him this afternoon and now one of the boys own parents was injured. To the extent that a dog can rationalize, Pluto thought it would have been better if his master was the one being carted away. He looked at his owners quizzically, *how do you tell one of your masters that the other is abusive?* He had watched the old man using his hands to talk to his lady. Somehow Pluto felt like she was getting the message. He looked back across the road as the stretcher reached the ambulance. A man had arrived, patted the boys head and the two disappeared inside.

Marcia called to him. Pluto raced to the bowl. He began devouring the chow. Marcia nodded to herself. "Haven't you eaten today boy? Mommy bought you the good stuff." She turned to her still bleary eyed and wobbly spouse. "You fed him today right? Beddy?" She searched her father's eyes sitting in the lounge chair. He opened and closed them twice. He had told her the truth.

Bedford now holding his head found his wife's term of endearment, a shortening and bastardizing of his name repugnant, but held his tongue.

He sighed inwardly, *well it'll soon be Beddy-bye. This move is going to be a short one.* He glared at the damn dog who seemed to be smiling up at him.

He hadn't answered the question.

"You did feed him today didn't you? It's all I asked you to do today, Beddy."

Their eyes met. Bedford puffed up, started to get up, red faced preparing blow up. Marcia's father noticed. He sat forward his eyes gleaming anger and disdain.

Pluto noticed too. He growled deep in his throat. Bedford looked at the bared teeth and shrunk back into his chair. He glared at the dog shook his head and went back to holding it.

Pluto noticed and understood. Tomorrow, with his lady master gone and the old man unable to intervene, would not be a good day.

FRANK and ALICE

"Well there. Those ambulance men didn't seem to think she's critical. I'm glad you got that off your chest Alice."

Alice continuing to recharge her air supply feebly rustled a curtain.

MR. KNEELY

A cold chicken sandwich and a cup of black coffee sat before him. The wine glasses were back in the cupboard. The rolls back in the freezer.

He picked at his sandwich and pondered the situation aloud. "What do I do now?" Something happened he was sure of that.

Wanda would have been there if she could? He tried to think logically. *The father is gone all day, the boy most likely had been in school. So what could have kept Wanda away*?

A piece of chicken sandwich lodged in his throat and he coughed. He swilled some black coffee burning his throat. His hand still bore the red from the burn at Christmas. *Christ the whole world is against me.* He rushed to the sink holding his throat, coughing, trying to dislodge it.

He gazed out at the darkness over the sink his eyes watering seeing his stricken reflection looking back at him. The bleakness of his own situation rose in his throat. The chicken dislodged and landed in the sink in a lump. He took a deep breath, his eyes glistened. He stared at the black screen outside the window, a blank slate, his blackboard at school. It all suddenly became clear. He needed a rare lesson plan. He studied his burned hand, he nodded his head. The burn would heal. He would heal. A sudden idea appeared as if written in chalk. He picked up the phone and called a substitute for tomorrow.

RYAN and his FATHER

They entered Wanda's darkened room. Wanda was moving uncomfortably in her blankets. A long sigh and low moan exited her coverings. A low cough moved her blankets. John Trussell cleared his throat as he approached the bed. "Wanda can you hear me?"

Ryan moved to the window.

Wanda managed a feeble response but it held no coherence.

"We just spoke to the doctor."

No response.

"There are no broken bones but you did crack several ribs."

Nothing.

"And you may have a slight concussion." John Trussell waited a beat. "Can you tell us how it happened?"

The poison that defined the woman was still intact. Wanda finally managed a response. "Why do you care?" She waited in her next declaration as if lighting up a cigarette. "It just happened."

She remained facing the wall.

John Trussell tried to take a high road. "Your son is here and he's very worried about you."

She coughed and moaned as the cough bounced off her injured ribs. In one painful breath she stated her case which would end her prosecution. "Hmmph, not as worried as about that yapping dog across the street."

Ryan could now make sense of what his mother had gasped out at home. He moved to the door. "Father, I'll be in the cafeteria drinking hot chocolate and worrying about that yapping dog if you need me."

John stayed another dozen minutes with nothing but labored breathing answering his questions. Finally frustrated and fed up he left, telling Wanda he'd check in tomorrow with her doctor to find out when she might be released. The minutes of silence, a reminder of their relationship in the best of times, sparked his exit line. "You sound nearly back to normal."

Ryan was just finishing up his hot chocolate and paper bowl of French fries when his father joined him at a table.

I'm sorry you had to hear that." He looked directly at his son as he dragged up a chair.

"You didn't do anything wrong son. This is all about your mother and I and which came first the chicken or the egg. " John Trussell took a deep breath. "When I first met your mother she was vibrant and alive and full of life." His eyes clouded over. "I know that's hard to believe but it's true. Let me get a cup of coffee and I'll tell you a bedtime story. John Trussell dragged the chair nearer his son. He took a sip of the coffee and began. "Once upon a time" he smiled. What emerged was a trip down memory lane. "I was working in the paper mill in Machias and she was living and working in Bangor. She was enrolled at the University majoring in music. We met at a music concert and she apparently liked my looks." He chuckled, "I know that's hard to believe but true." His eyes closed as a sigh left his lips, "I had two years of college under my belt and took a job in the paper mill as an internship. They liked me and I went to work full time."

He looked up to see if Ryan was paying attention. He was. "Anyway let me cut to the chase and bring these chickens home to roost." He shifted in his seat. "We started seeing one another, mostly me coming down to Bangor, she never made it to Machias until we moved there." His father shifted gears. "As if overnight your mother was three months pregnant with you. She didn't see any option but when the reality of what becoming a mother meant hit her, along with the remoteness of Machias, she became a different woman." John Trussell shifted once more in his seat as the discomfort with his life reached his backside.

He cleared his throat. "Did I make promises I was never able to keep? Yep, but it wasn't for lack of trying."

He met Ryan's eyes, "On the other hand your mother left it all up to me since to her mind I was the source of her uprooting from the ivory tower she had been accustomed to. So chicken or the egg, which came first I have no idea, all I know is the egg is scrambled and the chicken flew the coop a long time ago."

He patted himself on the arm. "As for me I'm not innocent in all this. I took the easy way out. Though I didn't begin to drink seriously until well after you were born. For the last six months of her pregnancy, which by the way was not an easy one, your mother blamed me for ruining her life. By the time you arrived it was pretty clear where I stood and where I was going to stand. My parents were not there when you were born because your mother did not want them there. They never became true grandparents because your mother didn't want them doting on you when she could barely stand being at your crib."

Ryan was hearing much of this for the first time.

"That's on me, I let that happen. I was busy with my work and happy with my job so I let a lot pass."

John Trussell stood up walked around the table then sat back down. His anger began to surface. "It was only when she made no attempt to bond with you or to be a good mother that I hardened."

Ryan's father cleared his throat. "I would come home from working a double shift to a baby that hadn't been changed or bathed since I left in the morning. A screaming crying baby that had been crying for who knows how long. I would clean you up, feed you and rock you to sleep then feed myself. Night after night."

A pleading look entered his eyes, "I tried Ryan, I really did." He threw open his hands as he offered what trying had looked like. "I suggested counseling which she refused. So then I thought maybe she is just overwhelmed so I got a part time housekeeper."

A wry smile reached his lips. "Two weeks in she accused me of having feelings for the woman." He shook his head, "Nothing I did was good enough. Sad to say, and there is no excuse, I finally gave up and in the process gave up on you."

He shook his head, "Even in our shared misery we stayed together, with you being the collateral damage." John Trussell's eyes filled, "I'm so sorry." He touched Ryan's arm.

"For years I've been either floating in a bottle or trying to float a bottle." I think my hobby was always about sailing away to an island where I could be happy." His eyes were glistening with tears as he continued. "Tonight has brought everything into clearer focus for me. I'm sorry for the kind of father I've been and if you'll give me a chance, and with your help if I'm not too damaged, maybe we can help your mother."

Ryan studied the hand that was reaching across the table. He nodded. "I'd like to try. I've met some people here I like a lot. I don't want to move." Ryan fidgeted, but couldn't bring himself to tell his father about their house guests. *Not yet*, he thought

The two left. The ride home filled with silence. On this night John Trussell did not go to the cellar to enter a bottle he sat quietly in the recliner in the living room with an empty hand and a lot on his mind. He made promises to himself that night.

Ryan sat across from him in the dark trying to make sense of all this. When it became apparent his father had to wrestle through this by himself Ryan excused himself to his room to have a conversation with his journal.

MR. KNEELY

Ed Kneely's mind was full of possibilities. He was on the throne emptying himself when the realization struck him that all he needed from this woman was her house.

The plan that emerged earlier at the table began to crystalize beyond an outline. *If he could convince her this was all real would she dump her husband and son? He thought so. Would it be possible to move into his old house*? This seemed possible as well. *And why do I think I need to be in that house, to be in control in that house? The answer came with the sound of water leaving the toilet. Isn't it obvious? It was in that house that I lost control, and my whole life was flushed down the toilet. What living in that house, spending days and nights there would actually do he wasn't clear on, but in this moment it felt right. In that house since coming back he had been able to sleep.* He came out of his head long enough to acknowledge the slight pain from the burn that remained. *A different form of healing might take place in that house. Tomorrow he would make a house call and find out what had happened.*

CHAPTER FIFTEEN

RYAN

Ryan sat at his desk and wrote what amounted to a letter to the resident ghost.

> *Sir,*
>
> *Something bad happened to my mother today. She is in the hospital with broken ribs and a bunch of scrapes and sprains.*
>
> *She's blaming me for it all. Now my Father thinks this is a sign and he's promising to change for the better to save our family. Do you know what happened to my mother?*
>
> *Your friend,*
> *Ryan*

FRANK

Frank gazed at the bed containing the boy. He read the words the boy had written about trying to become a family again. *Well that couldn't happen! At least not in the way the boy might be thinking. A plan was in place and if things worked out Ryan would have a better than new family.* Frank chuckled at that thought then grabbed his head. When his head cleared he was looking into his past in this place. Over the years trapped in the walls he had watched people come and go, seen the shirkers and the workers. If given a second chance with Alice at his side he promised he too could be a changed man. He wrote none of this down of course it would simply confuse the boy. He reread the message. Frank decided it might be best to wait on a reply.

One thing his own life had taught him; it was a lot easier to talk the talk than walk the walk. *Who knows what tomorrow might brin*g? Frank was betting a healthy supply of Jack Daniels, or Jim Beam or whatever the man drank would not give up their seat in the boat easily.

Alice, sitting nearby in quiet contemplation sent him an air message. She had taken an active role in determining her future and seemed happy about it. Frank caught the drift. "*You go girl, I might have to throw a monkey wrench or two myself before this is finished.*"

EDWARD KNEELY

It was eight in the morning, the snow had lasted most of the night. Six inches of new snow blanketed the town; sticky snow this time, snowball snow. Ed Kneely nursed his second cup of coffee gazing out the window. His first thought was the recess duty he would be missing today, shouting at the little bastards 'to put that snow down.' He turned his burned hand over and over studying the blisters while thinking about executing his plan. The gloves he had worn had irritated the burn while shoveling earlier, clearing a path to his garage. For the briefest of moments he thought about standing in front of his first period class he was missing and realized he didn't miss it at all. He rinsed his cup and put it on the drain board to dry. He looked around at his kitchen all clean and orderly with the morning sun coming through the windows. The spit and polish he had applied yesterday reminded him of why he had cleaned in the first place. He had not attempted a real relationship with a woman in years. *Why now?* He asked himself. The answer came in a flash of sunlight that had entered and moved to a spot on the wall. *Because it's not about the woman. It's all about the house. This might be my last chance.*

JOHN TRUSSELL

John Trussell awoke still in his recliner morning light lightening the curtain. He stretched and noted a clear head for the first time in a long time. He also noted he had slept in for the first time in a long time. Every muscle in his body groaned as he stood and moved to the kitchen.

Ryan had left a note.

John Trussell went to the bathroom took a shower then returned to the kitchen to make and drink a cup of coffee. He left a note of his own. He would be back to pick up Ryan at 4pm. to go to the hospital. He closed the door looked at the shoveled walkway his son had cleared earlier then picked up that same shovel and cleared his way to his garage

ED KNEELY

Mother Nature had delivered on her promise overnight but left before getting tangled up with the town plows. Ed drove the freshly plowed streets, glare from the sun and snow nearly blinding him. He parked down the street from his old house. He took a deep breath. How would he respond if either the boy or his father answered the door? He fingered the key to the house he had never relinquished. He was amazed that with the frequency of one tenant following another nobody ever changed the locks. Over the years this key had allowed him to enter at night, mostly when the place was vacant. Several times though when he felt the need for a fix he snuck in after all the lights were off and the tenants asleep.

Sneaking in and lying on the floor in his old bedroom when the place was empty knowing his father was dead brought the only peace he'd ever known. There were times he felt a cold breeze reach him but he paid it no mind. The sounds from the walls didn't frighten him but rather became a soothing salve. Was it possible that the evils inflicted by his father had not gone unpunished? Imagining his father trapped forever in these walls was comforting indeed.

Was it too much to hope for that he might be able to take up residence and get a good night's sleep on a regular basis. Thinking of what might await him when he rang the bell another thought entered his mind, a now distant memory. *Only once had he brought a guest. He had inadvertently scared the woman. Trying to calm her had ended with a terrible and tragic result.*

He climbed the steps noting someone had shoveled and there were tracks leading to both the garage and to the sidewalk. With luck no one but Wanda would be home. Ed climbed the steps and rang the bell.

PLUTO

All tied up once again across the street, Pluto was rolling little mounds of snow with his nose. His lady was long gone to work. She had shoveled her way to the garage and managed to navigate the steep pitch. Pluto had watched from the window. Fed and watered he was in the Livingroom dozing. What his master had in store for him today he couldn't know but you could bet it wasn't going to be good. It wasn't.

The old man was at his seat in the chair staring out at nothing. His owner was late getting up so Pluto missed the boy leaving. Pluto woke shivering remembering what he had dreamed. He was at the window waiting to be put out for the day when the boys master backed his car from the garage then spinning his tires as he attacked the new snow.

The morning sun brought rectangles of light to the kitchen wall. Icicles already grudgingly releasing their lock. Pluto was mesmerized by the drops that rhythmically left the roof. Suddenly his owner appeared and Pluto was dragged outside and tied up on a shortened leash. His master paced a distance then placed Pluto's food and water just beyond that distance.

He could wait this out. There was fresh snow to lick. The boy would be home in a few hours. Pluto continued to roll small balls of snow and sweep them up with his tongue. The sun was higher still when he observed a man walk up the shoveled path across the street to the porch. He could hear the doorbell chime.

FRANK and ALICE

Frank and Alice had been up all night. Truth be told ghosts never sleep which can make for a very long twenty four hours just to do it all over again. Alice was in Wanda's bedroom and Frank was in the recliner in the living room when the doorbell rang. Twenty seconds later it rang once more. A loud knocking followed, then a voice asking, "Is anyone home?" **Frank could hear a key in the lock. The door opened and a man entered. He looked to his right and left then called out,** "Is anyone home?"

Alice upon hearing the bell had joined Frank. He had not seen his son since he was a boy so Frank didn't recognize him. Alice did not know this man was Frank's son but she recognized him. It was the first time she had seen him in the light of day. She gasped and rustled Frank's sleeve. The air hissed. Frank struggled to understand.

Alice had experienced a man sneaking into this house in the dark over the years. They thought he was a harmless vagrant and left him alone. This morning she recognized his smell as the same man. In the light of day Alice was so clear in her messaging that Frank suddenly understood this was the man who had killed Alice. *What would he be doing here*? The two of them watched the man roam the house. He seemed to know the place. They were shocked to see him climb the stairs and enter Wanda's bedroom. He sniffed the air. He went through her drawers, finding the sleeping pills.

Alice could hardly contain her rage. Frank tried to encircle what appeared as a violent rush of air. "*Let's think this all through before we act.*"

MR KNEELY

He knew from experience how difficult it can be to find restful sleep. When he entered the room where the woman had died he felt a strange cold air current reach him only to quiet suddenly. He saw the one impression on the bed. Wanda did sleep alone just as she had said. He went through her dresser. He found the pills. Everything she had told him was being confirmed. Briefly he checked his old room. The boy slept here. He noted the books on shelves and what appeared to be a notebook on the desk. He walked down the stairs and opened the cellar door. He snapped on the light. Down there he saw for himself what Wanda had told him of her husband's obsession with boats and liquor bottles. Plenty of empty liquor bottles adorned the shelves, some sporting small boats with sails in their bellies. Everything Wanda had told him appeared to be true. Where could she be? He climbed the stairs and went into the kitchen. On the table he found the note. He had to read it twice. Wanda was in the hospital? Had there been a fight? The note indicated the man would return late this afternoon and pick up Ryan to go to the hospital. He checked his watch, just after 11 am. A million thoughts entered his head. He was suddenly exhausted. He sighed. He decided he needed to rest. There was what appeared to be blood on the first step of the stair. He climbed the stairs to his old room and laid down on Ryan's bed. He closed his eyes. He slept. He awoke at 1:00pm refreshed. He walked down the stairs and stared into the living room at the scene of his first crime. Anger replaced the calm that had followed him down the stairs. He looked once again at the first step on the staircase. Had another crime taken place? He slipped quietly out the door.

FRANK and ALICE

The two of them followed as the man roamed the house. Frank trying desperately to keep Alice calm. The man seemed unsettled when he read the note. He turned and re-climbed the stairs to the boy's room and was now fast asleep. *He killed Alice. Who can he be? Why is he here? Could he be the man meeting up with the boy's mother? What does he want?*

Alice had made it clear to Frank. *He's the man who killed me, I've tried to get that into your head for years. All those nights he visited and we didn't understand. Well now we do. Did you see he looked right at the spot in the bedroom where he smothered me? What does all this mean?*

Frank now understood the gasps of air emerging from Alice like balloon captions in a comic strip.

Frank had an idea. *Let the boy investigate.* He slipped into Ryan's room and sat at the desk. He opened to a new page.

Ryan, a bad man entered your house today. He seemed to be looking for your mother.

He studied your room, he slept in your bed

He creeped around and found your father's note.
Then he left.

I fear he has done harm here before. Find out.

PLUTO

It had been a brutal morning. His master had tied him up with just a short amount of rope giving slack. His master cussed him out while tugging on his rope, choking him. He purposely placed a dish of food and water just beyond his reach. His master had chuckled to himself as he walked off the distance Pluto would need to travel, then put the food and water down. He stared the dog down not saying a word then turned and walked away chuckling to himself. Pluto tried to free himself but the rope was thick and strong. He tried to reach his water dish. He tugged and tugged then lay down exhausted. He had managed to get water by swallowing little snowballs he had fashioned with his nose. A thought of the boy who had come to his rescue before seemed to relax him. He would wait for the boy to come home. He laid down and put his paws over his eyes. He would not give the man the satisfaction of hearing him howl. He slept. Upon awakening he stretched and yawned. He looked across the street. The boy was not home yet. The man who rang the doorbell earlier was just now leaving. The sun had moved a good distance in the sky. It had to be well into the afternoon. Pluto barked once and the man waved then hurried down the street. Pluto sighed and lay down once more.

WANDA

Wanda had spent the morning undergoing pokes and probes. She lay now semi-dozing facing the wall after a lunch of mystery meat, green beans, and mashed potatoes. The doctor had been in and said he thought she would be able to go home tomorrow since all the tests were back. The lights were down and the blinds pulled when her door opened and she heard what she thought was a nurse entering. Her name was spoken. She hadn't had a male nurse attend her. Her name was repeated. Through the drugs and pain came a voice she recognized. It was Edward

Kneely. She turned sharply which caused her ribs to hurt and she winced. She began blubbering. He reached her bed. He took her hand. "Wanda what happened? I knew you would have been there if you could."

Wanda continued to wail, her responses barely intelligible and strung together like a line of wash. "I'm so sorry, I fell, clumsy me, wasn't thinking, oh I just don't know." Her face was scrunched, her voice hoarse and helpless. She finally managed a deep but painful breath. "Fell down the stairs." She sighed, "I hurt my ribs." She groaned. "I'll be okay," she began coughing then groaned again, "So they tell me. Another cough, "Home tomorrow," she squeezed out. She tried to smile.

Ed Kneely studied this woman lying in front of him. Suddenly transported back to his own youth in that moment to a mother who had always managed to find excuses not to leave. A hundred little things; religion, money, insecurity, timing, taken together they kept the family together right up till his father was killed. Wanda in that moment even looked like his mother; weak, pitiful.

Ed shook his head. No this couldn't be his mother. He needed this woman to be strong. He handed her a tissue, squeezed her hand and sighed, "Let's hope for the best. Obviously you need time to heal. Call me when you get home and we will figure this all out together." He took her hand. He studied her wounded face. A final thought before he said goodbye. *Please don't let this woman be as weak as my mother.*

Wanda felt she had a reason to hope. This man was strong. She needed to form a plan for the three men in her life. She closed her eyes and thought again of what that afternoon might have been like if she had not fallen.

RYAN

Ryan actually enjoyed the walk to the library in the afternoons. No more exhaust filled bus rides. He noticed things he had never seen from the windows in the bus.

He looked in store windows as he made his way up Madison Avenue. He saw a dummy wearing some new clothes that might look good on him. He had money in his pocket from his paper route maybe like Violet with her new doo, he could use a makeover. He was day-dreaming when he reached those granite steps he looked up. All his hero's lurked in the stacks in there. He sighed. Today though it didn't seem any of them could help.

Was he abandoning his heroes? No he decided, he just wanted to go home. He began his walk. Were the five o'clock paper deliveries beginning to take a toll? He felt exhausted. The snow on the roadside was melting, speckled with sand and turning into a dirty gray slush. The sidewalks had been plowed. He didn't hurry the house would be empty and little to eat. He kinda figured he and his father would be going to see his mother and he wasn't sure how he felt about that. So there was no hurry in his gait. Then the dog came to mind and he picked up his pace. Pluto raised his head when he saw the boy reach his driveway. He began to bark furiously. Ryan looked at him, put his pack down and hurried across the street.

The dog wasn't wrapped up in his rope but Ryan noted the rope had been shortened. Ryan in his innocence first thought the man was doing a good thing. There was less chance of Pluto getting tangled up. He investigated.

Pluto's rope fully extended was out of reach of his food and water dishes. So that's the plan. *The man is a terrible human being*, thought Ryan. He brought the dishes closer, Pluto ate and drank with abandon, his tail wagging appreciatively. Ryan figured out in the moment that the meanness he had heard in the man's voice yesterday had made it through the night. He heard a noise from the living room window. He saw a weak tapping on the glass and wave of a hand seemingly thanking him before the blind closed. He patted the dog and reassured him he would check on him every afternoon. The dog whined and buried his nose in Ryan's glove. Ryan had done all he could do. He turned to go when his neighbor's door opened.

The words came in a remembered slur. "You should maybe worry about your side of the street, no ambulances over here." Then the man added, "Not yet anyway." Ryan made eye contact but said nothing.

"I'll take care of the damn dog." His neighbor turned and slammed the door.

Ryan did not respond. He had witnessed cruelty and indifference and he recognized it in this man. He was still shaking his head when entering his house. He suddenly felt as hungry as that poor dog. He went to the kitchen to find a snack. He found his father's note. He checked the time it was 3:45pm. He decided the hospital food would be tastier than anything he could put together here. He went to the bathroom then to his room.

His journal was lying open. Ryan always closed his journal when done writing. With heart racing he read the message. Someone has been sleeping in my bed? The line from <u>Goldilocks</u> reached his mind. This was no fairy tale. Could the ghost be correct?

Could this be the man his mother had been seeing? Should he tell his father? Nearly overcome by all this he realized he needed to talk to Violet.

Below, the door opened and his father announced he was home. Ryan was left like one of his father's boats, a ship at sea with no shore in sight. He would try to figure this all out when he got back home from the hospital. *I really need to talk to Violet.*

* * *

AWKWARD. That is the only word to describe the environment in the Trussell household two days later.

Wanda couldn't climb stairs so she now filled the couch. John Trussell took a week off from work to care for her.

This first morning he attempted scrambled eggs and toast. Ryan had delivered his papers but stayed home from school to help. He carried the tray in and placed it on the folding table. Wanda was lying down her face in the pillow. "Mother your breakfast is ready."

Wanda did not respond.

Ryan repeated himself.

Wanda groaned and hissed into her pillow, "Shouldn't you be in school?"

Ryan took the high road. "Actually yes," he sighed, "but I thought you might need my help today."

Silence.

"Father made eggs and toast. He's in the kitchen. He's trying, Mother."

Silence.

"Do you need help sitting up?" He was determined to keep things positive. Expecting more silence Ryan was surprised when his mother cleared her throat.

Wanda coming to a decision to bare her plan, barely turned her head. "Why don't you ask your father to come in here? I have something to tell the both of you."

With father and son standing in front of her, Wanda spared no feelings. "As soon as you can," she panted, "you need to pack your stuff. I want you out of here, the both of you." That effort had Wanda fading out.

John Trussell was taken aback. "We want to try to help, Wanda. Give us a chance. Ryan deserves better, we all do."

Ryan's father straightened, "I promised Ryan I would stop drinking and I promised to try to be a better father."

"It's too late for that."

"Why is it too late? You certainly aren't in any condition to be on your own."

Wanda didn't answer.

His father asked again.

Wanda didn't answer, she turned her head away.

Ryan made a decision. "Is it because of the man you have been spending time with in his car?"

Wanda didn't answer.

John Trussell looked at his son questioningly.

"That's right father, mother is seeing someone else. Isn't that true mother?"

Wanda turned her head back and looked at husband and son. She shook her head from side to side those locks she so religiously brushed one big tangle. "Yuh got me! Now pack your bags and get out." A long lingering cigarette cough ended her part of the conversation

"I'm not going anywhere mother. This is my home."

John Trussell spoke up. "I should have known this wasn't going to work. Ryan's right, if anyone is going to leave it will be you."

John Trussell spread his hands, opened his eyes wide and finished with a flourish. "But it looks to me like it might be a day or two so you might want to eat those eggs, they are getting cold. C'mon Ryan let me take you out to breakfast."

CHAPTER SIXTEEN

The door slammed and the house was quiet. She could hear the tick of the heat rising from the furnace. She sat up. The morning sun was lightening the shade. She looked at the clock on the wall. She needed to call Ed. Surely he would take her in. A change of plans maybe but what did it matter where they lived, they would be together.

She painfully got to her feet. John was right about one thing it would be a few days before she felt like going very far. She winced as she pulled the walker to the couch and stepped behind it. She began to sweat from the effort. *A few days for sure.* She dragged herself to the kitchen. Ed would be at work but she could call the school and get him a message. She saw her reflection in the toaster and she looked a fright. She gingerly grabbed the phone from the wall. She sat down heavily in a kitchen chair, out of breath. When her breath leveled she dialed.

FRANK and ALICE

Having heard the conversation from beginning to end Frank and Alice remained in the living room. Alice was wringing

her hands. Frank was holding his head. The blow that had ended his life left him with a constant headache which always intensified when heavy thinking was required and this particular fly in the ointment would require just that. After a healthy pause Frank was still without a solution. *"It's obvious the men of the house do not intend to leave. This is a disaster Alice. We can't let her leave. Any ideas?"*

Alice air mailed the message. ***Maybe she can be the one who leaves till we straighten this all out. That hospital seems to keep a close eye on her.***

PLUTO

Pluto was out and had finished his business and was presently on the porch. When she arrived home last evening Marcia's father conveyed the message that her husband was still mistreating the dog. Pluto watched Ryan and his father back out of the drive and speed away. Ryan made eye contact and waved. Pluto barked in return. He shook his head from side to side, he was still smarting from the whack in the head his master had doled out just an hour ago.

His lady master had not appeared happy when she came down the stairs to let him out for his constitutional earlier this morning. After finishing his business and about to scratch at the door he heard angry words in the kitchen. Words that had started upstairs where Pluto was forbidden to go. He was on his hind legs wondering if this might turn violent when he saw the lady pointing her finger towards the door Pluto had just recently exited. It was not lost on Pluto that the man of the house was being directed to use that same door. Pluto scratched and was let in. The man continued to raise his voice, his face reddening, veins in his neck bulging with anger. Pluto managed to dodge a slippered kick. When his tormentor's foot found air instead of fur the man snapped and moved suddenly towards Pluto's savior. Pluto reacted. He struck and bit right through the man's pajama bottom and found real meat on the bone. He was still tugging on the leg and material when he was hit by something that stunned him. When he got his senses back he was being talked to gently, a cold towel pressed to his head. Only after it was clear to his owner that he was okay was Pluto put out for the day. The man of the house was missing. Pluto noticed the old man was sitting in the lounge chair with a satisfied warped smile on his drooping face.

ED KNEELY

The eighth grade girl who volunteered in the office during her study hall delivered the message. It was a simple message. 'Ed please call at your earliest. W.'

Ed sat at his desk. The lecture part of the class was over and students were left to begin homework or just remain quiet. Half of them would soon be visiting Ed's desk to make sense of what they hadn't bothered listening to the first time. He took a deep breath. *No he hadn't missed the place.* He read the message once more. He looked at his class without really seeing them. *One desk was empty. Ryan was probably home trying to help his mother.* Fingering the message his mind formulated possible next steps. A noise then sudden laughter in the back of the room drew his attention interrupting his thoughts. He shook his head from side to side as students began to move away from the seat of the problem. One student raised her hand. "Mr. Kneely can I move please, it stinks up here." Mr. Kneely didn't answer. He thought to himself. *Sit in it you little shits, you all stink.* The bell rang, ending any needed response.

RYAN

Ryan and his father returned from a lengthy breakfast around 11 am. It had been a quiet breakfast, both lost in thought. His father went into the house, Ryan went across the street to talk to Pluto. He would surprise Violet and be outside her school this afternoon and tell her all that had happened. Right now he would commiserate with the dog. He was rolling in the snow with the dog when the door opened. It was not the man of the house who came out to check on the dog it was the lady.

"Well hello young man no school for you today I see. I don't think we have properly met. I'm taking the day off too." She arrived at the seat of Pluto's world and patted her pup. "Pluto has told me all about you though," she kidded, then smiled a warm smile. Ryan needed a smile just about now. She held out her hand. "I'm Marcia."

Ryan took off his gloves then took her hand, "Ryan Trussell. Very pleased to meet you. I love your dog."

"Well I'm glad. Would you like to spend more time with him? I could use your help."

Ryan looked at her questioningly.

"Would you like to dog sit for me?"

"Well yeah, sure, but what abouttttt...?""

Marcia knew Ryan had met the extreme of her husband but took the high road. "My husband suddenly was offered a job out of the area." Her eyebrows rose. "Gone already," she smiled. "Not sure when he will be back. So, do you want a job?" "I sure do." Ryan beamed. "I have never been allowed a dog" Ryan reached down and patted Pluto. "You know I have a paper route. Does Pluto get up early enough to walk it with me?"

"You just tell me what time and Pluto will be waiting on the porch. Most mornings he's wide awake and waiting for me to open my eyes and let him out."

Ryan suddenly thought of those two old men who still made his life miserable on occasion. He chuckled.

Marcia explained she would put food and water on the porch and when Ryan returned from his paper route he could tie Pluto up for the day. Every afternoon Ryan would walk Pluto, make sure he had food and water, pick up droppings and do whatever else might pop up.

"Can I take him into my house?"

"I don't see why not. By the way is everything okay with your mother? I don't mean to be nosy but I see that she's back home."

"Mother had a bad fall but is going to be just fine."

"Well good then," she cupped some snow and offered it to Pluto. "You can take Pluto for a nice long walk right now if you'd like."

"I'd like that just fine." Ryan untied the rope and a tail wagging Pluto walked down the street ready to explore this new territory, Ryan happily bringing up the rear. Pluto immediately began staking out his new found freedom stopping at a freshly dug out hydrant. Ryan thought, *Wait till you have to navigate the old men and the swinging bridge.* He smiled inwardly, *Things are looking up for this newspaperman.*

Inside Ryan's house it remained quiet, Wanda lay with her face hidden in her pillows. John after getting the silent treatment descended the cellar stairs to face a flotilla of demons.

FRANK and ALICE

***"Those two talk less than we do Alice.* Little joke there get it. I understand what you *have planned in the short term but how do we make sure it's the man that goes?"* Alice began rustling curtains much as a sail begins to billow in a strong wind. Frank caught on. *"Ah, the boats. So we will be visiting the cellar after all. Promises are made to be broken, you know."* Frank stood looking out the window at the boy and the dog beginning a walk down the sidewalk. His head began to throb. *That kid, a strange one. I don't think he has mentioned us to his father.* He closed the curtain and followed Alice. Below in the cellar John Trussell felt a sudden breeze enter and shivered.**

RYAN and VIOLET

When Violet left her school in the afternoon Ryan was waiting on the sidewalk. Violet looked up in surprise when Ryan shouted her name. "I could have hit you in the back with a snowball," he kidded, "but seriously I don't need a war right now Violet, I need some advice." Ryan reached to carry her book bag.

"You look serious. You didn't get caught skipping school again did you Ryan?" She wagged her finger at him with a big smile on her face.

Ryan thought of all the troubles emanating from his own house and the house across the street and he had to laugh, *Sometimes you have to laugh to keep from crying.* "Violet, so much is happening around and in my house I don't even know where to begin."

She blushed as she made a suggestion.

Ryan had no problem whispering in her ear as he hugged her, "I love you Violet Mooney."

Violet, still appearing not ready to say the actual words, broke away slightly and offered what she hoped would suffice. "Right back at you Ryan Trussell."

That was good enough for Ryan.

The two sauntered hand in hand slowly into the downtown. "I have money for a couple of hot chocolates if you'd like to hear all about it."

"So that newsman's job is paying off huh?" Violet took Ryan's hand and they small talked their way to Whittemore's Restaurant. "Yeah I'm thinking about a new wardrobe too. More about that later."

Seated, with a cup of hot chocolate warming his hands, Ryan opened up about the people across the street and the mean man who was now gone to a new job. He told Violet of his new job taking care of Pluto and how the dog was going to help him deliver the news. He had previously told Violet about the two old drunks on his paper route "Wait till they meet Pluto," he laughed. Ryan sobered, he let the heavy shoe drop. "My mother's insisting that my father and I leave the house."

Violet was shocked into silence.

"But I'm not going anywhere. I told my mother that and I think my father agrees."

Violet listened. “So you and your father are getting along?”

“Well, he says he’s going to quit drinking.” He rolled his eyes slightly. “That would be a good first step anyway. He tried to convince my mother.” Ryan rolled his eyes a bit more deliberately. “Mother shot that idea down. She doesn’t care obviously. So only one of them is even pretending to be trying.”

Violet wasn’t convinced this was all going to work out the way Ryan hoped. “Maybe you could come and live with me, my parents like you.” Violet wasn’t kidding.

“I can’t say I wouldn’t like the idea but what about our ghosts. Can I bring them with me?” Ryan continued, “Honestly, I think the ghosts have a plan of their own, I just need to find out what that is.”

“What about this man your mother has been meeting, any more idea who he might be?”

“None, but I think my mother intends to stay here and if that’s true, I don’t think she intends to live alone.”

“You have a lot to think about Ryan, newspaper man, dog walker, and detective, not even adding where you might live. Busy times.”

By the time the two got back to Violet’s house they had a plan for Violet to spend some additional time in Ryan’s room. “You need to read what was written in my journal, maybe you can make more sense of it. Supposedly someone was in my house and in my room. That’s creepy.”

Violet agreed with that assessment. “So I’ll see you at six?”

Ryan nodded.

FRANK and ALICE

Alice wandered the cellar freeing dust motes into the air. She had never had an interest in the man of the house but that all changed when Wanda told her husband to leave and to take their son with them. Alice and Frank had to make that wish come true.

Frank peered through glass liquor bottles at boats that had been launched, not with a champagne bottle broken over their bow, but rather with the residue of good old whiskey hastening their voyage. He had heard the man named John promise his wife he would mend his ways. ***Well, we'll see about that.***

But you go ahead first Alice.

John Trussell, absorbing those freed up dust mites, sneezed four times in succession, opening up his nasal passages. **Alice smiled as she watched her effort reach home.** John wiped his nose on his sleeve.

Then Frank went about his business. He found a half empty bottle and opened it. He motioned Alice and suddenly the smell of John's addiction began to fill the cellar. John, working with his head down suddenly noticed the aroma, his nostrils filled. He shook his head trying to ignore it. **Alice made sure a proper dose of smell rode right up his nose.** He closed his eyes even as he breathed in and could almost taste the amber. He began to quiver. He looked around. He found the open bottle and put it to his nose. He breathed in the smell that had dominated his life for nearly a dozen years. He studied his surroundings. Nothing but boats on the horizon. He put his tongue to the tip of the bottle. He gazed down at the riled waters almost wishing the bottle was empty. It wasn't. All that was going on up those stairs, over which he had no control, disappeared in that smell. He poured a drink for himself. It would be just a light one. He made a promise, speaking aloud.

"I'll start tomorrow, that's soon enough."

Frank smiled, *this was going to be a cake walk; though all this excitement was hurting his head.*

The two toasted themselves in their own way and returned to the living room to offer what comfort they could to the woman of the house.

CHAPTER SEVENTEEN

ED KNEELY

Ed watched the last class of the day dismiss. He stood at his open door and watched the kids scramble to lockers and then to busses or to the sidewalk. Every day was the same. He felt like he was being swept through life on a plane headed to a destination he hadn't bought a ticket for. It was only in the last several weeks he actually gave thought to where he might end up. Now that seemed uncertain. Standing there in the doorway watching all these kids leave to go home to mostly loving caring parents, he felt miserable. "Hey, no running in the halls." Eyes filled with hate returned his stare.

The power he held over these kids made him feel just a little better. He returned to his ponder. Mentally he flipped a coin. *Heads, it was going to work with the woman, and she got the man and boy to leave. Tails, he would have to take matters into his own hands and get everyone out including Wanda.* He had made a decision to buy the place years ago but always seemed to be a day late and a dollar short as they say. Late fall and winter was normally the worst time to try to sell a house in Maine. Ed had been banking on that. The place would still be empty come spring and he would have saved enough to buy the place outright. He had planned to visit all winter long at his leisure. Then the Trussell's, out of the blue, came on the scene and ruined his plan. So plan B. had taken root and now that was in jeopardy. Ed had called Wanda back during his free period. She didn't seem terribly convinced that the men would leave. She broached the idea of her moving in with him. Ed Kneely listened not quashing the idea but not promising anything either. "We'll work things out."

He went through the motions for the remainder of the day. When the bell rang and the halls were bare, the smell of a bunch of adolescents still hung in the air. Ed walked the corridor. Other instructors sat at their desks preparing for the next day. Edward Kneely, the professional, thought them fools. He didn't carry a briefcase, he didn't have a bunch of papers to correct. He prided himself on having all he needed to know in his head.

The system worked for him within his professional world; evaluated once a year, if that often, and pre-announced when it did occur.

He took a breath. Back from the men's room sitting on his leather chair like a king on a throne looking out on his minions five periods a day he dictated how his and their day would unfold.

It was only when the day ended and he entered the world at large that Edward Kneely, a failure as a person, felt he could use a lesson plan.

Leaving the building and sitting now behind the wheel in the parking lot, the winter sun glaring at him through his windshield, he was at sea. Inside, his day was governed by predictable bells and smells. Outside, sitting on a different leather seat, the car running, the radio playing whatever the station thought might hold a listeners interest, Ed wasn't interested at all. He snapped off the noise like he was admonishing one of the wise guys that filled his classes; abruptly.

He checked his watch: early afternoon once again with nowhere that begged his presence. His eyes sought the rear view mirror and he studied the man in the glass. *Who am I?*

I don't drink, so no bar to belly up to, no friends, no one to go spend time with. For some reason, a flash of the dog across the street from his old house came to mind. *No dog even.*

Still lost in thought he put the car in drive and left the parking lot of Skowhegan Junior High. He reached the main road at the end of the parking lot. Traffic was snarled with the factories emptying. Every afternoon he encountered a rush of two lane traffic trying to cross the two bridges. He worked on an island and he felt like he lived on one as well. He sat there playing head games with himself as strangers in their little cocoons, their own set of circumstances clouding their eyes, crawled by not moving their heads. No way were they going to let a car merge. *Not my problem, wait your turn, seemed to be the only rule of the road. Where were all these people headed? Does it matter? Eenie, Meenie, Minee, Moe, does it matter which way I go? Does it even matter if I I'm still sitting here an hour from now?* His head on a swivel he looked for an opening. Finally the universe aligned and a break in traffic forced him to make a decision and he entered in the direction of his apartment.

PLUTO

Pluto was at the window when the two young people reached the sidewalk. They appeared happy with one another. They stood there talking and touched hands and kissed lightly when they parted.

His lady owner announced that his dinner was ready. Pluto was at his bowl when the phone rang. Pluto couldn't understand much human language but he could read body language with the best of them. His owner was not happy with whoever she was talking to.

Given the way his day had unfolded Pluto surmised his two masters might be arguing like they did this morning and he had intervened. He rubbed his paw over the welt that had nearly closed his left eye. The phone was slammed down and his master went through a series of growls that even a dog could decipher. He smiled to himself. It looked like he might be on a longer leash and taking more long walks with the boy across the street. He was chewing on all this while he chewed on his dinner. The old man with the crooked smile was staring down at him from the chair in the living room. Suddenly the doorbell rang.

RYAN and VIOLET

An hour later Ryan was on the porch waiting when Violet showed up under a street light. He met her on the sidewalk. Ryan brought Violet up to speed on what was going on in his household. "Before I sneak you into my room, there's someone I want you to meet."

Marcia answered the door with Pluto a respectful but wary distance behind. Ryan and the young girl who Pluto had observed earlier were standing there. "Hi Mrs. Dennis, I wanted to have my friend Violet meet Pluto if that's okay?"

Pluto recognized that voice, his tail began to wag.

Marcia was still fuming from the phone call and her face revealed that fact.

Ryan noticed. "We don't want to bother you Mrs. Dennis. We can come back another time."

Marcia took a deep breath. Her face opened, "Come in, and please call me Marcia," she smiled. She motioned, "C'mon in."

Pluto looked at the girl. *Another new friend possibly*? He cautiously approached.

Violet noticed the welt over Pluto's eye and bent to offer soothing words and a soft touch.

Definitely a new friend, thought Pluto, his tail echoed his thoughts.

Within moments, Marcia, Ryan, and Violet were seated at the kitchen table with Pluto at Violet's chair gazing fondly up at her.

Ryan, meanwhile was studying Marcia. He thought to himself, *this lady needs a friend as much as Pluto does.*

Sitting there but lost in her own misery, Marcia absently watched the two kids. Recognizing she wasn't ready to be social, she remained quiet letting the two focus on Pluto. The laughter and genuine affection the two were showing made her feel a little lighter herself.

She stood up took a deep breath and introduced her father who was sitting in the lounge chair with a blanket pulled up around his neck. She explained the poor man had suffered a stroke early in the fall and had come to live with her. "He can't speak but somehow he still communicates. He has a walker but this time of year can't go outside obviously." Both Ryan and Violet could see kindness in his eyes. They smiled in unison.

By the time hot chocolate had been offered prepared and brought to the table, Marcia felt much better. She took the lead and told the kids that her husband would most likely not be returning so she was glad to make two new friends. "Pluto obviously loves you Ryan and the way he's licking Violet's hands it seems he has another new friend too."

"Ryan is going to walk Pluto, but if you need anyone for other errands or anything else, I'd be glad to help," offered Violet.

Marcia met Violet's eyes and smiled a genuine smile. "Well I'll keep that in mind young lady, just helping out with Pluto is going to be a lifesaver." Then she had a thought. She looked to the living room. "Maybe I could use some help Violet. I don't get home most days until after six pm. Would you like to check in on my dad in the afternoons while Ryan is taking Pluto for a walk?" Thinking ahead she suggested, "When the weather improves you could help my dad get out to the porch and later in the spring maybe even a few steps down the sidewalk."

"I would love to help, Mrs. Dennis."

Marcia took a deep breath and sighed, feeling much better. "So do you two go to school together?"

"No, but we're in the same grade." Violet motioned towards the window. "We met on this very sidewalk a couple months ago." Violet looked at Ryan, "we have a lot in common don't we?"

"Really," mused Marcia aloud, "way back in my day boys and girls were still avoiding one another at your age. So what's your common interest if you don't mind me asking?"

Violet and Ryan exchanged looks. Ryan shrugged thinking anyone who loved their dog probably has a good heart. He reached out and patted Pluto.

Violet let Ryan take the lead. He started in innocently enough. "We are both interested in the paranormal world."

Marcia sat back. She saw two serious intelligent young people across the table from her. "So are there any ghosts in this neighborhood I need to worry about?"

Ryan looked at Violet as if asking permission to continue. She nodded. "I wouldn't use the word worry, but yes I have two ghosts in my house."

Marcia smiled not sure if she was having a serious conversation, "So do they communicate with you in some way?"

Over the next half hour Ryan and Violet each in turn explained ghosts in general and two ghosts in particular. Violet even revealed that she thought one of the ghosts was her grandmother.

Marcia shook her head in amazement. "You two are something else. You have made me a believer. Would you show me their messages sometime?"

"Actually, I was about to sneak Violet up to my room and show her the latest message." Ryan had a sudden thought. "How about you and Violet stay here and I bring my journal over?"

Marcia smiled and nodded, "Since my husband took the TV with him we would love to have some company wouldn't we Pluto?" Pluto, happy that Violet would be staying awhile, wagged his tail and licked Violet's hand.

Ryan entered his house whistling. His mother was in the living room seemingly sound asleep. He went looking for his father. The light was on in the basement. Ryan went down to tell him he would be across the street if he needed him for anything. "Hey father," he announced when still on the last step. His father was asleep in his basement recliner snoring. Ryan saw the bottle on the floor at his father's feet, amber liquid an inch high in the open bottle.

Ryan studied his father's sleeping form. He looked around the room, history on full display. Nearly every completed launch had occurred in a whiskey bottle. One more false promise drowned in a sea of addiction. Ryan didn't bother to wake him. If he was going to stay in this house he would have to create his own plan. When he got back upstairs, his mother was stirring in her blankets. He almost spoke aloud to her. Instead he shook his head and climbed the stairs to his room where he grabbed his journal. He looked at the cover. Ryan's World. Now he was about to share his closest held thoughts, observations, and musings, as well as the writing of a ghost, with an adult he'd only recently met. *Wow*!

He entered the darkened street. He looked up and down. The trees and buildings with their edges softened hugged the darkness. He took a deep breath. The dark felt like an old friend. He crossed to Marcia and Pluto's house. As he climbed the porch and looked through the window the only ones who seemed to care about him were still sitting at the kitchen table. Pluto remained at Violet's feet.

FRANK and ALICE

"So he's seen that he can't depend on his father or his mother. Who does that leave but us Alice? We'll give him a day or

two then we'll allow him to become the hero in saving his mother from herself." A stab of pain reached Frank's eyes. He winked out briefly but his train of thought remained and he continued.

"We'll have the old man out of here long before that." Another stab of pain closed his eyes. Deep breaths followed, willing himself to finish his thought. "He's going to have a headache in the morning like mine; a sledge hammer." Franks own sledge hammer hit and he closed down.

Alice watched this poor wretched tortured soul. He is definitely not going to make it in the real world. *I'll just go up and try to bring some maternal instinct to the woman, let's try to instill some affection into her bones.*

Frank came awake with a start. "I'll let that boy know that he and his mother need to remain in this house." Frank checked the time. *"Eight pm. whatever that means."* His mind went blank.

ED KNEELY

Ed was semi-dozing, seated in front of the small black and white TV, lights off, darkness arriving unannounced, a crime drama playing. Four words that seemed to emerge every week in this long running TV drama spouted from a deep throated detective, filtered through Ed's consciousness. **'Just the facts ma'am.'** Ed shook his head vigorously from side to side.

Those four words hit him full force. Ed closed his eyes. *He was being transported through a dark abandoned building, a cold hand wrapped around his fingers. A musty smell riding just below the smell of something long dead reached his nose. He was being dragged along by a cold wind. He suddenly felt the woman he had taken to his family home. He remembered how it had all started; the chance meeting over spilled oranges, the car, the bar, the Ballantine ale.*

He remembered the woman drinking heavily while he nursed his Ginger ale, the music, the dancing, the offer, the acceptance; the car again. Reaching the darkened house the sudden kissing. He had no desire to force the woman, things would surely have ended quietly, but then the shaking of the walls started and panic, then the resistance, the scream, the struggle and its result.

Right now that woman seemed to be beckoning him. He awoke with a start, fully panicked. He was shaking, his hands felt clammy, his breathing ragged. This sense of the woman's presence had been with him since the day he visited the house trying to find Wanda.

A commercial suggesting he might want to change laundry detergents had replaced the detective. Ed sat up straight. He couldn't remember the last nightmare he'd experienced. He snapped off the TV and returned to his chair. Still shaking he asked himself aloud, "What was that all about?"

RYAN and VIOLET and MARCIA and PLUTO

Laughter and light heartedness filled the kitchen. When Ryan felt the time was right he opened the journal that lay in front of him. He began turning pages slowly. He skipped the earliest entries back when he first began writing things down. He did not share the pages that revealed the progress of a boy moving from early elementary school in Machias, to a teenager expressing the frustration of that move. The journal expressed his love of reading and his heroes. Like a trip down memory lane his eyes scanned his affection for the dark, the joy of discovering a new friend, and finally the revelation that more than just he and his parents inhabited his house.

It had taken him less than ten minutes to see his life pass before his eyes. He arrived at the place where he had first heard from the man he would later dub the *Ghost Writer.*

He told Marcia of his first encounter with the man who would come to be known as Frank. "I questioned myself at the time. I thought Violet had maybe planted the thought in my head. When the vision in the chair didn't return I was sure it was all Violet's fault."

Violet raised her eyes, her hands still ruffling Pluto's fur.

"Just kidding, Violet." Ryan patted her arm. The smile they shared indicated the two understood one another well beyond their years. Ryan turned pages to where he had recorded the first time the ghost spoke to him. "I wasn't positive if I heard him right but this is what I wrote down later." **That was me aggravating your father's favorite chair. I used to have a chair on that very spot. I want that damn chair back."**

Marcia was totally amazed at the maturity of this young man. A scientist in the making or a writer in the future. She remained silent. This was Ryan's show.

Ryan moved ahead to when he and Violet spent time in his room trying to make sense of all this.

Violet took command of the conversation then, telling Marcia about the air current in the attic kicking up and seemingly shuffling newspapers, with the exact one that included an obituary of a death on this street. Violet cleared her throat.

"I'm convinced my grandmother was making contact with me. That's how she tells me stuff, through the air."

She looked at Marcia who remained silent. "She has been telling me stuff for a long time, about my mother and lots of other things. Sounds crazy right?"

The jury was still out for Marcia. Then Ryan revealed the first time someone else wrote in his journal. "I think that's when it really hit me. I mean, look at that writing, a kind of creepy poetry, scary stuff."

Dirty darkened dreary winter snow.

Bleak though chances be we have to try to go.

Plans have been made so leave this alone.

Well-meaning yes but we'll do better on our own.

The old man stinks of whiskey and glue

The woman seems addled but that's nothing new

On the girl's special day we'll contact you

Marcia read the poem and found herself taken aback. This was not the writing of a fourteen year old, not even one as mature as this boy sitting across from her.

After a general discussion of what the words might mean, Ryan turned to Frank's next journal entry. ***There is danger lurking. Keep your eyes wide open!***

Ryan, for the first time brought up Mr. Kneely's name. "I don't trust that man."

Violet gave Marcia a little back ground on Ryan's experience with his teacher.

Ryan found himself nodding along with Violet's description of his math teacher's actions toward him.

Ryan pointed to his house across the street. "My mother has been going through a bunch of stuff that I don't understand. She is telling my father and I that we have to move out." He pointed to the part of his journal where he had written the ghost for assistance.

Finally he opened to the last message from the ghost.

Ryan, a bad man entered your house today. He seemed to be looking for your mother.

He studied your room, he slept in your bed.

He creeped around he read your father's note.

Then he left.

I fear he has done harm here before. Find out.

Ryan closed his journal. He took a deep breath. "Now you know as much as we know." Eyes locked around the table. Pluto had taken all this in without offering an opinion but his mind was spinning.

Marcia checked her watch. A lot to digest. What she did believe in the moment was these two young people were not crazy and they firmly believed there were spirits in Ryan's house. "Wow, lots to digest." She breathed in deeply and rose. "Let's call it a night. Violet, would you like a ride home?" Violet, with the last hour swimming through her head, thought that was a great idea. "Let me tuck my father in and I'll get my coat. That should give you two a chance to say good night." Catching the drift the two teenagers smiled.

Violet waved good bye from the passenger seat. Ryan in the street turned back to the window, Pluto seemed to be sending a signal that he intended to watch over him with the same caring Ryan had shown him. Ryan crossed the street to his house carrying his past, present, and possibly future with him. He had no idea what awaited him inside but with a deep gulp of fresh air and one look back at the dark and the doggie in the window he made the plunge.

The house was shrouded in darkness. Ryan carried the full weight of what had been summarized earlier. The furnace started and Ryan jumped. He was still just a fourteen year old kid with no family support and it seemed the only one in this house he could share his new found hopes and fears with was a ghost. Ryan climbed the stairs in the dark and went to his room. He placed his journal back on his desk. Tomorrow would be soon enough to write about all that was going on across the street. He crawled under the covers, glad to have an adult joining his team; oh yeah and what seemed like his first dog.

FRANK and ALICE

Frank watched the house across the street from the living room window. He could see the three of them at the kitchen table, mouths moving, smiles blossoming, and head nods of understanding. The dog too seemed to be a focus of attention. Between flashes of pain and near blackouts, he watched the boy leave the table, cross the street, and reenter his home. Frank blacked out for minutes this time. When Frank's headache settled he resumed his watch. The boy was leafing through a book of sorts, talking all the

while. Frank went to Ryan's room: the journal was missing. Frank became unsettled. He began pacing which got Alice all worked up. She attempted in her own breezy way to downplay the significance.

Frank was having none of it. "Secrets shared are secrets bared," he rumbled. "This kid is beginning to remind me of my own son way back when, never knew enough to just shut his mouth."

Alice persisted. Settle down she seemed to be saying in her unique way and the air filled with the smell of flowers in spring time. Frank's nose began to tickle and he couldn't avoid the smile that began to form.

His grimace faded along with his anger. "I suppose you're right, we'll just have to wait and see. I have to admit the boy has been loyal to a fault. I don't like what's happening with that dog though. I hate dogs, they can't be trusted." Between shards of pain causing pauses to his ranting and rambling, Frank went on and on about his own experiences with dogs back when he could place his feet on concrete and walk the streets in this town.

"I never gave in to that little shit of a son begging for a damn dog. That was about the only thing my wife and I ever agreed on. She was a bitch. Did I ever tell you about the time..."

Alice pretended to listen as Frank droned on and on. She had calmed the beast at least. But, in fact she too was concerned about how all this newness across the street might impact her finding a way back into the world. All this darkness, Alice preferred the light of day, bad things happen in the dark. Tomorrow perhaps she could raise the shade on all

this darkness. Right now the boy was sound asleep. Alice suddenly thought of Frank's ravings about boys and dogs, *Let sleeping dogs lie.* Somehow that seemed an appropriate thought.

{Authors aside} Sometimes things happen in bunches. The good, the bad, and the unexplainable.

CHAPTER EIGHTEEN

These sometime things that happen began in the dark of an early morning. Ryan introduced Pluto to Stan Tuttle, the night watchman at the spinning mill. This was Pluto's first adventure. He was waiting on the porch just as Marcia had said. The walk to pick up the newspapers had been leisurely with Ryan letting Pluto stop and stake out his territory at every fire hydrant along the route. Pluto looked back at Ryan after each squirt. He seemed to be saying, 'we got this.' Stan confessed he hadn't run into Pop and Whitey yet but he would. Ryan patted Pluto's head. Armed with a capable companion Ryan told Stan that might not be necessary.

When Ryan and Pluto reached the Swinging Bridge, Pluto got to experience the same off-kilter dance steps that Ryan shimmied to seven days a week, twice on Saturday when he had to collect his paper money. Pluto held himself back as Ryan tossed papers on to the porches. The first several times a paper left his hand Pluto ran to retrieve it. *Isn't that what dogs do?* Ryan laughingly told him he had to curb his enthusiasm. Pluto got the message and now simply watched the folded paper arc and land with a thud. They finished their delivery and were half way back across the bridge when Pop and Whitey started across from a night of revelry. Ryan stopped abruptly. Pluto ran into his backside. Suddenly Ryan smiled, patted Pluto's head, took a deep breath and went to war. He began jumping up and down causing the bridge to start its rise and fall. Pluto seemed confused. Then Ryan ran as fast as he could toward the men, jumping up and down on every third step. When he was within twenty feet of the two men he stopped but continued to bounce. Then he spoke, "Go get 'em, Pluto, these are **bad** men." Pluto understood the word **bad:** he had been labeled that early on by his past master. Pluto charged roaring.

Pop and Whitey, already unsteady from last night's drinking, were now being bounced side to side and up and down. Pluto hit them like a bowling ball, and they both went down. Ryan passed them and looked down. He didn't say a word. The message had been delivered. At the end of the bridge he stopped and looked back. Both men were still rolling around unable to right their balance. Ryan patted Pluto's head. "Good boy."

When he turned into his street, Pluto bounded toward his own porch. His food and water had been set out. Pluto, savoring the sweet taste of victory, ate ravenously.

Ryan waited until Pluto paused then walked him to his spot and tied him up. He placed the food and water close and promised to check on him later. I'll be home all day. He crossed the street and entered his darkened house. It was quiet, his father had left for work. Two days of trying to reason with his wife was all he could manage. Ryan had been given the responsibility of taking care of his mother for the remainder of the week. Ryan peeked into the living room. It was dark and he sensed no movement. He went up to shower. Wrapped in a towel he entered his room and snapped on the light. As he sat on the edge of his bed and got dressed, he was chuckling about the events of earlier. He had already captioned a journal entry in his mind. He would highlight it and call it **Pluto's Plunge.**

He fairly skipped down the stairs and was shocked to see the entire downstairs lit up like a Christmas tree. The windows stood wide open as if welcoming a winter morning in for a visit. The shades and blinds were swinging freely in the breeze. He could hear the heat ticking feverishly trying to keep up. Every light in the downstairs glowed fiercely.

He let his eyes roam and was seeing his house in the full light of day for the first time. Dust that had clung to lampshades now appeared in freefall, the blinds and curtains had also given up their collective dust as if taken out side for a good shaking. It was like a windstorm had taken place in the downstairs. In the living room his mother was half sitting with her back against a sofa arm. Her face was drooped, a shocked look on her face. She seemed frozen in place. The furnace had been unable to keep pace and Ryan freshly showered with wet hair, shivered. Ryan ran to her side. She didn't blink, her breathing was shallow. She seemed unable to speak. She was either in shock or had experienced one. For the second time in less than two weeks, Ryan was calling for an ambulance.

FRANK and ALICE

Frank seemed alarmed. He had never seen Alice like this.

She told him in her own unique way to calm his hemorrhoids, she seemed to be signaling that she was taking charge, though she seemed out of breath at the moment.

RYAN and JOHN TRUSSELL

As the ambulance disappeared down the street, Ryan looked across the street. Pluto seemed to be feeling Ryan's stress, pacing from one end of his tether to another whining all the while. With his father at work, Ryan needed some support. He had placed a call to his father's workplace. He checked his watch. His father should be home soon. Ryan walked across the street and freed Pluto. Together they crossed to Ryan's house and entered. Pluto immediately knew he and Ryan were not alone here. Ryan was starving. Stress always seemed to do that to him. He filled a bowl with cereal, and smelled the milk bottle. At the table he added sugar and sat down in all this new light entering the kitchen. Pluto came to the table and allowed himself to be petted, then he left Ryan to explore. He sniffed, *someone else was in this house.*

FRANK and ALICE

With Alice still out of breath, Frank had the opportunity to rant unabated. "I hate dogs. Look, he can smell my hate, I just know it. Look at him sniffing around." Frank raised a pant leg. In his mind he could see the tooth marks inflicted many years ago.

As Pluto moved about the living room, Frank became more and more agitated. His head began to throb and his mind closed then reopened to a different time and place. Suddenly he was back on the milk farm where he had been raised by a mother and stepfather. It's amazing what the memory bank conjures up as the truth, nothing but the truth. *Frank's memory was of a stepfather who cared more about the dog that herded the hundred or so milk cows to the barn every evening.*

Frank remembered having to sit on that little stool smelling cow shit while coaxing each cow to give it up. He hated everything about the process. The cows sensed and fought his efforts. Franks stepfather observed the boy from a different stall and shook his head in disgust. The dog, during the milking, having done his job, sat at the foot of his owner's stool and listened to the belittling of his son. "Why don't you take a lesson from Dick Tracy here and enjoy your work. Don't be lazy." Wayne Ketchum reached down and roughed the dogs coat playfully. Frank glared first at his stepfather then at the dog who had been named for the man's favorite radio show. Wayne Ketchum continued to pat the dog and confirmed the reason for his name. "You always get your man, don't you boy, not a single stall is ever empty. You could learn from him Frank, if you had a mind to. It never pays to be lazy." Praise for the dog didn't end in the barn. It extended to the kitchen table where a soft voice and a pat on the head accompanied a piece of meat or chicken. The dog listened to the radio at his stepfather's feet in the living room and slept outside the bedroom door. Frank came to hate that dog. He had bite marks to reinforce that hate. Criticism from his stepfather didn't end in the barn either. It followed like the stink of the cows right into the house and into every room the boy found himself. He had never in all the time he lived there warmed to the man since his mother picked up and moved onto the hundred acre spread. Frank was a city boy with no feel for farming. When his mother had a kid with the man, Frank realized she was here for the long haul.

Frank fought his stepfather, the farm and the dog for five years before leaving at age seventeen. His school experience was nearly as miserable. Sitting with his head down avoiding a swinging tail while staring at protrusions that wouldn't cooperate became pencils that wouldn't produce the results his teachers wanted. Meanwhile his classmates followed the ever present lingering smell of cow right back to his desk. Kids could be as cruel as his stepfather. He took it for as long as he could then quit school and joined the armed service. But with no direction he simply traded the muck of a cow pasture for the muck of a foot soldier.

If he learned one thing from that experience it was that he was terrible at following directions or orders. He lasted eighteen months and was dismissed with a duffle bag of bad memories. A long line of half-hearted attempts to be normal followed but with a legacy of neglect and out right malevolence in family matters, things had finally ended in this very living room with a bashed in head.

Frank grunted, the pain reaching through all this light in a normally darkened house had him getting a queasy feeling. *I'd throw up but there's nothing in there. I remember the feeling though.* He had just held it together long enough to cover all those years though, *having a good day*. He hadn't thought about any of all that for years, not until the dog entered and began sniffing around. He had seen the boy walking him and praising him. This morning the boy took the dog with him and was gone for over an hour. Frank had no experience with a dog showing him affection. Frank fairly shouted to the rafters "I hate friggin dogs."

Pluto looked in the direction of Frank, he cocked his head he bared his teeth.

Frank looked in Alice's direction, alarmed, "He can't hear me can he?"

CHAPTER NINETEEN

Ryan closed the windows turned off the lights and lamps then finished his breakfast. Pluto had remained upstairs. He hollered for Pluto. Pluto, who had been sniffing out the place, came down the stairs with his fur sticking straight up, a low growl exiting bared teeth.

"What's wrong boy, you look like you've seen a ghost."

Pluto looked directly into Ryan's eyes. Ryan suddenly realized Pluto had sensed something in these walls. "Let me get you home boy. I'll tell you the whole story when we walk the paper route tomorrow." Ryan ruffled and patted down Pluto's fur as he reassured him in a calm voice. "My father should be here soon I have to go to the hospital to see my mother."

Ryan continued to pat and comfort Pluto as they made their way to the sidewalk. A police car pulled into his driveway with lights flashing. Ryan waited for the officer to get out. The man sat stock still in his cruiser. The officer seemed to be studying Ryan. Was it more bad news about his mother? They hadn't found out about him skipping school had they? The officer continued to sit there, cruiser running, staring; finally the flashing lights were turned off and the door opened.

The officer didn't look like he was delivering good news. "Is your mother home?"

"No sir, she was just taken to the hospital a half hour ago." *So that can't be it,* thought Ryan.

"Are there any adults in your house right now?"

Ryan was getting a funny feeling. He reached down and put an arm around Pluto. He shook his head.

The officer cleared his throat. "There has been an accident."

Ryan already knew his mother had been taken to the hospital, did she get in an accident on the way. "Is my mother ok?"

Now the officer seemed confused. "I don't really know anything about your mother, I hoped she'd be here."

"Something happened to my mother and she was taken to the hospital a short time ago. My father should be here soon. I called him right after calling the ambulance."

"What's your name son?"

"Ryan, Ryan Trussell."

"Ryan, I'm afraid your father has been in an accident." The officer nodded to himself. *Now I understand why the blue lights were on.*

"Is he going to be okay? Can you take me to him? I'll just go and tie up Pluto." Ryan started across the street with Pluto.

He reassured the dog even as his own stomach was churning carrying a hundred questions.

The officer seemed at a loss as he a watched the boy and dog go to the yard where the boy tied the dog, talking constantly. He got back into his cruiser. He called his lieutenant to find out how to handle this.

Ryan knew the way to the hospital. This wasn't the way to the hospital. He looked across at the officer.

"We need to stop by the station. My lieutenant wants to speak to you."

Lieutenant Magoon met them at the station door. There was a woman with him. He held out his hand and introduced himself. Then he introduced Mary Fallon. The three left the officer twisting his hat in the corridor and moved down the same corridor to an office with frosted glass and Mary Fallon's name on a brass plate. The name plate did not indicate what Mary needed a name plate for.

With the lieutenant seated behind Mary's desk, which too bore Mary's name on a hunk of wood, Mary sat with Ryan and suddenly took his hand. *She seems kind*, thought Ryan. She smiled the kind of smile that says what I'm going to tell you next is not a joke.

"The officer told you your dad was in a car accident." A sheen of moisture dampened her eyes. "Ryan, your father was killed in that accident. I'm so sorry." Her grip tightened.

Ryan took a deep breath. He wasn't sure of what to make of all this. He looked around the office. A book case filled with some of Mary's possible heroes sat across the room. A picture of Mary and a man and two little children and a dog sat atop the book case. Diplomas of some sort were on the wall behind the desk. Ryan saw and absorbed all this even as his father's cellar filled with boats and booze bottles floated by in his mind. He felt sad but not devastated.

Ryan couldn't muster words because he had no idea what to say.

Mary noted his silence but misread. She patted his hand. "I'm sure this is all a shock Ryan." She sighed and twisted in her chair. "And I understand your mother was brought to the hospital a short time ago? Are there any adults who can come and stay with you?"

Ryan immediately thought of Violet and her parents. *A possibility.* Then he thought of Marcia across the street. He nodded, t*hat might work.* "Let me think about that. Just get me to the hospital."

Mary suggested if Ryan wanted she would help him break the news about his dad. Ryan was struck by the irony of what was taking place. *It had appeared his mother was the parent who might not survive and he would be living with his father. With his father dead he would be left with a mother who clearly didn't want him.* Also thinking about how things had been left between his parents, Ryan decided he needed to tell his mother the news. He straightened with his next thought, *but before that he needed to talk to Violet.*

A little white lie wouldn't hurt right about now. "My cousin is in school, can you take me to see her? I'm sure if I talk with her I'll have a place to stay."

When Violet reached her principal's office greeted by a police officer with her friend Ryan at his side she knew enough to go along with any story being peddled. It didn't hurt that Ryan greeted her with a wave and a "Hello cousin."

After a brief discussion and a tearful, "We'll pray for you both," from the head sister, Violet and Ryan shared the back seat of the cruiser on the way to the hospital. The two whispered and locked hands. Left alone in a waiting room, as the formal part of his mother's admission was underway, Ryan tried to make sense of all that had happened this morning.

"Violet, when I came down the stairs all the lights in the house were on. Every window wide open, curtains and blinds all twisted like a hurricane had come through, and my mother frozen in place."

Violet, picturing what Ryan was describing just knew her grandmother must be involved.

Ryan remained in the waiting room while Violet went to the cafeteria to get them both a hot chocolate. When Violet returned they sat sipping, gazing at one another over the lids, two kids lost in thought. The seriousness of what was happening was reinforced with the shrill sound of an ambulance arriving, followed by the intercom barking orders.

A nurse found them several hours later. "Are you Ryan?"

Ryan wondered how she knew his name but nodded.

"Your mother has suffered a cardiac event. We won't know how serious this is for several days. Right now she seems unable to speak and one side of her body is not moving. She can hear and see and blinked her eyes in understanding when she was told what had happened." The nurse set her shoulders, "I'm sure you have a hundred questions." The nurse smiled then. "Your father has been in to see her. He said to let you go in after he had time alone with her. I believe he has left so you can go in now."

Violet's eyes widened, Ryan sat there too numb to react. *My father?* Violet ran to the window, two floors below a car was just now leaving the parking lot.

Ryan recovered and without another word the two followed the nurse to an elevator, then to his mother's room. The setting was exactly the same as before. The room dimly lit his mother nearly invisible white blankets pulled tightly around her. Violet stood at the window which faced the woods in the distance. From the fourth floor winter was on full display. From this height with naked trees moving in the breeze Violet could feel her grandmother's involvement in all this. Ryan approached the bed. His mother, melted to a puddle of her former self, looked helpless and hopeless. Gazing at a sagging face that twisted into a half grin and two black holes for eyes that held no life staring upward at nothing, Ryan wasn't sure how to begin. Should he ask who had just been in her room pretending to be his father or should he just let her know his father had been killed in a car accident?

Her eyes told him what to say. There was no recognition, no love coming from those eyes.

"I'm sorry you're hurt mother." No response or movement of even an eyelid which seemed to signal Ryan to get on with his business. "Father was killed on his way to see you."

Wanda Trussell's eyes didn't blink, no moisture built up behind them, two black holes resisting enlightenment.

"Did you hear me Mother? Father was killed on his way to see you." Either she was drugged or the news didn't matter. Ryan decided to get right to it. "Who was in here pretending to be father? Was it that man from the supermarket?"

Wanda moved her head slightly towards the wall.

Ryan stood there breathing deeply staring down at a woman that in the moment he never wished to see again. He turned away took Violet by the hand and they left. The elevator ride was quiet but during the mile walk from the hospital back to Ryan's house they talked about the car Violet had seen. Then they talked about Ryan possibly moving into Violet's house. Pluto was tied up outside. He barked his own needs. Ryan hollered he'd be over in a bit.

The windows were still open and the lights remained on. They were sitting at the table, still hashing out what it might all mean when a cruiser pulled into the driveway. Ryan looked out.

Mary Fallon was a passenger. Ryan took a deep breath. *Was she coming to take him away to some agency or another*?

Ryan invited her and the officer in and they all sat around the kitchen table. The officer started the conversation. "I am very sorry about your dad, Ryan"

Ryan nodded.

"Mary will discuss what that might mean for you." The officer fumbled with his hat.

Ryan thought, *do they all do that when they bring bad news*?

"But before that, I have questions about what happened in this house this morning." He stood looking at what had been described. "The ambulance people say all the windows were open, every lamp was on, and the curtains and blinds in disarray when they got here. They also said it was freezing cold. Can you explain any of that?"

Ryan saw no reason to lie. "It's still cold I haven't touched a thing." He motioned to the open windows. "That's exactly what I came downstairs to. It was like someone had broken in opened every window and shocked my mother."

"You didn't hear anything?"

"I was in the shower I didn't hear a sound."

A deep breath followed another twirl of the hat. "Okay then. He's all yours Mary."

Mary cleared her throat. "I'm sorry to drop all this on you Ryan. Would you like your aunt here to hear this?"

Ryan looked at Violet then shook his head.

"Your father's body will be with the medical examiner until they rule out anything and everything that could have contributed to the crash. It seems he hit a patch of ice and the car slid into a tree. Still, tests have to be conducted."

Ryan thought of the last time he had seen his father, passed out with a whiskey bottle at his feet like a favorite pet. *Could his father have been drinking at work and in the car?*

"There are two different funeral homes in town. You might want to talk with your aunt about all this. I am going to leave my card and if you have any questions you can reach me at this number." She rose and patted his hand. "I am very sorry all this is happening to you Ryan, it's a lot for a kid to handle."

Ryan nodded and showed them to the door. The officer had a final announcement before the door closed on his back.

"Someone else might be by to follow up on that possible breakin. Just so you know. We'll also be monitoring your mother's progress. We would like to speak to her as well."

"Can I close the windows?"

The officer nodded.

Ryan and Violet were overwhelmed and decided they need to walk and talk this all through. They gathered the pooch for a walkabout.

FRANK and ALICE

"What the hell. The father is dead? I didn't see that coming. Too bad I couldn't have been there I might have had my ticket out of here." **Frank winced.** ***"On the bright side, that's one we don't have to account for,"*** **he mused.** ***"What do you suppose will happen to the boy?"***

Alice had concerns of her own. Had she overdone things a little? The ambulance drivers seemed a little more skeptical when they picked the woman up this time.

In a worrying little breeze Alice asked Frank to write to Ryan. ***Ask Ryan when he thinks his mother might be back home?***

EDWARD KNEELY

Edward was back in his apartment. He was still in wonder at the serendipity at play that allowed him to be on scene when Wanda was carted away once again. He had been out for a ride with his head in the clouds. The car seeming to have a mind of its own ended up driving by, just as Wanda was being placed in the ambulance. He shook his head as he stirred a cup of coffee. He chuckled then. It wasn't serendipity that got him to the hospital and placed himself first in line to see the woman.

When Wanda's husband wasn't on scene he figured the odds and headed straight to the hospital. He managed to stay close enough to the action to see Wanda admitted to a room. He then instructed the nurse that the boy, his son Ryan, not be allowed in until after he left.

Wanda's face was certainly distorted but her mind was keen when he visited her.

She couldn't explain but insisted 'there must be a ghost in the house.' She did not intend to go back there.

Ed was thinking, *if you only knew.* "Well let me help you figure all this out. Act like you are in a coma or something. Don't tell anyone anything. Pretend you can't speak at all."

Wanda nodded. This man would help her through all this. "Thank You Edward."

"I'll be back tomorrow after I think all this through."

At his kitchen table, digesting his conversation with Wanda for the second time, Ed needed to make some serious plans to gain ownership of this house.

* * *

At six-thirty the next morning having read his newspaper, Ed was armed with the knowledge that Wanda was now Wanda the widow. He didn't know if she had been told but for now he intended to play dumb. Just before shift change occurred, when a nurses' station resembles a bee hive with all the nights' war stories being shared, Ed Kneeley reentered Wanda's hospital room. Her face had stopped melting. She seemed almost buoyant. Her smile was closer to the one that had sat across from him in his car. There was not a trace of sympathy or regret in her announcement, "My husband is dead, killed in a car accident, Ed, isn't that the best news?"

Ed sat there thinking, *I hope she never gets angry with me.*

FRANK

Frank sat at Ryan's desk, his head in his hands lost in thought. Frank didn't often think beyond his open mouth but this might be important. *I wish Alice could talk. I could use some help with this.* Well here goes nothing.

Ryan, I'm going to level with you, your girlfriend's grandmother is here in this house. I will even tell you her name, it's Alice. She's trapped. I've already told you who I am. If you agree to help, write back and I will give you instructions.

RYAN and VIOLET

It was in the gathering darkness that Pluto was returned to his house. The lights were on and Marcia was sitting at the kitchen table, her father sitting across with a napkin tucked into his sweater neck. Ryan and Violet felt like they needed to talk to an adult. When Marcia opened the door, Pluto rushed in tail wagging as if to signal, Mom I'm home.

Marcia had yet to hear of all that had gone on today. She just knew Pluto was gone with his two friends and they would all be hungry when they got home. She invited them to supper.

Seated around the table, bowls of beef stew and freshly baked biscuits in front of each of them, Ryan seemed quiet and contemplative. He worried a biscuit and dipped a small piece into his stew. He studied the people around him; his best friend, his new best friend, a warm caring adult, and a father who obviously loved his daughter. He waited until they had all had a chance to eat up and then without preamble began his story. Half-way through Ryan's telling, Marcia rose and stood behind Ryan's chair and placed her hands on his shoulders.

Across from Ryan, Marcia's father's eyes filled with tears. Violet had one hand on Pluto's shoulders carrying the same message. Pluto understood and walked to Ryan's feet and warmed them with his body.

When Ryan finished, Marcia responded. "I am so sorry Ryan, what can I do to help?"

It was decided that Marcia would help with all funeral arrangements and identify as Ryan's aunt if asked. Ryan would stay with Marcia in the short term, at least until his mother was home from the hospital.

"You can go back and forth to your house as necessary for clothes or whatever you need."

Ryan was sad but not overwhelmed. The smell of good food and the caring that radiated from this house gave him hope. "Violet and I need to visit my room to see if we have any new messages. Then you know what I feel like doing? How about a card game?"

That broke the ice. Ryan would be fine. Laughter filled the kitchen.

Ryan and Violet and Pluto walked across the street. The house was dark. Ryan turned on the hall light and they climbed the stairs to Ryan's room. The journal lay open with the new message lying there waiting to be read.

Violet was the first to react. "I just knew it."

"So what do we say? How can we help?" What does that even look like?"

"Slow down Ryan, let's talk this out."

While the two of them sat on the bed talking things out Pluto was sniffing and growling his way through the house.

Something wasn't right with this place and he sensed it. He strolled into Ryan's room and looked up at these two humans who had treated him so kindly. If there was something they needed to do here he would help. He inched between them, lay down on the bed and let his instinct guide him.

After a lot of discussion the two went back to Ryan's journal. Violet was charged with writing in his journal for the first time.

> *Hello, my name is Violet. Alice is my grandmother.*
> *Ryan and I will help if we can. Let us know how.*
> *Tell my grandmother I miss her.*
>
> *Sincerely, Violet Mooney*

Ryan and Pluto walked Violet home. Somehow even amidst the trauma of the day a long lingering hug and kiss promised a future. Violet scratched Pluto's shoulders and went inside to tell her parents what had happened at Ryan's house.

Pluto took the lead on their way back to Marcia's house. Ryan was lost in the stars. To his mind, stars simply showcased the dark, making it even more vibrant. He looked across at his own darkened home which darkened further when a passing cloud snapped off the night lights. *Tomorrow will be soon enough*, nodded Ryan. I'll stay with Marcia and you boy, tonight.

EDWARD KNEELY

Edward Kneely was having evil thoughts. With the father out of the picture and Wanda out of the house, it made sense to keep the house empty. With no parent on board the kid, Ryan, would have to live somewhere else. Given the history of the place added to what had taken place in the past two days, he should be able to pick the place up cheap. *So first things first: what to do about Wanda, and her kid, permanently.*

FRANK and ALICE

A light mist accompanied the breeze in Ryan's room. Frank had shared Violet's message aloud. Alice was being emotional. Frank couldn't identify with emotional, he had a bull in a china shop approach to everything. His days on the farm in his youth soured him on life and these eternal headaches did nothing to soften his attitude.

"We have to be careful in what we say. We can't let them know what we have planned for Ryan's mother. Now that the man of the house is gone we simply need Wanda back here. We also might need to take care of her new beau." **He winced but continued,** ***"I might actually have a plan for that."*** **Frank nearly fainted when a mega-migraine struck with no warning. He couldn't catch his breath, his eyes watered. He was flat on his back with Alice standing over**

him wringing her hands when he recovered. Still out of breath he had a sudden thought, *now I know how you feel Alice.* Another thought followed. *Was this empathy?* When he had his breath back the real Frank returned. *Nah, he decided, probably just heartburn.*

RYAN and PLUTO

Ryan slept in a strange bed and tossed and turned throughout the night. It was like his mind was throwing spaghetti at the walls hoping something might stick. Marcia woke him by sending Pluto into his room. He dressed for a newspaper delivery kind of morning in mid-winter.

A cup of cocoa and a piece of toast awaited his seat at the table. Marcia was busy getting ready for her own day. Ryan could smell the fragrance pushed from the shower, he could hear Marcia singing in a soft voice. The old man was already in his chair, a cup of coffee warming his gnarled hands. This was the first morning Ryan wasn't excited about doing his job. Stan frequently reminded him during the worst of weather that 'the mail must go through.'

Pluto was feeling Ryan's reluctance to start the day and brushed against Ryan, whining just loud enough to get Ryan's head out of himself, Pluto had places to go and fire hydrants to see.

They headed down the steps. Ryan looked across, his house still dark and cold looking. A couple of hours from now he would go in there and try to communicate with his house guests. He would take Pluto with him.

When he got to the Spinning mill, Stan was standing at the ready just inside the door. He had a concerned look on his face. He was holding one of the newspapers. Ryan nodded good morning. Pluto took it a step further and moved toward Stan for a good old fashioned fur rubbing.

"I am very sorry about your father, Ryan."

"Thank you Stan, I'm sorry too."

Stan had the same hundred questions Ryan realized he'd be asked today by anyone who knew him: Do you have someone to help you through all this? Where will you live? How can I help?

Ryan remained just inside the front door with Stan. He answered Stan's questions as best he could then asked to see today's paper. A picture of his father's car with a smashed front end was just to the right of the main headline of the day. Below the picture was a caption referring to the story on page 3. Looking at the picture of the car brought Ryan's first real understanding that his father was really gone, never to return. Stan touched his arm. "You sure you're okay?"

Ryan took a breath, rubbed Pluto's fur, and smiled up at Stan. "You have said it yourself Stan, the mail must go through." Inside, Ryan was furious and he didn't really know why. He knew one thing though and he voiced it, "We would really like those two old drunks to show up this morning wouldn't we Pluto?"

Back at his own home an hour later, Ryan and Pluto walked up his walkway.

He entered with Pluto padding behind. He put out some water for the dog and he climbed the stairs to the bathroom. He flushed, washed his hands and went to his room. He opened the door. Sitting there on his bed was Frank, (kind of anyway) he wasn't three dimensional, more like a shadow but he was clearly sitting there with his back against the bed pillows. Ryan gulped. His heart began beating rapidly.

Frank made himself present without a word being spoken. Ryan's door suddenly closed. ***"I don't need that damn dog rushing up here and putting his mark on me.*** Ryan's desk lamp turned on. ***"Sit down at your desk. We need to talk."***

ED KNEELY

Ed was missing another day of classes. *He wasn't missing it* he told himself *just missing it.* He was armed this morning with a plan. By now everyone in town knew Wanda's husband was the man killed in that car crash. So this morning Ed made his presence known to the nurses by claiming to be Wanda's brother. He had on a suit and tie and in his best professional demeanor was clearly convincing. Once in the room he nudged Wanda's arm. She turned. She smiled. She could count on this man. Ed told her he was ready to move in to her home and take care of her. Wanda told him she wasn't sure about returning to the house, she felt it was haunted. Ed reassured her. "If it gets to be too much, as a real-estate salesman, I will handle selling. Given all the rumors about the place it might need to be bargain priced." He took her hand. "I will take care of you and your son if you let me."

Wanda readily agreed.

"In fact I planned to go there later today." He affected a look of contrition. "I know it might seem cold with your husband's recent death but the sooner things are settled the better, don't you think?" He actually leaned in and gave her a peck on the cheek. "You already told me Ryan knows you have a special friend. It should ease his mind to know that your friend is a beloved teacher."

Wanda had not said a word. For the first time she felt there was a man in charge in her life. A professional man, a respected member of the community. She looked up at that man and nodded her assent. Ed ruffled her pillow making her comfortable. "I will be back this evening and let you know how the day went."

RYAN and FRANK and ALICE taking it all in

Frank continued to occupy the bed while Ryan had moved to his desk. Frank sketched out his life in this house like he was filling out his taxes using short form trying to avoid another migraine. He didn't leave an opening for Ryan to ask questions. He moved onto how Alice had come to join him. ***"Bottom line, Ryan, we are stuck here and need you to help, the girl too."***

It was finally time for Ryan to speak. "What can we do, we're just kids?"

Words appeared. Ryan held his breath.

"All you need to do is get your mother back into this house. I can 't tell you why but she needs to be part of this. I have promised Alice."

Ryan observed the shadow figure with what appeared to be a dent in the head suddenly grab that area and rock back and forth in the desk chair.

"Well I'll be going to the hospital later. There should be an update. What does my mother have to do with any of this anyway?"

Frank looked over at Alice who was holding back any comment. So far Frank was handling things just fine. The journal came alive again. ***"All I can tell you is your mother is***

not well. She has tried to commit suicide in the past month and we stopped her. And now all this. We need to watch over her."

Ryan stared down at his journal. When he raised his eyes Frank was gone.

Pluto had left his water dish a while ago. He was roaming the upstairs when suddenly his fur stood on end. He growled deeply just as Frank found refuge in the attic. Ryan was confused and angry. Confused by what the shadow figure sitting on his bed had to say and angry with his mother, Ryan held one finger up to Pluto. "Wait right here boy. I just need a moment." Ryan descended the steps to the basement, the smell of liquor rode along with a lingering smell of glue. Ryan went to his father's work table. He grabbed a hammer. With every blow that shattered a boat in a bottle, Ryan's anger dissipated just a little. The smell of glue got stronger and Ryan's sense of loss grew. He loved his father, he had never truly understood him but he loved him, at least from a distance.

The longest conversation he could remember was the recent one at the hospital. *I think he was sincere that night,* thought Ryan. *He couldn't follow through but I think he meant it when he said it.*

Ryan left the sea of glass where it lay. He hated the time those damn boats took his father's attention away from trying to get to know his son and how this move to a new town and this house had changed his life. *I wish I had told him about the ghosts.*

The morning had turned bright and sunny. The icicles were melting like an ice cream in summer. Ryan walked Pluto to his own work space. While he readied Pluto for the day he spoke aloud to his canine friend. "I need to see Violet. I can't wait for 4 o'clock. I'm going to see if I can get her out of school early." Ryan walked back into his house and found the number for Violet's parents.

When Ryan reached Violet's school she was already in the foyer waiting for him. He took her hand.

Outside, Violet quizzed him. "I don't know what you told my parents, but whatever they told the Sisters had them treating me much nicer than normal. One of them even hugged me." Violet wrinkled up her nose, "She smelled like garlic."

Ryan laughed. "Your mom is so understanding Violet, she can't do enough for me right now. When I told her I didn't think I could face going to the hospital alone she even offered to drive us." Ryan gently nudged Violet away. "Oh, and by the way, guess who was sitting on my bed when I got back from my paper route this morning? You'll never guess what he wants. He told me my mother has been trying to kill herself."

Violet's face showed she had absorbed all this. "How come I miss all the action Ryan?"

"I don't think you are going to miss any more. Our house guests are asking for your help too. And that's how I have spent part of my morning, I sunk a few ships too."

Violet looked confused.

"I'll tell you all about it on the way."

After hearing the whole story Violet still had questions, "What did he look like Ryan? Did you get a glimpse of my grandmother?"

When they got to the hospital Wanda was out of the room undergoing more tests. The two kids went to the cafeteria for hot chocolate and a donut. "So, they want your mother back in the house. What do you suppose that is all about?"

"I can't be sure but **Frank** said it was to help your grandmother. In what way I don't have a clue. He told me they have saved my mother's life in the past so maybe they want to be able to do that again if necessary."

When they got back to his mother's room, Wanda was once again wrapped like a mummy in her bedding. This time when he approached she turned her head. She actually spoke. "Someone is going to be coming to see you soon Ryan. You need to hear them out. It's for the best." She turned her head away and refused to answer any of Ryan's questions.

After sitting there enduring the silence, Ryan took Violet by the hand and they left frustrated.

The two kids walked back to Ryan's house. On the street was a vehicle. Violet was the first to react. She nudged Ryan, "I think that's the car I saw at the supermarket. Hmm. She walked to the back of the car. "I think it's also the car I saw heading out of the hospital parking lot. Why is it parked outside your house?"

The two were about to go find out when Marcia hollered from across the street. "Ryan, there is someone inside who wants to talk with you, he says you know him."

CHAPTER TWENTY

FRANK and ALICE

Frank was still remarking on the destruction in the cellar. *"That boy is pissed Alice."* His blow by blow description had brought on a migraine and he lay now resting his eyes. Alice ruffled his feathers.

Stop worrying about the damn cellar, what is that horrible filthy man doing out there? She made it clear to Frank that her killer had been looking in the windows. *When the woman across the street drove into her garage this horrible man walked over to talk and is now in her home. And now the kids are here and going over there too. Oh my poor granddaughter. What can we do?*

"Alice, easy now. Nothing we can do but wait. You heard the bottles break down there. I don't think the boy is in the mood for a lot of falderal. This might be headed to an ending that works out for both me and you." Frank grabbed his head. *"Any aspirin Alice?"*

RYAN and EDWARD KNEELY

Ryan remembered this car too. It was the same car that traveled his street occasionally. It was clear to him even before he entered Marcia's house that there to greet him would be his math teacher, Mr. Kneely.

Ryan had Violet by the hand but in the moment thought perhaps an extra layer of support was in order. Before going in he went to Pluto and untied him. The dog was pleased to be included in this conversation.

Sitting at the kitchen table was Mr. Kneely all dressed up in a suit and tie. He rose immediately. "Hello Ryan." He smiled a smile Ryan had never seen on that face. *Might even fool you if you didn't know better,* thought Ryan.

Edward Kneely didn't allow for a response but moved to pat Pluto who was sizing him up. Pluto tolerated it for his owner's sake but wasn't buying it. "I was just telling Marcia what a good student you are and how difficult it must have been to move here in October, but how well you handled it." Mr. Kneely looked directly at Violet, "I don't think I have had the pleasure of meeting you miss, I'm Mr. Kneely, Ryan's math teacher."

Violet, who knew this man's history with Ryan, nodded politely but without comment.

Mr. Kneely continued. "I am very sorry about your dad Ryan. Actually that's why I am here. In the past few months, Ryan, your mother and I have become close friends. I went to visit her in the hospital and she has asked me to look in on you."

Marcia spoke up, "I think it's kind of Mr. Kneely to step up don't you, Ryan? I'm sure you would like to stay in your home and not have to run back and forth for everything you need."

Ryan's eyes widened. "But I thought I was staying with you?"

"Well you are welcome to, but Mr. Kneely tells me your mother has asked him to move in and take care of things at least until she is able to come home. Has she spoken to you about any of this?"

"Kinda, she just didn't say it was going to be Mr. Kneely."

"I'm here to help, Ryan, in whatever way I can."

Violet thought, *this man is the devil.* She exchanged looks with Ryan and they read one another's mind.

Ryan had to try. He was just a kid and adults rule the world but he had to try. *I have to keep this positive until I know what he wants*, thought Ryan "Mr. Kneely, Marcia lives across the street so with a little help from her I can manage on my own. Mother knows I do very nicely on my own. I'll talk with her later today. Thank you for the offer. It's nice to know you care for my mother but I'll be fine."

Mr. Kneely wrung his hands. "I'm simply doing as your mother asked. Go on about your business. You won't even know I'm there but your mother will rest easier. I was about to go over and acquaint myself with the place. Would you like to give me a tour?"

Marcia's father sat frozen in his chair, but his eyes revealed that he didn't believe the man either. Ryan made eye contact. The old man nodded.

Ryan had no choice in the immediate. He didn't have enough ammunition to accuse Mr. Kneely of anything except spending time in a car with his mother. Ryan's life was taking another turn and he had no idea what was around the next corner.

Ryan scraped his chair back from the table and in a daze, rose to follow Mr. Kneely. Pluto rubbed some warmness against his leg. Violet stood and took Ryan's hand. Marcia offered a smile. He felt love in that room but he had no idea what he was facing from this man who had belittled him since he had arrived. He reassured Violet he'd be back shortly. His feet didn't feel that assurance however and he could barely place one foot after another as he crossed the street, an inner sigh accompanied each step. He looked up and a flash of shadow crossed the living room window. *They know we're coming.*

Back across the street, Marcia responded to a whining canine who was insisting he be let out to do his duty. As soon as the door opened Pluto bolted across the street and was at Ryan's feet when he opened the door to his house. Ryan looked across at an agitated Marcia and signaled it was fine. He patted the dog. *I'm glad you're with me boy.*

Mr. Kneely hollered across, "It's okay, I love dogs. I always wanted one."

FRANK and ALICE

That terrible man is coming in here again, what can he want? He gives me the willies. **Alice shivered the curtains.**

Frank pondered the possibilities. ***"You know that boy is pretty clever, let's listen to the conversation. I have a strong feeling he's going to get the man to reveal just what he intends."*** **Frank blinked back the pain,** ***"Then we can act. Remember, Wanda needs to be back in this house one final time. Just two weeks till show time."***

Alice patted Franks hand with a blow kiss of air.

RYAN and MR. KNEELY

Ryan opened the door.

Mr. Kneely with his smile locked in place waved his hand in a grand gesture, "After you Ryan, it's your home."

Ryan got right to his plan. Somehow he knew Frank was listening and he intended to give him an earful.

As soon as the door closed Ryan began, "So how did you meet my mother?"

Mr. Kneely went right to the heart of his deception. "I was concerned you weren't fitting in, I thought your mother should know. I called her."

Ryan knew this wasn't true but played along. He began the tour even as he thought of how to get to the truth. "So, do you intend to stay here when my mother comes home?"

"Actually your mother asked me to stay here and watch over you until she gets back home, then we will decide."

"Why you Mr. Kneely, I mean she hardly knows you, right?"

"She says she doesn't have a single friend in this town except for me. Ryan you can trust me. Your mother called me at my office and asked for my assistance even before she became ill." Mr. Kneely offered the most sincere look he could muster. "We only want what's best for you."

Pluto spent this conversation looking around. He sensed there was someone or something lurking in the living room. He growled deep in his throat. He was struck with a blast of air. His fur raised and his lips curled back in a snarl. Another even colder blast of winter weather stung his eyes. He darted back to the kitchen and between Ryan's legs.

"I think what's best for me is to stay with Marcia. You can stay here if you like. Would that work? You can check on me whenever."

Ed pretended to think about this. In his mind though, he was thanking his lucky stars. He could come and go as he pleased with the boy's blessing. He would bring some of his things over and by the time Wanda was home he would have effectively moved in. "Ryan, you seem to be a mature young man. I think your idea is sound." He looked beyond the kitchen. "What say we have a look around? Where do I sleep?"

"You can stay in my parent's room. Just stay out of mine please, all my things are in there."

Mr. Kneely merely nodded.

The two walked up the stairs.

When they opened the door to his parent's bedroom, knowing what the ghost writer had written, he popped the question. "Have you ever been in this house before?" Ryan watched his face.

Mr. Kneely lied in the immediate but revealed more than he could ever know with his answer. Mr. Kneely had no way of knowing his distant past was sitting on the edge of his seat waiting for the slip of a tongue.

"Years ago I lived in this house. But I haven't been here since."

Alice didn't agree with that statement. She laid a whisper to Ryan's ear. She had a mind to lay a blast across Mr. Kneely's head but Frank held her back. Frank, while holding Alice in a death grip, took a longer look at this math teacher. His

mind riffled his through past renters, nothing there. He went back further, what did years ago look like? Suddenly he arrived back to a time when he breathed real air. He reached the time of his last breath. He met the eyes of his assassin. *Could this be happening?*

So he has been here and he slept in my bed, and he's lying about it, thought Ryan. *It's worse than I thought.*

They finished the tour at the cellar door. "You might not want to go down there. There's quite a mess to clean up. I'm going to get a few things from my room then I'm going back to Marcia's."

"I'll close up when I leave offered Mr. Kneely. If you would like a ride to the hospital just be here at 3pm." He continued to display his plastic smile.

FRANK and ALICE

Frank continued to hold Alice tightly. She was fairly swooning with pent up rage. There was only so much he could do so he ushered her up into the attic then let her unleash. The room became a tornado of moving debris. The sounds of books and magazines and odd bits of furniture rumbled the walls. Frank needed to let her vent. When Frank finally calmed Alice, he would reveal that this man who smothered her to death, also killed his own father.

EDWARD KNEELY

When the boy and his dog left, Ed went quickly back to Wanda's room. He lay down on the bed with his hands behind his head. *Yes, he was home at last.* He closed his eyes. Anger began to dissipate with the memory of the brief time he lived here after his father's death. He and his mother never mourned what happened almost by accident when her young son came to her aid while being physically attacked by an abusive man. Edward hit him alright. He meant to stop the abuse but he didn't intend to kill him. If only his mother had stayed. They could have been happy here. Ed might have gotten the dog he wanted. Her religious fervor and accompanying guilt divided mother and son, sending her to Florida and her son claimed as a ward of the state. A deep sigh left his lips.

Suddenly the ceiling above him began dropping bits of plaster on his head. The noise accompanying the falling debris was like nothing he had ever heard. The walls shook, the furnace came on adding its own unique sound and suddenly Wanda's babbling about the place being haunted and causing her injuries didn't sound quite so unrealistic.

He rode out the storm lying there with eyes closed, curled up in the same fetal position he remembered from his days in a similar bed.

When what felt like an earthquake had subsided he continued to lie there. He never wanted to get up. He felt drained. An hour passed. He dragged himself up off the bed dusted the plaster from his clothes and went to find the source. The hallway was undisturbed. He washed his face in the bathroom sink. He never made eye contact with himself. He was still shaking when he reached the attic door.

The knob would not turn. His hand felt an intense cold. The door seemed frozen shut. He felt an even stranger sensation as his hand once more tried to turn the knob. A different memory reached him and he suddenly had his hands and arms around the woman he had brought here that night. Ed Kneely fairly reeled.

He needed this house to be his salvation not his greatest nightmare so he lied to himself once more. Haunted? *Just an old wives tale*, he told himself on his way down the stairs.

RYAN and VIOLET

Back in Marcia's house Ryan was trying to make the case that Ed Kneely was not looking out for anyone but himself.

"What could his motivation be, Ryan? Don't take this the wrong way but your house is not exactly Beverly Hills, so I don't think he wants your house. Maybe the two of them really care about one another." Marcia thought suddenly of her own situation. "Maybe it's as simple as that."

Violet had been quiet in all this. She listened. She studied this young man she had declared her love for. She trusted his instinct. People don't change overnight and this Ed guy had treated Ryan poorly from the beginning. She spoke up.

"I think Ryan has that man pegged. He might not want the house but I'm telling you right now he wants something from that house. There is some connection we just aren't seeing."

Ryan nodded. "Well, I asked some questions that I believe were overheard by Frank and Alice. The ball is in their court now. I left my journal in my room. I plan to go over and read it when we get back from the hospital."

FRANK and ALICE

Alice finally calmed down and Frank told her they both were killed at the hands of the same man. *"He was just a teenager but always a bad one."* Once again Frank couldn't look the truth in the face. During his lifetime and for the

full time he had walked this house as a ghost, he continued to portray himself as the victim. *"So my son has come back here, but for what?"* He looked in the direction of where he thought Alice might be balled up trying to regain her breath. *"The good news Alice, is he has no idea we are here within these walls."*

Frank made a bold prediction, *"He's going to get a taste of his own medicine. Now wouldn't it be ironic if my own flesh and blood got to carry on in my absence."* He chuckled at his little private joke. The two went into Wanda's bedroom. *"My head hurts right now Alice but when I'm thinking more clearly this just might turn into a two for one."* Alice, partially recovered blew the debris off Wanda's bed.

"I'll write to the boy after I rest Alice"

CHAPTER TWENTY-ONE

RYAN and VIOLET

The trip to the hospital was a waste of time. Ryan pleaded his case to his mother who never turned her head. It was clear Ed Kneely had affected her mind. The one response she managed was her wish to have Ed in the house until she was discharged.

Ryan insisted he would not stay in the house with that man.

Ryan and Violet took the long way home. Ryan directed Violet to the Chevrolet Buick dealership.

"Why are we here Ryan are you getting your license?"

"Look in that window at the latest models, aren't they something." Ryan smiled to himself keeping his dream of taking Violet to a concert in Bangor years from now was still fresh in his mind. When Violet looked at him strangely Ryan smiled.

"You had to be there Violet." Then Ryan laughed right out loud.

Violet just shook her head thinking what a strange young man I have fallen in love with.

When the two reached Ryan's house, thank the lord, Ed Kneely was not there. "I can only hope Frank and Alice have an idea how to end all this. Come on in let's check my journal. If there is a message we'll let Marcia know the latest. We need to convince her he's a bad man."

The journal lay open to a new page. Frank had left a clear message that sent chills through both Ryan and Violet.

This man is a killer of both Alice and me

What he wants of us now we'll just have to wait and see.

He bludgeoned me and smothered poor Alice

Plans for your mother remain unclear

We sent him a warning but the pull seems too great

It's this house he seems to hold dear.

This man used to live here years ago a beloved trusted son

He killed me in a fit of rage,

Yes your teacher, he's the one.

"OMG! Ryan, what can we do?"

"I have no idea. I do know I won't be sleeping in this house with Mr. Kneely in the next room." He opened his closet. "Help me get some clothes together." Ryan stormed through his bedroom, draws opening and closing even as he continued to speak. "We have school tomorrow. Sleep on it. We'll meet at Marcia's house tomorrow afternoon." Ryan's mind was running a mile a minute with no safe place to land. In a flurry of activity an overnight bag was located, filled, then with Violet ahead of him on the stairs, he cast one last look into his room. He shook his head in frustration. His journal, safely tucked under his arm brought comfort, and he squeezed it to his chest. He spoke to the room where he knew **FRANK** and **ALICE** were paying close attention. "This man should not be in my house."

MR. ED KNEELY

Ed didn't mention the turbulence he had experienced in Wanda's bedroom. He spent the half hour reassuring the woman that he had everything under control at home. The doctor came into the room and spoke to Ed with Wanda's permission. The doctor motioned Ed to the corridor. He told Ed he was mystified as to what had caused the bruising and swelling around her lips, face, and neck. "She had all the symptoms of Frostbite. Her skin was cold and the first two layers of skin are burned." The doctor shook his head, "Very odd." He looked to Ed for an explanation. "Has she spoken to you about it?"

Ed told the doctor Wanda was just beginning to be responsive he would try to find out.

When he went back into Wanda's room he did not tell Wanda what the doctor had asked. He stood to the side rethinking the disaster of plaster that had rained down on his head earlier. He said his goodbyes and left determined to visit the attic when he got to Wanda's house. One question remained in his mind that echoed the doctor's diagnosis. *Why was that door knob so cold? And why did it bring back memories of that terrible night?*

Ed needed some time to think. He drove by the school without a glance. *Least of my concerns* he said to himself. He continued across the second bridge and took a right turn. He soon found himself entering the small town of Norridgewock. A restaurant on the right side of route 2 caught his eye. He pulled into the parking lot. He entered and took a seat facing the roadway. A waitress approached swinging a pot of coffee offering a refill to those already dining. When she reached Ed's table. She stared him straight in the face. Ed didn't speak but the waitress did.

She pointed the pot as if it were a magic wand. "This will fix you right up, I can see you have a lot on your mind. You look almost haunted."

Ed had to chuckle in spite of himself. "Lady you don't know the half of it. Sure, pour me out of my misery."

Ed watched the waitress move about the room. He ordered eggs toast and home-fries, what would normally be a breakfast meal. The waitress kidded him about his choice, "Is your life that turned upside down?" Ed said don't even ask. He began nursing his coffee. The ease with which the woman worked the room, filling and refilling cups, taking orders and laughing with the patrons was not lost on Ed. His mind began to wander. Thoughts of what lay ahead in the coming days filled his head even as the waitress returned to refill his cup. Right now, in this place, he thought he too could balance his life. Ed spent the afternoon in the restaurant managing to drink four cups of coffee while wool gathering his future. He seemed reluctant to leave the place. Things could work out he could reclaim his old house. When the waitress finished her afternoon shift, Ed followed her out the door. He was about to ask her a personal question when an automobile entered the parking lot and the woman waved. A window rolled down and a smile intended for the lady emerged.

Oh snap thought Ed I really liked her style. Never the less his buoyancy lasted all the way back to Skowhegan. When he turned into the driveway and the house loomed above him reality returned. It was getting dark out. Shadows teased him. He walked slowly towards the front door glancing up at the attic window. Something seemed to move beyond the glass. Ed shivered took a deep breath and entered.

The house was dark and cold. Ed turned on a light in the kitchen. He shivered once again. He could see his breath. The thermostat registered 72 degrees and the heat was running.

Then why am I so chilled. He continued to shiver in his coat. He turned up the heat to 75 but left his coat on. He checked the fridge. Nothing looked edible. He went into the living room and sat in the recliner. A strange vibration emanated from the chair made it through his clothes; a probing feeling like he was being examined by a doctor. He stood. He faced an empty wall. And a closed curtain. This house had no television. Ed checked his watch. Too early to call it a night and he was not a reader so that left little to do but explore the place.

He decided to visit the cellar where the man of the house had plied his hobby. When he reached the bottom step he saw that all the boat models had been smashed. The floor was littered with glass. The only sound came from the roar of a furnace that seemed to be trying to keep up. Confused by the destruction he climbed back up the stairs. He looked briefly into the boy's bedroom. The closet door was open and hangars were empty. Drawers had been pulled in the dresser. In Wanda's room the plaster remained, covering everything. The outline of his body where he had lain formed a snow angel on the bed.

He'd have to sweep all this mess up if he intended on sleeping in here. It seemed even colder in here than down stairs. Only now did it register the temperature in the house had dropped since he arrived. He shivered. Even with the furnace running full blast it was damn cold. He moved on to the attic door. This time the knob turned easily. He snapped on the light. From above, shadows creeped down the stairwell, the bottom three steps filled with newspapers and magazines that looked for all the world as if they had tried to escape a storm. Ed took a deep breath and made a decision. He looked up, he wasn't climbing those stairs. He turned and closed the door. There was nothing up there he needed to see he rationalized. He used the bathroom and while gazing at himself in the mirror, made one more decision. He closed Wanda's door and turned to Ryan's room he would sleep here. He tossed himself beneath the covers, sleeping fully clothed with his coat on and buttoned to the top.

FRANK and ALICE

"So he plans to stay here. I'm not sure exactly how we get rid of him." Frank was struck with a brainstorm. "Alice, you can make his night a night to remember. With no sleep and bad dreams his day in the classroom might just be a bitch."

Frank added his own recipe for disturbing dreams by placing himself on the bed right next to his son. Alice smiled

as she watched Frank snuggle up to his son. *This should be one hell of a night.*

MR. ED KNEELY

For nine hours, every emotion Ed had ever felt emerged in a continuous nightmare. In a twist of blankets, shivers, hot flashes, cold sweats, and what felt like actual physical nudges, Ed heard himself cry out. At times his breath felt squeezed from his body like toothpaste from a tube, he was left gasping like a fish out of water. Amid the physical discomforts were feelings of guilt for ending that woman's life. And for the very first time, he was left feeling a little bit sorry for causing his father's death.

In the morning sobbing uncontrollably he stood in a shower with the water running from cold to freezing. Shivering, the new normal reached clear into his bones. The towels were cold and stiff.

He had slept in his clothes which were wrinkled beyond repair. He would need to go home and change. He checked his watch, he had time.

His car was sitting in the garage with the door closed. When he got into the car the windshield was a block of ice. *How is that possible*? He sat heavily behind the wheel; he tried to turn the key, it wouldn't turn. On his third attempt he snapped the key off in the ignition. He sighed deeply. Frustrated, cold, and forlorn, he slammed the car door then the garage door. Swearing constantly, at a level that was heard by more than one neighbor, he made it to his apartment.

He tried to reach the school but the line was busy. *Of Course it was.* Slamming still another door he hoofed it to school arriving twenty minutes late for his first class. When he opened the door to his class room, much to his chagrin, the assistant Principal was covering.

He gave Ed a glare, handed him a planner that was not written on, and said he would like to meet during Ed's free period.

Edward Kneely, the professional, the veteran, the man who seemed to be above all school laws, was left feeling suddenly vulnerable. *What a friggin nightmare this is. All of it.*

When the door slammed behind the Assistant Principal, Edward breathed deeply and sought to regain control. In a demanding voice he told his charges to open their books.

A hand went up. A reasonable question was asked. Ed Kneely, who had missed a good number of days recently, had no idea what page they were on. A look of confusion clouded his face.

Funny thing about kids, they can sense any weakness and right about now the back row sensed Mr. Kneely was on the ropes.

The class had been through a bevy of substitutes over the past several weeks and in general had their way with them. Even the studious one's found there was a certain joy in being in control. One of the vocabulary words from their English class took over the room; **emboldened.** Mr. Kneely, at the moment at least, knew less about what was going on in his class than they did. Time to test the waters.

First a series of farts fouled the air. Several paper airplanes took flight. When the planes all landed safely, the clucking sound of tube ends of chap sticks being manipulated, circulated the room. Mr. Kneely's head remained down. Even without the cold that plagued his night and delayed the start of his day, Mr. Kneely remained in his seat as if frozen.

Ryan, quiet in his seat, witnessed all this and suddenly Mr. Kneely didn't seem such a formidable foe. He seemed to age right before Ryan's eyes. Not once during or after the class did Mr. Kneely make eye contact with Ryan, or with anyone else for that matter. At the bell the students noisily, laughing among themselves, simply left the room. *Wait till I tell Violet what happened in math class. I can't wait to write all this down.*

RYAN and VIOLET

Ryan walked home set his back pack on Marcia's porch and with a new bounce in his step walked to free Pluto. He couldn't keep the smile off his lips as the day continued to play in his mind. Upon their return from a walk, a happy to have you aboard pup was constantly rubbing against Ryan's leg. He fed, watered, and tied the pooch back up.

From across the road Ryan could see through a side window that Mr. Kneely's car was still in his father's garage. He wondered if the man was inside. He was about to go inside to write in his journal when Violet showed up to care for Marcia's father. The two sat at the table as Ryan described what a difference a day makes.

"I am going to move back into my own house, Mr. Kneely doesn't frighten me anymore. He patted his journal. I need to hear from Frank and Alice. Whatever they did to him last night is working.

Marcia's father heard everything that was said as he sat waiting to make a trip around the living room, maybe a walk out onto the covered porch. The poor man couldn't talk, could hardly walk, but he could hear with the best of them. He had that Mr. Kneely fella figured out the minute he had walked in the door. Kinda reminded him of that no good, do nothing, husband his daughter had recently shed.

Violet could see the poor man getting antsy. "Let's get a jacket on you it's a beautiful afternoon to spend some time outside."

Ryan rose, determined. "Well, I don't know if Mr. Kneely is in the house or not, but I plan to sit at my own desk and record what happened today."

Ryan was in his bedroom. Marcia's father was seated on the porch with a blanket pulled up over his waist. Violet had gathered Pluto to frolic with when meandering down the street like one of those two drunks Ryan had to contend with on his paper route, came Mr. Kneely.

He walked to the garage, got in his car, and sat there briefly. He got out and slammed the door. Even from across the road

Violet could hear all the swearing. Pluto barked but Mr. Kneely did not acknowledge him. Edward Kneely walked to Ryan's porch and sat down heavily. Five minutes later a tow truck entered the street and backed up to the Trussell garage. Mr. Kneely walked back across and conversed with the driver.

When the car was attached, Mr. Kneely got in the truck cab and left along with his automobile.

Violet took Marcia's dad back inside with Pluto at her heels.

Ryan, was well into his journal recording the events of the day. He put his pen down when Violet entered his house and hollered up the stairs. Pluto stayed near Violet, this place was starting to get to him.

Violet described what she had just witnessed.

Ryan told her that his mother's room looked like it had come through an earthquake. "Something happened here overnight that has unhinged Mr. Kneely, you just saw it for yourself."

Violet had an idea. "Marcia left another beef stew she made in the refrigerator, I think it's her father's favorite. Let's heat it up. Did you know I can make biscuits? When she gets home we'll fill her in."

CHAPTER TWENTY-TWO

ALICE

Alice looked at the rectangle on the wall. The picture gracing the calendar in the kitchen showed the boy's father had boats on the brain even when he wasn't placing them in an empty liquor bottle. February in Maine doesn't usually conjure up much interest in being out on the water but Ryan's father had found a calendar that celebrated boats year round. A giant ship breaking through ice floes on one of the Great Lakes seemed to be headed directly towards her date of demise. It was just a week before Valentine's Day, February 14, her granddaughter's birthday, and hopefully Alice's resurrection.

Alice was feeling a little bit guilty. She glanced at Frank sitting in the recliner with his head bent forward, nursing a head ache that seemed to be visiting with more and more frequency. Alice had her travel plans well underway. They did not include Frank.

She thought back to her life before her death. As her mind captured the past, Alice unconsciously wrung her hands.

She had been married once, had a daughter. Much later she watched her granddaughter be born. She honestly tried during the first five years of the girl's life to be a better grandmother than she had been mother.

She became a mother before the first anniversary of a marriage which took place only because both kids were Catholic. As soon as the seed was sown a union of the two was a done deal. Once their parents had made the two kids do the honorable thing, they left them to their own devices.

There was never enough money to pay the rent and put the proper amount of food on the table. Blame was placed and tossed back and forth across a kitchen table that was as unsteady as their marriage.

When their daughter was colicky from the start, even the infrequent visits from both sets of grandparents became sparser still. Alice was trying to work a job and be a mother and was failing at both. They all attended church though, every Sunday morning faking a working relationship.

When the little girl constantly cried through the priests weekly attempt to save the congregations collective souls, Alice and Warren Beaulier were discouraged from attending.

The Priest actually had the gall to have Alice's parents deliver the news. If God didn't want them in his seats, what chance did the marriage have? Their tiny third floor apartment was forever too cold.

The local bars however provided heat from multiple sources, warming a body inside and out. The two seemed to be in competition, one sitting with their kid and one sitting on a bar stool. When Warren added even more heat by inviting a lady to join him at the bar, Alice flat out gave up. Her daughter eventually was left with her husband's parents as the two teenagers went their separate ways.

Alice was forced to stay away from her daughter who was raised a staunch Catholic, complete with all the trappings of guilt.

When Violet was born, Alice felt like she was given a do-over. Her daughter was resistant at first but soon found out how difficult it was to raise a daughter on her own.

The church had about given up on forcing two people who hated one another to stick it out for the kids' sake. Just as her mother before her, Violet's mother found that the love of her life was living a double life and she was suddenly a single parent.

Alice began to take the little girl Violet, one night a week which turned into two and then became 'any time you want just call first.' Grandmother and Granddaughter bonded in an intense way right from the start. The little girl seemed to read Alice's mind and never a cross word passed between them.

Alice looked again at the calendar. That damn boat didn't seem to be making much progress.

Frank hadn't moved a muscle from the chair, his eyes remained closed. Alice went right back to reminiscing.

Caught unaware, defenses down, yes too much hooch, a weak moment, the walls suddenly trembling, a panic attack, a scream leaving her mouth; suddenly Alice was dead. Killed on her granddaughter's fifth birthday.

Alice took in some air and looked at Frank. She shook her head. With that dented head of his, he was lying to himself. Now she knew his past and suddenly she liked him even less.

This was all his fault. If he hadn't been such a miserable father, his son would not have felt the need to end his life. When you looked at in total, three lives had been destroyed. It was obvious this terrible man Edward Kneely was the apple that didn't fall far from the tree.

She managed another deep breath and allowed air to reach a curtain. Within that whisper of movement was a new truth.

When she left she would be leaving alone. *Can't have a man like Frank out there.*

One week until Valentine's Day

Ryan had not heard back from Frank. It was a Sunday morning. He managed the heavier Sunday editions of the newspaper while Pluto stood guard following closely across the bridge. Ryan carried all the news fit to print on that Sunday, February 10, 1960.

Along with the news, Ryan carried in his head the annual celebration of all things scented and chocolate. Ryan was buoyant, the bridge seemed to hold steady as he fairly sailed above the ground. This was the first time Ryan had ever thought about Valentine's Day in a serious way.

Since he first began school the day had stood out as different. Kids bringing in and handing out little cut outs, asking, "Will you to be mine?" Heart shaped candy with a message that disappeared when you popped it in your mouth was left on every desk. This year was different, Ryan was in love. He ruffled Pluto's coat and said it aloud to Pluto and to the world almost as if testifying, "I am in love with Violet Mooney."

* * *

Ed Kneely had not spent another night in the Trussell house since he had car trouble. This Sunday morning he was back in his own kitchen trying to figure out where he had gone wrong. Somehow his personal life had invaded his professional life and he was in trouble in both. When he met with the Assistant Principal he was not allowed to speak.

'Just listen Ed. You need to get it together. You have missed too many days, and frankly you look like hell.'

Ed winced.

'If I can help I will but this can't go on.'

Ed tried to speak.

The assistant Principal held up his hand. 'The Principal has even noticed.' He nodded gravely, 'He's giving me the opportunity to straighten this out before he has to bring out the big guns; the school board.' He raised his eyebrows. He sighed aloud. 'Get it together.'

With that conversation fresh in his mind, Ed tried to muster a little warmth out of his coffee cup but even that showed no sympathy.

One glimmer of hope remained. Wanda would be going home this week and she wanted him in her life. The past few days she was looking better. She wasn't allowed to smoke and she seemed to be coughing less. Her color was coming back and all in all, she wasn't a bad looking woman. He could do worse. Maybe it was time to try to put all these demons to rest and finish out his career and life like a normal person. She had told Ed there was some life insurance and if they sold the house, and he continued to work, they could build a life together.

He got up and walked to the calendar tacked to his kitchen cabinet. He counted the days till February vacation. Christ, Valentine's Day was Thursday, always a sugar fed nightmare and tomorrow he had to go back and face those little demons. He studied his hands. Hands that were beginning to shake without provocation. In that moment he wasn't certain he could face a future with anyone, hell he wasn't sure he had one.

* * *

Ryan broke the news in his journal. His mother was coming home Tuesday. His father's funeral was going to be tomorrow afternoon. Burial wouldn't be until spring so a simple service acknowledging the fact that his father had indeed been alive at one time and was now dead, summed up what the pastor intended. His father had not attended any church so Violet's parents had intervened with their Parish priest to use some influence to get the man's body into a holy place for his sendoff.

FRANK and ALICE

Frank read Ryan's journal to Alice. The only part that interested them was the day Wanda would be back in the house. Frank's son Ed, had not stayed since being given a cold shoulder by Alice, so he shouldn't be a problem. *"So Thursday, Alice, the day for lovers and lovers of life, very appropriate. We'll get you up and running then you can help me out of my fix."*

Alice had a question. When she got through to Frank, he had a ready answer. *"Why, my son of course. With you being the new woman of the house it should be easy to bring on his demise. We'll make it look like an accident of course. I don't want you getting into trouble, you have a whole new life to*

live."* Frank went right to his knees when the pain struck him. Alice just shook her head. *This was not going to go as he hoped. She wanted no part of it.

Ryan and Violet spent Sunday, an absolutely beautiful day, walking with Pluto having lunch with Marcia and hearing of a concern she had just been apprised of; her husband wanted to come home.

Marcia's father nearly fell out of the recliner he had claimed when he heard those words. He got their attention. He wanted to get up and go out onto the porch. The snow was mostly gone. The walkway was clear to the concrete. Marcia's father showed his intent to get down those steps and feel ground under his feet. Marcia stood on one side and Violet on the other as the old man navigated the steps and the walkway, all the way to the street. The revelation that his son-in-law might becoming home seemed to energize him. They could read his outside but they couldn't read the rage he was feeling.

He got back to the porch and sat down with a self-satisfied look on his face, ***he could do this.*** As perceptive as the group cheering him on were, they had no idea what ***this***, meant to the old man.

* * *

Monday did not go well for Edward Kneely but he gutted it out. He managed to be on time to school, but success seemed to end there. The outlaws smelled blood. They had figured out that Mr. Kneely would not send them to the office no matter the infraction, so bedlam reigned. Ryan almost felt sorry for the man; almost.

* * *

Ryan's father's funeral was at 4pm. Violet and her family met Ryan at his home at three.

The service was as brief and as impersonal as advertised and they were back in Violet's parent's kitchen by five. Ryan was tired out. He excused himself, hugged Violet tightly, and went home to an empty house. Pluto wasn't out. Oh well, he'd be waiting on the porch in the morning.

* * *

Bedford arrived back at his home at 3:15 pm on the same Monday. Marcia was at work. Pluto was tied up. Ryan had promised to walk him as soon as they returned from the funeral.

Pluto was nothing if not patient. The dog watched a car he didn't recognize drive up. When Bedford exited the vehicle he immediately walked to a point just beyond Pluto's tether. "Honey, I'm home," he said in a mocking tone. Pluto, hearing the cruelty of his voice and the anger in his eyes, backed up a step. From the living room Marcia's dad watched and read Bedford's lips.

Not for long you're not, thought the old man. He moved back to the recliner and resumed lifting the five lb. weights that were already strengthening his arms, his grip, and his resolve. *He's not going to put my daughter and that dog through another round of cruelty. He'll never see it coming.*

Bedford was seated at the kitchen table when Marcia arrived home early. He had already thrown a murderous glare at the old man. For some reason the old man just smiled back at him. *Stupid old coot,* thought Bedford.

The strange auto parked at the curb was a dead giveaway. *Well at least he warned me, I'll deal with this.* Marcia set her shoulders, gathered Pluto, and went inside.

The tea kettle was singing, Bed ford had the largest of smiles as he rose to embrace his wife. Marcia stiffened but let him have an un-returned hug. "What are you doing here Bedford, I thought I made it plain this is not going to work out." Bedford went to the cupboard and brought out two cups. "I couldn't find the tea so I waited. Water's hot though."

"Bedford, you can't stay here. More pointedly I don't want you here."

Bedford went to the table and handed Marcia a red envelope. "Just open it. This is our special week you know."

Marcia tore open the envelope. A Valentine, a simple heart on the outside in which Bedford had written his name. A larger heart graced the inside, with a smaller heart centered. Marcia's name was written on the larger heart and Bedford had written his name once more on the smaller one.

He had penned a simple message.

<u>With you in my life, Marcia, two hearts beat as one.</u>

This was Bedford's attempt at a peace offering. If this didn't do the trick, he had another envelope he would hand her.

Marcia had a simple question. "Have you found work Bedford?"

Bedford eyed her warily, the teapot continued a dull whistle.

"You look like you could use a shower."

Bedford scowled but said nothing.

"And Bedford, if you want to sweep a girl off her feet you might want to remove the price tag from the back of the card." She moved to turn off the heat. "Now please leave. Valentine's Day might have been our anniversary but all the love associated with the day ended a long time ago. It just took moving here to make it register."

Bedford stood. Marcia wasn't sure what would follow. He reached into the bag on the table. He handed Marcia the second envelope. It was from a lawyer. The lawyer explained that Bedford was unable to work because of an unspecified condition. That being the case he would be asking for a good part of Marcia's earnings and half of any money in the bank when the divorce was settled. Marcia read all this aloud.

Pluto read Marcia's body language as she asked Bedford to leave. The man didn't react in anger which surprised Pluto. Pluto glanced at Marcia's father who seemed to be hanging on every word. The old man had recently put all his money in Marcia's name. A fair amount. *Was Bedford asking for half of it?*

"Well, we'll see about that," responded Marcia. "For right now just get the hell out and don't come back."

As Bedford slow walked to the door with a big smile on his face, he offered, "I heard you recently came into money." He winked at the old man. "Don't you think you should share your good fortune?" He glared at Marcia's father. The old man continued to smile that smile and thrust those weights skyward. *Stupid old coot*, thought Bedford once again. He opened the door.

"You will be getting an envelope from me, Bedford and it won't be a Valentine." She slammed the door. Pluto moved to her side to offer comfort.

On Tuesday morning Marcia called a well-respected lawyer in town, Carl Wright. He gave her a simple fix. "You have to money of your own, correct? And your father is still alive? Just have your father put his money back into his own account. Divorce this leech then your father can give it back to you?" A busy man, he rose and was already calling for his secretary.

"I'll do all the transferring necessary, just get me the account numbers. I'll send divorce papers by the end of the day. Do you know where he's staying so he can be served?"

"He left a number to call if she had a change of heart," said Marcia.

Tuesday evening, expecting Marcia to be the one knocking on his motel door, Bedford was shocked and surprised to be handed a simple white envelope. In a matter of moments he was seeing Valentine red.

Only one way to handle all this, determined Bedford, sitting in the one chair in the room. He needed to get the old man out of the way. If Marcia's father died before the divorce went through the inheritance would be automatic, and so would Bedford's share. His mind flipped ahead to Thursday, Valentine's Day, their anniversary.

His mind raced. Surely Marcia would honor one final meal together. He would call her. Of course the wait at the table might be over long on such a busy night, plenty of time then to get his cousin to enter Marcia's house and take the old man out. Hell, the old guy could barely move.

He called Marcia and apologized. He didn't want any of her money. He understood why she wanted a divorce and he wouldn't contest it. Could they have one final dinner together at a nice Restaurant in Waterville? Heck, they could meet early on

Valentine's eve so she wouldn't even have to come home first. "If you don't believe me you can call my lawyer. I've already called and he'll be changing things over the next couple of days."

Remembering why she had married Bedford in the first place weakened her resolve. If he was truly having a change of heart why not part on better terms. She agreed to meet him at the Jefferson Restaurant on Wednesday, at five pm.

RYAN

Tuesday began as just another day. Paper delivery without a hitch. Pluto seemed a little restless, but together they got the job done. School was school. Mr. Kneely seemed to perk up and actually reprimanded several students. They were one step from being sent to the office when they decided their teacher meant business and straightened out.

Ryan walked Pluto when he got home then tied him up. Violet wouldn't be coming to care for Marcia's father today. Ryan had agreed he would stop in. He checked in and asked the old man if he wanted to walk. He shook his head. He just set there lifting his five pound weights and had the same look on his face he'd carried the other day.

Ryan crossed the street, entered his own house, and went directly to his room to check his journal. Nothing! He hadn't heard from **Frank** in days. He lay back on his bed thinking. He heard a car door slam. He went to the window. His mother was being helped out of Edward Kneely's car and up the sidewalk. He heard the door below close, followed by Mr. Kneely's voice. Ryan went to the head of the stairs. He could hear them move to the living room and the sound of the recliner squeaking. They continued to converse. Ryan needed to know what he should do. He sat down and wrote once again to **Frank**.

This is Tuesday February 12,

Frank,

If you are listening, or watching, I need some help here. What is the plan? This man cannot stay in my house.

FRANK and ALICE

Frank and Alice watched the same action from Wanda's bedroom. They heard the same sounds that would indicate their killer had ingratiated himself with the woman of the house. Frank couldn't be happier.

Alice had a different take on all this. She was prepared to deal with Wanda. She wasn't so sure Frank could deal with his son. He needs a different target. *He just might need to wait until the new me is up and running. I don't want to be here when he does what will surely fail. I'll tell him tomorrow.* She could see Frank trying to think this through, and already he was holding his head.

WANDA

Ed placed a pillow behind Wanda's head. She looked up at him lovingly. "I'm feeling ever so much better, would you see if Ryan's in his room I'd like to talk with him?"

Ed climbed the stairs, he opened the door to Wanda's room where plaster still covered the floor. The door to Ryan's room was partially open so he spoke from the hall. "Ryan, your mom is downstairs. She is feeling much better. She asked me to get you to come down and talk with her. I'll leave so you can have some privacy."

By the time Ryan reacted, used the bathroom, descended down the stairs, and entered the living room, Ed Kneely was gone.

His mother was now on the couch looking up at him. She actually did look better. All her lines had softened. She even had the blinds raised. She smiled a smile Ryan hadn't seen in years. "Ryan, it's so good to be home. I am terribly sorry about your father."

Her smile grew even larger if that were possible. The news fairly gushed out. "We have a chance for a new beginning. I know I said some terrible things but that was in the past. I feel better than I have in a long time." Her eyes widened, "Can you believe it? I quit smoking while I was in the hospital. What a terrible habit. I plan to start teaching music again."

Ryan watched as she jumped from one topic to another, like Pluto worried every new smell. He wasn't ready to enter the fray just yet, so he let her continue to ramble.

"Your father left some money you know. He did have some good qualities. He left you a trust as part of his insurance policy. We're going to be just fine."

She continued to ramble but still had not mentioned the elephant who had just left the room. *Now was the time to get right to the heart of the matter,* thought Ryan. "Where does my math teacher fit into all this?"

Wanda cleared her throat without coughing, "Well Ryan he wants to care for me; actually you and me. He has a good heart, as well you know. He's told me how fond he is of you and what a great student you are. Don't you see? From misfortune springs hope, and opportunity. I can be happy again. We can be happy again."

Ryan, who had not been able to talk to his mother in years, realized he'd be wasting his breath. He also knew he could not live under the same roof with this man. "Mother, I had no idea you would be home today. I have been staying with Marcia across the street. I think I need a little time to get used to the idea that someone is going to be replacing my father. You understand don't you?"

Wanda smiled brightly at the common sense her son was showing. Of course he needed some time.

"You've had to be on your own for some time now so do what makes you happy."

* * *

Ryan excused himself gathered his journal once more and crossed the street.

Marcia was home already. She explained that Bedford had indeed come home and the couple would be divorcing. "I'm meeting him one last time on Wednesday for dinner, then he's out of my life. Believe it or not Thursday is our anniversary." She shook her head, "Yep, Valentine's Day."

Marcia's father heard the plan and didn't like it one bit. He did not trust that man. Ryan explained there was drama across the street as well and reluctantly made his pitch.

"Right about now it's nice to have two strong men I can count on, so yes please stay as long as you like."

* * *

Tuesday night Bedford was holed up in a no-tell motel on the outskirts of Skowhegan. At 7:30 a cousin from Vermont showed up. "No one knows you're here do they?"

Bedford's cousin assured him he had told no one of his trip to Maine.

"You didn't stop for gas or for anything else, right?"

Bedford's cousin once more gave the answer Bedford wanted to hear.

Bedford's cousin had a single question. He got the answer he wanted, so plans were laid and promises made.

* * *

At Ryan's house, Edward Kneely returned and spent the night in the recliner while Wanda slept on the couch. Edward didn't bother to tell his new roommate of the mess in her bedroom above.

"I'll just sleep down here in case you need me in the night." He kissed her on the cheek, tucked the covers around her, and tried to get comfortable in that squeaky chair.

* * *

At Marcia's house the old man insisted on sleeping in the recliner. He just knew Bedford was up to something and he would be ready. The five lb. weights rested on a folding tray. Pluto slept at this feet.

Above, Ryan sat on his bed with his journal on his lap. He felt helpless. He looked back over the four months he had been in this town. Some entries brought a frown to his face but even early on, the one bright spot had been Violet. Pluto too, had been a good addition and Marcia. He would just have to wait this out. It seemed like **Frank** and **Alice** had something up their sleeve but Ryan couldn't figure out what. He got up and used the bathroom then turned off the lamp. He gazed across the street at his own house. His mother was in there with Mr. Kneely. **Frank** was in there with **Alice.** Ryan thought about being a fly on the wall watching what might be taking place over there, then remembered the hundreds of bodies he had swept up and the countless victims of his rolled up newspaper. Yes indeed, a lot had taken place in that house in four months. A final thought as he closed his eyes, *Violet's birthday was Thursday, he needed to do something special for her.*

* * *

Frank watched his son sleeping in his chair. Alice had indicated that for tonight just let sleeping dogs lie. Somehow she intuited Frank's fear of dogs and communicated that fear in her message. ***Tomorrow night as the clock strikes a new day, we will act. Now leave me alone. I need to save all my breath.***

CHAPTER TWENTY-THREE

Wednesday morning Ryan gathered Pluto sitting at the feet of a wide awake old man, still seated in the recliner. The old man seemed to want to say something to Ryan. In the end the only thing Ryan could decipher was that something bad was going to happen. Pluto could read body language; the old man was scared. Pluto whined and licked the old man's hand. Ryan offered the only solution available to him. "Pluto will stay with you inside today, starting now. I'll just let him out to do his business then I'll water and feed him. He can be right by your side all day until I get home from school."

When Ryan reached the Spinning mill Stan was surprised to see him alone. Ryan thought a million thoughts. Part of him wanted to tell Stan what was going on but really it was just too much. "Pluto is taking the day off. He's being company for an old guy who needs him right now."

"Those two old geezer's aren't bothering you any more are they?"

Ryan shook his head.

"Good, I warned em' you know," a puffed up Stan announced.

Ryan thought back to Pluto's confrontation with the two, but said nothing. "Thanks Stan."

The morning light was just beginning to emerge when Ryan got back to Marcia's house. The smell of coffee and bacon hit him as he opened the door. Marcia was up and ready to leave.

Ryan explained he thought it might be a good idea to leave Pluto with her father inside today. He didn't go into detail but said her father seemed to need Pluto's company.

"Well sure, that sounds fine. Dad can get up and get to the door and let him out when he needs to."

She glanced at her dad. She spoke to Ryan but really wanted her dad to know how proud she was of him. "Have you seen how strong he's getting, lifting those weights all day long?" She took her father's hand and then hugged him.

"There are some scrambled eggs and bacon in the oven staying warm if you are interested, I won't be home for dinner." Maybe you could fix something for my dad and yourself." With that she touched Ryan's shoulder and went to work.

Ryan was eating his eggs and bacon when he saw Mr. Kneely leave his house across the street. His math teacher, who never seemed happy, was whistling and bopping his head like a teenager as he walked to the garage. When the car backed out of the garage and disappeared up the street Ryan made a decision. After he showered he would stop in and see his mother. Had she possibly come to her senses? If not, Ryan had nothing to fall back on. What could Frank and Alice have in mind and what did Violet's birthday have to do with anything? The old man said goodbye in his own unique way. Ryan could see he was grateful Pluto was at the foot of his chair.

* * *

His mother was wearing the same happy face she'd used yesterday. She was sitting at the kitchen table nursing a cup of coffee, no ash tray in sight. "Good morning Ryan, what a glorious day it's going to be. Her smile broadened.

"Are you on your way to school dear?" She looked slightly sheepish but she asked anyway. "Honey, don't you think you ought to give Ed a chance? He really would like to make us a family."

Ryan was stuck on the words dear and honey and was at a loss for words.

His mother moved on when Ryan didn't answer immediately. "I'm going to get a cleaner in here and get rid of any lingering cigarette smoke: Clean the drapes, the rugs, the walls, the windows, the cabinets, that cellar. We're going to start brand new, Ryan, honey."

Who is this woman? Thought Ryan.

He decide to stall. "Give me some time Mother." He struggled but announced, "if you're happy I am happy for you. But-but I need to work through some things. The lady I'm staying with, Marcia, she can use my help right now so I'm just not ready to be back here." *There, I've said it.* He rose and moved to the door. "I'll stop in every morning after that man is gone and we can talk, fair enough?"

Disappointed his mother might be, but the smile never left her face. She simply nodded.

At school that man did not reach out to Ryan in anyway whatsoever, neither negative nor positive, so apparently an unspoken truce had been struck; (don't bother me I won't bother you.) He had regained control of his minions, however, and the iron fist was back.

Ryan left his math class in a daze. He spent his day in a daze. It seemed like his world was upside down. His mind reeled.

He hadn't written in his journal in days, he was effectively homeless, he was in love for the first time, for all practical purposes he now had a dog, two guest ghosts who had gone silent, and oh yeah, a possible new step-father. Like he had thought earlier, it was all too much.

A small sense of normalcy returned as he gathered Pluto after school for a walk. Marcia's father was still at it. Pluto visited his same old haunts as they walked the sidewalk checking fire hydrants along the way.

Violet was at Marcia's house when they returned from the walk. She was sitting with Marcia's father on the porch. The old man was pushing those weights of his straight into the sky like a man possessed. Ryan sat down. He told Violet about the new house guest living with his mother and her comments this morning. Violet didn't seem surprised. "When my mother met my step dad it was a game changer. The man can do no wrong. I mean my step dad is a nice guy but he isn't the savior himself." All was quiet for a moment as each went into their own heads and checked in with their household.

Ryan suddenly brightened, "Hey let's go get something to eat. There is a lot more to tell. Marcia won't be home for dinner. She's meeting with her husband one last time for a farewell dinner, I guess you'd call it." The two kids rolled their eyes at the absurdity of supposed adults. They rose in unison, their hands coming together as if magnetized, matching smiles bloomed.

"So we'll feed Pluto and her dad, then go get a burger and a soda." Ryan stammered, "I- I need to make one stop if you don't mind, at the drug store."

Violet looked at him oddly but stifled a question.

Watching and listening and lifting, the old man took all this in. His eyes glistened.

WANDA and ED

Ed brought to Wanda's house all the fixings for pasta and a salad.

Wanda asked how the day had gone with her son.

"He was pretty quiet, I'm sure he has a lot to think about. Have you spoken to him?"

"He came over this morning and said he needs a little time to adjust. I can understand that. He didn't say anything negative."

Wanda put water on to boil as Ed cut up veggies for the salad. Ed turned, "Look at us like an old married couple sharing household duties," he smiled.

Wanda was over the moon. "I have cleaners coming in on Friday to air this place out." She looked around the kitchen. "What do you think about a whole new color scheme in this kitchen?" A do-over just like the two of us.

FRANK and ALICE

"Look at them Alice, all lovey-dovey-dovey."* Frank checked the time. *Just a few hours left till this little farce comes down around their heads.

Alice was just putting the finishing touches on her action plan and did not offer comment.

BEDFORD and MARCIA

The sun was just moving to the horizon when Marcia reached The Jefferson Restaurant. The parking lot was filling up already, early birds trying to take advantage of smaller plates and smaller prices. Chinese food was the specialty of the house. Marcia loved Chinese cuisine. Bedford watched her arrive and met her at the door. "We have reservations for six pm. I know that's an hour from now, but maybe we could have a drink at the bar."

You could have told me this earlier, thought Marcia, but she sighed and said nothing. Looking at him now she wondered how it had lasted as long as this. *One last evening to get through.*

Bedford ordered a beer and a girly girl drink for Marcia. She excused herself to the ladies room just like she always did when they went out. Bedford had been banking on this and with a sleight of hand swipe across the top of her drink added a little something to what he deemed a sickeningly sweet mess.

Small talk rose to a crescendo as the number of patrons increased and Bedford's promise of doing the right thing was heard only by Marcia. To a casual observer they were one of the invisible. By 5:45 pm Marcia was overcome with a feeling of nausea and dizziness. "I need to leave Bedford, cancel our reservation."

In truth there was no reservation and no paper trail. He followed Marcia to her car. "Are you ok to drive?"

Clearly Marcia was not. Bedford, who had arrived by taxi earlier helped Marcia into the passenger seat.

Behind the wheel he looked briefly into the rear-view mirror at himself. *No going back now Bedford*, he nodded.

RYAN and VIOLET

Violet thought it strange when Ryan went into Holland's drug store and bought chocolates right in front of her. *Not very romantic, I have work to do with this boy. And no card?*

When they got to their favorite place, the place where they had looked deep into the future and saw themselves as an elderly couple, Ryan took her hand with a funny smile on his face. Seated, he simply handed over the box of unwrapped chocolates with no message attached. *Clearly there is work to do,* she thought once again.

Ryan started, "aren't you going to offer me one?"

Violet removed the wrapper with just a touch of frustration and disappointment.

While she was unwrapping the chocolates Ryan was removing a small rectangular package from his coat pocket.

As she passed the open box to Ryan, he in turn handed the wrapped in Valentine red rectangular package to her. Violet was stymied. Then suddenly she got it. It was weird because in history class they had just been discussing a term called a <u>red herring;</u> (a ploy to divert from what is really intended.)

She laughed right out loud. "Ryan, I hope you don't mind but I am going to tell my teacher you threw a red herring at me."

Now it was Ryan's turn to seem puzzled.

Violet explained a Red herring as she unwrapped a brand spanking new Sony TR63 transistor radio. Violet was flabbergasted. “Ryan, my god, those are forty bucks at Wallace’s.”

Ryan took in the glee Violet was feeling and knew he’d made the right choice. “What I was thinking Violet, was maybe we could go to your house later and listen to some music on your new radio.”

“I would like that Ryan, I would really like that.”

WANDA and ED

Ed was missing his television shows he watched every night after dinner. On a whim he invited Wanda to come to his apartment and they could watch together. Wanda had never really watched TV. Maybe this was going to be part of her new normal.

“I’ll have you home and on the couch by 10:00pm, how does that sound?”

Wanda thought it sounded fine indeed.

FRANK and ALICE

Sounding for all the world like a nervous parent, Frank was sputtering, *“He damn well better have her home by 10: 00. We don’t need this shit Alice, should I stop him?”* That burst of anger put Frank right on his knees.

Alice didn’t even respond, *hell he won’t even remember what he was thinking by the time he’s back on his feet.*

10:00 pm works just fine for me, Ed whoever you are. You won’t know who or where you are come morning.

BEDFORD

Bedford drove slowly, aimlessly. Marcia was out of it in the passenger seat. He checked the time, 8:30 pm. His cousin should be at Marcia's house just about now. He visited the plan in his head like he was following his cousin through the door. *A ring of the bell, the old man inside not able to answer. His cousin opening the door with the key Bedford had given him. Pluto sure to rise and get all defensive. There was a plan for that. A nice hunk of sirloin with just enough seasoning thrown in would change the dog's attitude while his cousin stood just outside. With Pluto down for the count cousin Jim would simply go in and take care of the old man.* By the time Bedford arrived with Marcia, Pluto would be back on his feet and the old man off his, permanently silenced by a pillow. The inheritance would automatically revert to Marcia and she would have to share her good fortune.

He looked over at the sleeping lady. If only you had given me the opportunity this could all have worked out differently.

PLUTO the OLD MAN and COUSIN JIM

Just as planned and imagined, Cousin Jim parked down the street and left the motor running. The damn car was so old and beat up he was afraid it might not restart when called upon. He looked around. The street was deserted, a heavy cloud cover dampening sight and sound. Bedford had mentioned a kid that hung around but Bedford had assured him he should be in his own house by now. Cousin Jim kept to the shadows and arrived at the house bearing the proper number. He walked up the steps holding a paper bag of freshly seasoned sirloin. He rang the bell, nobody answered just like his cousin Bedford had promised. He fingered the key and placed it in the lock. He turned the door knob. As he opened it slightly, he saw the dog enter the kitchen, hackles raised. He could make out a pair of slippered feet just beyond the kitchen. He threw in the meat and closed the door. *Now we wait. Three minutes should do the trick Bedford had promised. One Mississippi, two Mississippi, three Mississippi...* Cousin Jim prided himself on following orders.

FRANK and ALICE

Frank, with nothing to do but wait, and Alice seemingly preoccupied, was staring out the window as Cousin Jim walked up the sidewalk. He turned up the shoveled path to the house next door. He was carrying a paper bag. He looked off to Frank; scruffy was the word that came to mind. *He better not open that door* Frank thought, *that damn dog will eat him alive.* What? The man barely opened the door and tossed whatever was in that bag inside. Now he's standing outside like a damn fool counting on his fingers. *"Alice, you have to come see this."*

The OLD MAN and COUSIN JIM

Exactly three minutes later, Cousin Jim gingerly opened the door. Silence greeted him. He peeked his head around the door and saw the dog lying between the kitchen and living room.

The old man was seated in a recliner just like he was supposed to be. Confident now, Cousin Jim entered and moved around Pluto, making eye contact with the old man. He looked feeble and helpless, a blanket pulled up over his shoulders, his hands beneath. Weirdly he had a wide smile on his face. *Must have had a stroke*, thought Jim as he moved closer.

Pluto still lay quiet. *This should be easy* Jim concluded as he grabbed a couch pillow and advanced. The old man didn't move a muscle. He continued to smile, his eyes gleaming fiercely.

Cousin Jim, a coward and a bully, couldn't resist. "So old man you ready to find out what's on the other side, huh?"

He had never killed anyone. But how hard could it be?

Especially an old decrepit cripple. Jim's heart was beating fast though. His hands were shaking. He gripped the pillow. "Why don't you just close those eyes old man? It'll be over before you know it." Cousin Jim didn't like the look in those eyes; two black holes that looked challenging. His heart racing, Jim stepped back and turned off the light. The darkness seemed to calm him. He reached across to remove the blanket.

FRANK

Frank couldn't take his eyes off that house. Now the man was entering the house. Now suddenly the light has gone off.

"Alice, will you get over here, something strange is going on over there."

CHAPTER TWENTY-FOUR

RYAN

Ryan and Violet were in Violet's bedroom listening to music on her new Transistor radio. Violet's mother said nothing when Violet showed her the radio Ryan had given her for Valentine's Day and her birthday. She looked oddly uncomfortable though. The kids listened to the latest hits, held hands, and exchanged an occasional kiss though the bedroom door remained partly open. Violet's mother kept finding excuses to tap lightly and enter immediately; cookies and milk, a reminder to their daughter she had homework, and at nine pm. the announcement that the show was over followed her mother into the room.

He was actually relieved. He had stayed longer than he intended. Violet seemed to keep his mind away from all the drama in his life but he needed to have a long conversation with his faithful companion. One more hug on the porch and a promise from Violet that she intended to cook him a Valentine dinner sent a very happy Ryan on his way.

He began his five minute walk home. As he came down the street he noticed a car a few doors down from his house parked on the street with its motor running. Ryan had never seen this car before. Curious, but not alarmed, he reached the house where he was staying. He glanced across the street at his own house, no light no movement. No light showed in Marcia's house which in itself was odd. The old man didn't like the dark. The street appeared as a ribbon of black, framed by a ghost-like off-white bank of snow. Ryan paused. This time of night happened every twenty four hours. He checked the time. Six and a half hours from now, at four thirty am he would be up and delivering his newspapers. He was tired. He should go in. He looked back at the car; it was an old bomber, the engine rattled. A wisp of exhaust rose eerily from the tail pipe. No one appeared to be in the car. Ryan decided not to let his imagination run wild. Ryan walked up to the house where he had recently begun staying, he found the door ajar. He opened the door. Inside it was dark. Pluto didn't run to greet him. Ryan snapped on a light. The old man was sitting right where he always sat, in his recliner. Pluto was a few feet away lying down eyes closed. It was what lay near the feet of the old man that shocked Ryan.

FRANK and ALICE

"Alice, the boy is just heading up onto the porch. He just snapped on the light. That man is still in there I think." **Frank's head began to hurt as he tried to imagine what was going on over there.**

WANDA and ED KNEELY

Wanda was suddenly craving a cigarette. She had been told this would happen. When all the medicine left her system her old cravings would return she was told, her heart began to flutter and she suddenly felt nauseous.

Ed had his eyes glued to the TV. He didn't seem all that interested in talking or listening. Wanda eyed him curiously. The drivel being expelled from that idiot box held more interest than she apparently.

Wanda's cravings were back but the medicine was gone from her system. She began thinking clearly for the first time in a long time. When had this man entered her life? The answer came quick and decisive. When she was at her most vulnerable.

Ed's eyes remained glued to the screen. Wanda's eyes remained glued to his profile. *What did she really know about him? He seemed impressed with her son but her son was obviously not enamored with him. What was the truth?*

Ed suddenly turned his head and met her eyes. He seemed able to read her mind. In a burst of uncontrolled honesty unsolicited, he mouthed two of his fathers' favorite cutting remarks; "Get over it. What's the big deal?"

Wanda might not be able to read minds but she could hear just fine. "Take me home Edward. I despise TV and all that goes with it."

"Well, let's just get you home then." He checked his watch and smiled a smile with no humor attached. "This show will be done in about ten minutes." He shrugged. He shrugged again returning to his show, repeating, "What's the big deal?"

VIOLET

As Ryan began his walk home Violet's mother was pacing her kitchen. *I don't want to upset the girl but this is not acceptable.*

She and her husband had spent the evening deciding how to best handle it. It was decided in the end that she would address this in an adult manner. Violet was nearly an adult. She would be able to understand their concerns.

Mrs. Mooney climbed the stairs. "Violet we need to talk."

Violet was doing her homework with the latest hits riding shotgun. "Sure Mom, what do you need?"

Mrs. Mooney sat on the bed facing Violet's desk. She sighed. She sighed again.

"What is it Mom?" Violet turned the radio down.

"Turn it off please."

Violet noticed her mother's tone seemed odd. She shrugged and turned off the radio.

The reasonable discussion disappeared when Mrs. Mooney pointed towards the transistor radio and said, "You have to give it back."

Violet was lost in the trees. "Uh, why would I give it back it was a gift?"

"Because, first of all, it's too expensive a gift for a boy to be giving a girl at your age. Second of all, we don't have a radio in this house for the same reason we don't have a television. They get in the way of conversation."

"Mom, Ryan makes his own money with a paper route. It's his money to do what he wants with and he wanted me to have a radio. I can turn it off whenever you want to talk."

"Your stepfather and I think you two are getting too serious. This gift simply proves we're right."

Violet wasn't backing down. "Mom, I follow all your rules get good grades and show you guys respect, but you're being ridiculous. Ryan and I are just two kids who are getting to know each other. We haven't even thought about going beyond kissing. He gave me a radio, not a ring."

Mrs. Mooney followed the script laid out in the kitchen. "It has to go back."

Violet felt her face flush. "Mom, I am keeping the radio."

Mrs. Mooney reached for the radio.

Violet slapped her hand away. "It's mine and I am keeping it."

Mrs. Mooney colored. "Don't make me call your step father up here."

Now Violet was angry. She got up from her desk and in a moment was down the stairs. Rushing past her stepfather, she grabbed her coat and was out the door.

Mrs. Mooney reached the bottom of the stairs and looked at her husband angrily; "Why didn't you stop her?"

BEDFORD and MARCIA

It was 9:20 when Bedford reached the edge of town. Marcia had come full awake. She looked at Bedford accusingly. "What happened back there Bedford? Did you spike my drink?"

"Of course not! Why would I do that?"

Marcia was confused. It actually didn't make any sense. She was on her way home. Bedford hadn't tried to change her mind about the divorce. He really had no reason to drug her. Maybe she just had a bad reaction to the alcohol.

As they came down the street, Marcia noticed the car at the side of the street with its motor running. She had seen that old bomb before. Bedford saw the car and panicked. *What the hell!*

His cousin should be long gone. When they reached her house, the lights were on.

"Just let me set here a minute to get my head clear." In the back of her mind she was still trying to place that car.

"Fine. When you're ready to go in, I'll just hoof it back into town and get a taxi. Bedford's head was spinning with possibilities, none of them good.

WANDA and Ed KNEELY

Ed pulled into Wanda's driveway and began entering the garage. Wanda turned, "You are not spending the night Ed. I think I need some alone time.

"Well just let me help you settle in, then I'll go. I'm sorry about earlier."

Wanda was tired and did not want to argue. Besides she needed a cigarette. She nodded, "Just to get me settled then."

FRANK and ALICE

Frank still had his head in the window. He had one hand on that head trying to keep the pain at bay. He watched the

neighbor lady pull in across the street. Good, maybe she could figure out what all that was about.

At about the same time, Wanda and his son pulled into her driveway. They were not smiling as they closed their car doors. His son didn't take her arm, he just followed behind as she moved to the porch. He heard the door open.

Alice was sitting in the dark in the recliner saving her breath.

RYAN

Ryan looked at the man lying prone at the old man's feet, blood pooled on the rug. The old man began lifting his five pound weights above his head. One showed blood stains. The smile he had worn earlier was wider still. Ryan didn't know what to do. Should he call an ambulance or the police or both? Pluto raised his head weakly. Ryan noticed a piece of meat at his side. Pluto began to vomit. Ryan realized this man had come to do something bad.

Ryan rose, touched the old man's arm, and went to dial the number for the police and the ambulance. The man groaned so Ryan knew he wasn't dead. Pluto heard the groan and moved to the prone body and stood over it. This man would not be getting up any time soon if he could prevent it.

BEDFORD and MARCIA

Marcia took a deep breath, clearing her head further, got out of the car and climbed the porch steps. Bedford got out of the car but made no move to follow her. "You can come in for a minute if you want Bedford, I'll call you a cab."

"That's ok Marcia, it's just a five minute walk. I'll call you tomorrow."

Marcia turned and opened the door. The first thing she saw was her father with his arms pumping the air with those damn weights. Ryan was kneeling over something Pluto right beside him. She took another step and saw Bedford's Cousin Jim, half sitting up holding a towel to his head.

Then she heard the sirens. She quickly went back to the porch and looked out into the night.

Bedford was barely out of the driveway when he heard the sirens and caught a flash of blue light mixing with the reds turn into their street. He high-tailed it across and took refuge in a garage.

VIOLET

Violet was half way down the street when she too saw red lights followed by blue stop in front of Marcia's house. Her first thought was that Marcia's father had another stroke. She hurried her pace. She saw just a fleeting glimpse of someone running across the street then disappearing into Ryan's garage.

By the time she got there the police were entering the house, followed by the ambulance attendants.

Standing on the porch looking in the window she could see Ryan explaining to an officer what he had come home to. His hands were flying. Marcia was speaking with a different officer and pointing at a strange looking man with a towel on his head. Marcia's father was still in that recliner and he had not given up on those weights. He was smiling like a hero in a comic book. She waited, taking all this in from the porch. When Ryan finished she tapped the glass. Ryan looked up. He appeared shaken. He moved to join her on the porch.

WANDA and ED

Across the street the beacons of color illuminated the shade like flashes of lightning. Ed peeked out. "Something's going on across the street, there are two police cars and an ambulance."

Wanda's eyes widened. "Ryan is staying over there, would you go over and check on him?"

Ed knew in the moment he hadn't been able to pull any of this off. He was just going to have to empty this house in a different way. He'd check on the kid and be on his way. He looked at Wanda. *Christ, if she wasn't the spitting image of his mother.* He shivered. "Yeah I'll check, get back to you, then I'm gone."

Wanda aimed a look of finality at him. "Amen to that."

As Ed started down the walk he glanced at his car. From the corner of the garage he saw a man. He hollered to him. The man disappeared into the garage. This was all nuts. Ed crossed the street. Ryan was on the porch.

"Your mother asked me to check on you, you ok?"

"I'm ok, it's nothing that concerns you."

"Righto, good night then. By the way Ryan, the house is all yours."

Violet could sense the bad blood between the two. She had her own tale though. "Ryan we need to talk. Can we go over to your house?"

"Sure, just let me tell Marcia and grab my journal. I don't think I'll be staying here tonight. She's going to be busy for a while in there. She thinks her husband set this whole thing up. That's what she's telling the police."

EDWARD KNEELY meets BEDFORD

When Ed came down the walk from delivering his message to Wanda, he got in his car. He checked his mirror. Bedford immediately sat up from the back seat. He had a hammer in his hand. He met Ed's eyes in the rear-view mirror. He held the hammer above Ed's head. "Pull this car into the garage and close the door. We're not going anywhere just yet."

FRANK and ALICE

"Alice, the boy is ok. He's on the porch. Your granddaughter is with him." **Alice sat up straight. Now she was interested. She had been watching Wanda return to her original state even without Alice's help. The woman was smoking up a storm and talking to herself. The clock now read 9:34 pm.** ***What about that creep son of yours*** **she managed to convey without expelling** ***much breath.***

"He's getting into his car." **Frank gasped,** ***"What the hell?! He just drove into the garage and now he's closing the door."***

Alice shook her head. This night was taking twists and turns she couldn't keep up with. The only thing she could bank on was Wanda. And she was right where she needed to be.

RYAN and VIOLET

Pluto heard the kids on the porch and asked to be let out. Ryan opened the door and went in to speak to Marcia. One officer kiddingly told Ryan not to leave town, as he closed the door behind him. Pluto was on the porch with Violet when he came back out. The three of them crossed the road.

There was a light on in the living room. Wanda had the room in a blue haze already. She rose as if to speak then waved him away parting the smoke like a curtain. She went into a coughing fit which summed up their conversation.

Ryan and Violet and Pluto went to Ryan's room. The two huddled on Ryan's bed swapping stories and hugs. Pluto, just getting his feet back under him, couldn't muster the energy to explore. He lay listening to the kids describing their new personal experience with things that go bump in the night.

* * *

At 11:30 pm the blue lights were turned off and the cruisers returned to the station. An All-Points-Bulletin was issued for a Bedford Dennis, age thirty-two, five foot nine, 145 lbs., blond hair moon shaped scar over his right eyebrow. Last seen on foot in the Summer Street area of Skowhegan, Maine he may be desperate and dangerous. Approach cautiously.

* * *

Mr. and Mrs. Mooney drove the streets of Skowhegan, looking for their daughter. They drove past both of the houses on Summer Street that had seen recent drama.

They knew of the on-going drama in Ryan's house and didn't want to bother him unless necessary. Now it seemed necessary. They had no idea what had happened across the street. They also had no idea what the rest of the night would bring.

BEDFORD and ED

Through the garage window Bedford watched the blue lights turn off and the cars leave. He had a million thoughts, ideas, excuses, and escape plans running through his head. This was not the time to try to reason with Marcia he realized. He had seen his cousin wheeled out to the ambulance. He knew his cousin; he'd squeal like a baby, so there was that.

No traffic this time of night in this little burg. Any car traveling would be stopped. So what to do? He wasn't watching when Ryan, Violet, and Pluto crossed the street. He turned to a tied up Ed Kneely. "Who is in that house? Ed saw no reason to lie. "Just a woman fresh out of the hospital."

"What does she mean to you?"

Ed saw no reason to lie. "Absolutely nothing, I was just checking on her for a friend. Her husband recently died."

"So, she's in there alone."

"She is."

"Well, what say we join her in her mourning? If you aren't too tied up that is," smirked Bedford trying to lighten his own mood.

"Honestly, I'd rather not but it looks like you're are in charge just now."

"I is."

FRANK and ALICE

Frank didn't see the two men leave the garage but heard the door open below. He had left the living room when that damn smoke got to be too much. He heard a strange voice appearing to direct someone to sit down. He heard Wanda asking, 'what's the meaning of all this?'

He turned to Alice. *"It appears we have visitors."*

Alice looked once again at the time. In a rush of air, Alice expressed concern. *I'm going to lock the kid's bedroom from the outside. It's almost show time and I don't want them hurt. You might want to write the boy and tell them to just stay put.*

Frank immediately joined the kids in the bedroom. The boy was already at his journal. Frank wrested control. Frank had to smile when the boy sat back in horror.

STAY IN THIS ROOM UNTIL THIS IS OVER!

Below, Wanda continued to demand the men to leave or she would call the authorities. She was coughing hard now, her emotions already in turmoil from earlier in the evening; now some man she didn't know storming into her house holding a hammer and a knife to Edward's head. "Get out," she managed before the man pushed her roughly back onto the couch.

Bedford had just gotten things under control when the doorbell rang. Whoever was on the porch could see there were people inside, so ignoring it was not an option. Bedford prayed it wasn't the police.

He told Ed to get rid of them. When Edward opened the door slightly, the couple on the porch introduced themselves as Mr. and Mrs. Mooney. They were looking for their daughter and hoped she might be here with a young boy she was fond of. Ed did not know Ryan and Violet were in the boy's bedroom upstairs so he did not lie when he said they were not here. He had seen them earlier across the street though, he said. The two looked across at what was now a house completely in the dark. "Can we come in and speak to Ryan's mother? She's home from the hospital I believe?"

* * *

Alice recognized that voice. She hadn't heard it in years. My god, my daughter is in the house where I was killed and my granddaughter is upstairs. She began to gather all the breath she could muster, her eyes going wild even as she tried to form a plan on the fly. Well, here goes nothing. Alice unlocked the bedroom door and got in Violet's face. Violet understood immediately.

Violet got to the top of the stairs and heard her mother speaking below.

"I'm up in Ryan's room, mom. Come on up so we can all talk."

* * *

At that moment a police cruiser continuing to search for Bedford Dennis passed the house across from the crime scene.

It was lit up, with people on the porch talking. *Maybe they have seen something*, thought the officers. They flashed their blue light briefly and pulled to the curb.

Inside, Bedford was stricken with fear. The woman on the porch, hearing her daughter's voice entered the house and began to climb the stairs. Bedford appeared and immediately ordered everyone but Ed up those stairs. He warned Ed to get rid of the cops. If anyone but you comes up those stairs, people are going to get hurt. Ed nodded.

Bedford shoved Mr. and Mrs. Mooney into the boy's bedroom, shook the knife and hammer in their face and told them to stay there. Ryan's mother would suffer the consequences if they left that room. Ryan and Violet and Pluto were all shocked. Pluto, still not at a hundred percent, tried to muster a growl. Bedford immediately locked the bedroom door from the outside. He saw the door leading to the attic and asked Wanda what was up there?

"The attic I guess, I have never been up there. Its cold I know that."

"Well let's check it out shall we?" He noted all the magazines and junk lining the steps but with the light turned on they managed.

Alice was happy this man had chosen to place her daughter and granddaughter out of harm's way. She sent a message to Frank to join her in the attic.

Ed didn't have much luck trying to convince the police that all was well on Summer Street. "We saw a man and woman on this porch, where are they now? And are you the owner by the way?"

Ed admitted he was just a family friend.

"Then you don't mind if we come in and look around, make sure everyone is safe. It's been quite a night of excitement hasn't it Mr. Kneely? You say you are a teacher at the local junior high?"

The two officers looked through the kitchen and the living room. One went down the cellar steps and came back with a questioning look. "There's dozens and dozens of broken liquor bottles strewn all over the floor down there. Little boats sticking up out of the broken glass. Any idea how that happened Mr. Kneely, teacher at the junior high?"

Mr. Kneely shook his head. He was feeling very uncomfortable.

Suddenly he blurted out, "The man you are looking for just ordered a man and two women up those stairs. There are kids up there too. That's all I know. He kidnapped me and made me come in here."

One officer went back to his cruiser to call this in. The other, not waiting for his partner began to climb the stairs.

In the attic, Bedford took a chair to the middle of the room reached up and turned off the overhead light. He hugged himself to his chest. "You were right lady, it is cold up here."

They waited in silence. Ten minutes passed. Then they heard the attic door opening. A man's voice hollered up the stairs. "This is the police. We know you are up there. Come down with your hands above your head. Send the lady down first. You stay where you are until she's out."

Bedford had a different plan. He whispered, "Lady, I'm going to let them know we are coming down." He tapped her back with his knife. "You are going to be directly in front with a knife at your back." He tapped her again. "If they get any funny ideas or they're anywhere in sight when we get down there, they will be responsible for how this ends."

Pluto, refused to leave the room when the officers located them and sent them down stairs to safety. The dog heard all that was being hollered up those steps. In a flash he was by the officer up the attic stairs at the same time Alice began working her magic. When a ball of fur in a frenzy collides head on with a tornado in transit, something has to give.

Alice and Frank listened to the entire conversation. Alice in the time they had been up here had already lowered the temperature in the room. When the officer called up the stairs she lowered it still further. The window began to frost over.

Wanda was shaking like a leaf from fear and the cold. Her arms were beginning to stiffen up. Her legs too could hardly move when Bedford pushed her closer to the stairway.

With the promise from the officer that they would not be visible and he could have the car he was demanding ready and waiting, Bedford shaking from the cold pushed Wanda down the first step.

Alice told Frank to wait on the fifth step down. If the two had not fallen by then he was to give them a little shove. It was dark and the steps were lined with debris.

At the moment Alice conjured up a storm of the century, the stairwell debris began pelting the two. A mind numbing cold accompanied the wind.

At the same time, the dog from across the street charged upward with Frank standing on the fifth step. Frank, who was scared to death of dogs, saw Pluto charging and panicked, hitting Bedford just below the knees in his own dash to escape. Bedford fell and took Wanda with him.

His knife entered Wanda's back and she twisted in pain. Bedford landed on the third step from the bottom his neck broken, he died almost instantly. Almost, being the key word here. Frank recovered his balance and his courage, attaching himself to Bedford's last breath, absorbing his soul.

Alice joined Wanda in her own death dance. She took a deep breath for the first time in years.

Writing in his journal weeks later

July 10, 1960

They burned down the house yesterday. I inherited the place but it held too many bad memories. The town paid me a small amount to use the place for fire training, enough for my first year of college. I have lived with Marcia and her dad and Pluto since that night. Mother is buried in a different plot than father. I think they would have wanted it that way.

I have no idea where Bedford is buried, or if he is buried. His body disappeared from the funeral home; another mystery unsolved.

Mr. Kneely seems to have aged a dozen years through all this. His hands shake continually. He has a very hard time sleeping, which is actually nothing new.

Before they burned the place down the police did some more investigating. This house seemed to have a history. Nothing can ever be proven but Mr. Kneely is now looked at by the town as a possible bad man. Knowing kids will haunt him daily, never letting up, Ed has put in for early retirement. I saw him recently, he looked like a ghost.

I haven't heard a word from Frank or Alice since that night. I hope they managed to get out before they burned the place.

Violet and I have remained close, though in the fall she will be going to high school in Waterville. She is a good horse trader. She will live at home, but by agreeing to attend a catholic high school, her parents allowed we can be high school sweethearts. She even got to keep the Sony TR63.

Marcia and her father and Pluto are my new family. Her dad is improving and he can talk, though you have to really listen to understand him. He is a hero in this house and Marcia treats him that way.

Violet and I continue to walk with Marcia's dad and Pluto remains my faithful companion, bouncing people off the swinging bridge when necessary.

Something odd happened last week and I just have to make note of it. Violet and I were sitting in Leako's having a soda when a lady approached. She seemed wicked nice. She said she was new to town.

'I just had to come over and tell you two that you look like an old married couple.'

Violet and I looked at one another remembering in that instant the conversation we had had in Whittemore's months ago. I had kidded that the old couple we were watching across the room might be us in sixty years, and Violet had kidded that it couldn't be her because she doesn't have a red dress.

Anyway the lady asked us a little about ourselves; what we wanted to be when we grew up. When we told her she nodded her approval. Then she turned to leave. Her final comment seemed to enter our ears through our bones;

'I'll always be there for you two.'

Violet seemed shaken, me not so much.

Violet was quiet for several minutes then she smiled, 'I think we just met a ghost in the flesh Ryan, maybe two.' She smiled even wider, 'you just wait, you'll see.'

I had my doubts until I saw the lady stop outside the window. She coughed into her sleeve. In that moment I saw my mother.

Then she was gone.

Anyway, I am going to a concert in Bangor on the weekend. Out of the blue, my boss, Scoop Plummer offered me two tickets. When I told him

I had no way of getting to Bangor, he invited me to walk with him. He lived on a side street in a very lovely section of town. He took me to his garage and he proudly showed me the carriage that would transport us. Yes, he would drive Violet and me to the concert. You won't believe this but it is a 1947 Buick Convertible, the exact one I had found in that LIFE *magazine up in the attic.*

He said the paper received the tickets for some advertising they had done and he was too old to enjoy that kind of music. Any way, it's a dream that I had that came true that wasn't a nightmare and the mystery woman in that dream, is in fact Violet.

Write to you soon,
Ryan

Ryan closed his journal. He didn't write in it every day now with all the other things filling his life. In fact it wouldn't be until after going to the concert on the fifteenth that he sat to describe what fun he'd had. When he sat down at his journal it opened immediately to a new page.

Scrawled in a hand he didn't recognize was a message.

Things worked out well for Alice. As for me I ended up with a loser so its same shit different day. See yuh when I need yuh. Christ, I don't even know my own name any more.

Ryan sighed. He closed his journal without penning a word. There was nothing left to say.

The End

www.ingramcontent.com/pod-product-compliance
Lightning Source LLC
Chambersburg PA
CBHW071414200726
48294CB00002B/392

9781961250888